*Carter didn't wait anoth
at the window. "Tom! (
trigger. The first bullet smashed the window to pieces, shards falling
to the ground. They caught the light from the fire and dazzled
Carter's vision again.*

*Inside, Green Shirt responded with amazing rapidity. He turned
and fired twice at the window. His aim was deadly accurate, and
Carter had to slam himself on the ground to avoid being ventilated.*

*By Carter's count, Green Shirt had fired six times. Unless he
had another gun, he would have to reload. Carter stood and pressed
his body up against the side of the gin. He peered around the edge of
the broken window, trying to catch sight of Green Shirt.*

*Two bullets slammed into the window siding. Splinters blos-
somed from the wall and Carter spun away to avoid being blinded.
So much for that question. Green Shirt clearly had another gun.*

*In his approach along the east side of the gin, Carter hadn't seen
any horse in waiting. That meant Green Shirt's only avenue of
escape was to the north. Crouching low, Carter scurried under the
window and avoided any more flying lead. He raced the fifty-foot
long side of the gin's wall, his feet pounding in the damp ground.
More shouts from the loading bay. Jackson must have been calling
Celeste for help or telling Carter to get the bastard. Carter needed no
encouragement. He only needed speed.*

*He rounded the north edge of the warehouse and what he saw
seemed like it was Hades itself. A bottle was arcing through the air
in his direction. Liquid filled the bottle nearly halfway to the top. A
cloth was shoved inside with part of the cloth hanging out of the
bottle.*

And the cloth was on fire.

ALSO BY S. D. PARKER

CALVIN CARTER: RAILROAD DETECTIVE

Empty Coffins

Hell Dragon*

The Aztec Sword*

Brides of Death*

The Senator's Daughter*

Iron Knights*

WESTERNS BY S.D. PARKER

Mosaic Law

A Father's Justice

The Killing of Lars Fulton

The Box Maker

The Agony of Love

The Naked Con

MYSTERIES BY SCOTT DENNIS PARKER

Wading Into War

The Phantom Automobiles

Ulterior Objectives

All Chickens Must Die

*Coming Soon

EMPTY COFFINS

Calvin Carter: Railroad Detective

S. D. PARKER

Quadrant Fiction Studio

Empty Coffins
Calvin Carter: Railroad Detective
By S. D. Parker

Copyright © 2019 by Scott Dennis Parker
A Quadrant Fiction Studio Book

Cover Design by Scott Dennis Parker
Cover Photos:
Top: Arndt Buthe
Bottom: John C. Bielick

www.ScottDennisParker.com

All rights reserved.

❀ Created with Vellum

NEWSLETTER

Join my email list to receive updates on new books and videos, and get an exclusive **Catalog Sampler for 2019** with a special offer: *Buy One Book (of your choice) and Get a Second One Free.*

Sign up at ScottDennisParker.com

To my grandfather who loved westerns

JAKE DENHOLM CONSIDERED himself the luckiest man in Waco. Not only did he have pocketfuls of cash, he also had evaded all the lawmen who tried to capture him. He had shot one, a sheriff's deputy out in Big Spring. He even slipped by those pesky railroad dicks in Dallas. As far as Jake was concerned, he was free and clear.

Jake studied himself in the glass reflection of the Little Elm Saloon. What he saw made him think no one could possibly identify him. His clothes were not fancy, even though he had the cash to buy the best clothes the town had to offer. His brown shirt was dirty, giving him the air of a ranch hand newly arrived in town to burn a few bucks playing poker. The work pants were equally nondescript. His boots were scuffed and he told himself that the first order of business after he crossed the border into Mexico was a complete overhaul of his clothes.

He scratched his chin, his fingernails rasping on the three-day scuff of whiskers. His blue eyes sparkled under the brim of the old, beat-up hat that had seen much better days. He took off the hat and inspected it. The brim showed the white stains of years of sweat and toil, the ribbon fraying at the edges, the inner lining long since gone. This was a good hat, and it had one more ride. He ran his fingers through his scraggly hair, unkempt and long down to his shoulders. He idly considered visiting a barber before he departed on the southbound train to San Antonio, Laredo, and freedom, but discarded the idea almost as soon as it entered his mind. He didn't want anybody even having a passing thought that he might be the same Jake Denholm who ran guns from Fort Worth to Big Spring.

Jake chuckled at the thought of how thoroughly he had outwitted the star packers. They were all down in Big Spring or somewhere along the westbound track to New Mexico and beyond. The clues he had left along the way — and the dead body to reinforce the point — was a grand scheme.

"You're one lucky son of a bitch," he told his reflection. He put his hat back on and pulled the brim down low. He pointed at his reflection, his forefinger extended like a pistol, his thumb in the air. At the pull of his thumb trigger, Jake made a soft gun sound. "Damn lucky."

He lowered his hand and brushed the cold iron of his Colt revolver. The worn oak of the butt had also seen its fair share of duty. His fingers touch the smooth metal of the trigger and down to the cylinder. Sure, the gun was merely a tool for someone like Jake, but he had begun to think of it as an extension of himself. Like a judge with a gavel or a lawyer with his words, Jake's gun was justice. It delivered him from evil and showed him freedom.

Satisfied with the way he looked, filled with the finest whiskey his money could buy, and emboldened by relating his tale to a fellow drinker at the saloon who listened with rapt attention, Jake Denholm stepped off the boardwalk and made his way down the street. The townsfolk were going about their mundane, daily lives. Women walked up and down the boardwalks, ducking into shops and buying essentials. The men driving the passing wagons had their lives already dictated to them. They couldn't get out of their lives if they wanted to. Jake chuckled to himself. He smiled, beaming at what he had taken from life, and turned his face up to the sun.

Jake didn't see the man who stepped up to him until the stranger put his arm around. "You look like a man who has the world by the horns." The accent was pure Irish. "I bet I can beat you."

Halting abruptly in his stride, Jake shrugged off the man's hands. Instinctively, his hand reached for his gun. His palm rested on the weapon as he studied the newcomer.

The man sported a thick red beard and sideburns. He wore a brown suit with a plaid vest that was a size too small for him, but he wore it like it was the best suit in the world. Atop his head sat a brown derby. The evidence of old dents being fixed were obvious. The man's shoes were polished and they caught and reflected the sun. The man's eyes sparkled in the late afternoon light. More to the point, he wore no holster on his leg.

"What do you want?" Jake muttered. His palm still graced his pistol.

"The name's Seamus O'Grady," the stranger said. The lilt of his accent sounded odd to Jake's ears. Out of place here in Waco, Texas. "And I'd like to offer you a wager."

Jake wet his lips. If there was one thing he liked more than running guns and earning money, it was winning money out of the pockets of suckers like this Irish dude. A part of his mind sounded an alarm. All he had to do was make his way to the train station a few blocks away, board the train, and get out of town. Another part of his mind made his mouth say, "What kind of wager?"

The Irishman's mouth, hidden behind the thick whiskers, creased into a grin. In a meek manner, O'Grady backed up a step. He gestured over to the boardwalk in front of a tailor's shop. A barrel rested on its end, the top serving as a makeshift table upon which sat a sign advertising a sale. O'Grady walked around the barrel, turned, and faced Jake. He reached into his jacket pocket and pulled out three playing cards. These cards were slightly bent long ways so that when the Irishman removed the sign and placed the three cards on the table, their faces were raised off the surface of the table. All three cards were lined up, like three rectangles, the blue backs of the cards a stark contrast to the brown of the barrel.

O'Grady lifted the first card to reveal an ace of spades, the black symbol large on the face of the card. The second card was the king of diamonds, while the third was the ten of hearts.

Jake squinted his eyes. "What's the wager?"

"Find the ace."

O'Grady began to shift the cards around. He picked up the first card while simultaneously picking up the third. He switched their places, then repeated the movement with the third and the second card. After a few more shifts, the idea was that Jake was supposed to identify the ace after having watched O'Grady shuffle the cards.

"First, let's practice." O'Grady stopped and held out his hands. "Where's the ace?"

Jake pointed. O'Grady turned over the card. It was the ace of spades.

"Very good, sir. Very good." O'Grady turned the ace back over and shuffled the cards again. While he did so, he started talking. "I'm making my way down to Mexico," he began. "Things aren't looking for good for me here in Texas. I'm, um, what you could call a little light on greenbacks. I don't have a proper job so I'm having to play this game to earn money to get me out of the country."

Jake barely heard the Irishman talk. His concentration was solely focused on the cards. "What kind of trouble?"

"The law. They're looking for me, and well, look at me. I'm an Irishman in Texas. You don't get more out of place than that." O'Grady stopped shuffling and presented the cards to Jake.

The outlaw paused a moment and chewed the inside of his cheek. With nearly the same confidence, he pointed to the card that now sat on his right.

O'Grady overturned the card. The ace of spades.

Jake actually barked out a laugh.

O'Grady inhaled deeply. "Now, how about that wager? I need some money to get out of the country. I've been askin' around, but no one wants to deal with an Irishman. So I've resorted to this. I have a few dollars, but I'm needing some more. How about we make a wager? Five dollars." He reached into his pocket and pulled out a small wad of paper greenbacks. He peeled one off and placed it on the table next to the cards.

Studying the single bill, the rational part of Jake's brain again implored him to walk away. He had more than enough money. When he got across the border, his American money would go a long way. But the other part of Jake's mind, the one that couldn't resist a good wager, over-ruled logic.

The outlaw pulled out his larger wad of cash and plunked down his own five.

"Say, that's a mighty large amount of money," O'Grady said, whistling under his breath. "Where'd you get it?"

"None of your damn business. Let's play."

Shrugging, O'Grady started to shuffle the cards. He

seemed faster this time, but Jake's eyes followed. After nearly ten seconds, O'Grady stopped.

Jake pointed to the middle card. O'Grady revealed the ace. The Irishman cursed, eyed Jake, and then placed another fiver on the barrel. "Again?"

"Sure." Jake removed one of the five dollar bills and left the other one. O'Grady pulled another from his stack of money and the process repeated itself two more times. Jake won every time.

O'Grady cursed under his breath. He scratched his forehead, slightly tilting back his derby. "I'm not gonna win any money losing like this." Thinking of something, he snapped his fingers. "Why don't we increase the wager?"

"No way," Jake said. "It would be like taking candy from a baby."

"So confident are ye?" There was a glint in O'Grady's eyes that hadn't been there before. "Then let's do something really big." He reached in and placed all his money on the barrel. "Let's bet everything."

A muscle in Jake's cheek twitched. That rational part of his brain started screaming. It told him he didn't need to do this. He already had more money than he needed. Just walk away.

Jake's hand reached into his pocket, grasped the wad of money, and placed it on the barrel. "Let's do it."

O'Grady nodded sagely. He made a big show of stretching out his shoulders and neck, as if he were about to start a game. He adjusted his jacket and brought his hands to the cards. He inhaled deeply and let it out slowly. With a last glance up at Jake, he said, "Okay, let's do this."

The Irishman started moving the cards. This time, he was fast. Very fast. In fact, he was faster than Jake had ever seen it. Panic charged through him as he kept his eyes trained on the cards.

As he shuffled the cards, O'Grady started talking. "I'm not sure if you realize this or not, but you made three mistakes." His hands kept flying from card to card. "The first mistake was the theft of the guns themselves. That's a bad idea, especially considering the guns were the property of the US Army. They don't take kindly to their weapons being used against them." After a pause, he continued. "The next mistake was the murder of the deputy out in Big Spring. He was a friend of my commanding officer. As soon as you did that, Jake Denholm, one way or another, you were gonna be tracked down." He tut-tutted his mouth.

Jake was so fixated on the cards that O'Grady's words slowly filtered into his brain. He frowned. How did this Irishman know about the guns? How did he know his name? Jake wanted to look at the Irishman but he knew if he took his eyes off the cards he would lose. Involuntarily, he eased his hand down to his gun and rested his palm on the handle.

"Your third mistake," O'Grady continued, "was playing with me. You see, I knew you couldn't resist making a wager. It's in your nature. Hell, I even bet my partner that you'd fall for this little ruse. You can't refuse a good wager." He stopped and presented the cards. "And here we are."

The words finally registered in Jake's head. With a confused expression, Jake tore his gaze from the cards and turned furious eyes on O'Grady. What he saw surprised the hell out of him.

O'Grady now held a pistol aimed at Jake's midsection.

"My commanding officer," O'Grady began, "really wants you to try and resist arrest. That'll give me all the reason in the world to ventilate you."

Curiously, O'Grady's accent had disappeared. Now, he sounded completely American.

"My partner here thinks you'll come quietly."

At that, a man walked out of the tailor's shop and came to stand next to O'Grady. He, too, held a pistol aimed at Jake. The man looked familiar. It took Jake a moment before he realized this newcomer was the man back at the Little Elm Saloon, the one to whom Jake related his story.

Jake studied the man who he no longer took to be an Irishman. O'Grady held his gun in his left hand. The gun didn't waiver at all. It remained steady, its black eye staring at him. Thoughts of prison and the hangman's noose flooded into his mind. Other thoughts of Mexico and freedom began to fade. The seething hot anger at this man cheating him out of everything he had worked for made his lose all control.

"Who the hell are you?" Jake yelled.

The man formerly known as O'Grady took off the derby hat and tossed it casually aside. Next he reached up and, to Denholm's astonished eyes, peeled the beard off his face. The face underneath was handsome in a suave manner with a well-defined chin and jawline. The mouth was curled in a grin of amusement. Finally, he pulled open his suit jacket and revealed a shiny silver star pinned to his vest.

"The name's Calvin Carter. This is my partner, Thomas Jackson. We're railroad detectives, and you're under arrest for gunrunning and the murder of Deputy Randy Meyer."

White hot rage took over all thought in Jake's mind. Somewhere in the back of his brain, he knew he wouldn't live, but he sure as hell would never be arrested.

His hand tensed over the grip of his pistol. He yanked it upwards, but it never cleared leather.

The guns from both detectives spoke loudly. Two nearly simultaneous booms filled the air. Flame geysered from the barrels. And two slugs slammed into Jake Denholm's body, throwing him backward. The lifeless corpse fell down the steps and landed in a heap on the dirty street.

* * *

CALVIN CARTER HELD out his right hand, palm up. "Pay up."

Grudgingly, Thomas Jackson shoved his hand into his pocket and pulled out a ten dollar bill. He slammed it into Carter's hand.

"How'd you know he'd take the bait?" Jackson asked.

Carter put his Colt back into the shoulder holster positioned inside his coat and under his right arm. He preferred a shoulder holster because it often put people off guard if they didn't see a holster strapped to his leg. His partner was the complete opposite. "Show the iron and make'em know I'll use it" was one of Jackson's familiar sayings.

The townsfolk who witnessed the altercation looked at the two detectives warily. A woman shielded the eyes of her two young daughters as they passed by the corpse lying in the street. A cow puncher dressed in ragged range clothes looked on laconically, a large wad of tobacco wedged in his cheek. Occasionally he launched a thick, brown stream of spit through the air and onto the ground.

"You have to know people, Tom," Carter said. He scooped up the money from the top of the barrel. He folded the greenbacks and slipped them into his jacket pocket. He took the three playing cards and also secreted them back into his pockets. "Jake Denholm didn't become a thieving murderer by chance. He was molded that way. He planned out every step. He may not have matched my wits, but he certainly bested the local lawmen in west Texas."

Jackson moved down to inspect Denholm's body. He put a finger on the man's neck to verify no pulse coursed through the outlaw. "I know a few sheriffs who might dispute your claim."

"And yet, here we are. We found our man, gave him a

chance to come peaceably, and, when he refused, brought him to justice. Now have some spare time on our hands." He rubbed his hands together and looked up and down Fourth Street. His heart beat faster when he spied a particular sign. He motioned Jackson who stood and followed his partner's gaze.

"What?" Jackson said.

"The McLelland Opera House is staging Julius Caesar. The Colonel is certainly not going to make us take the evening train back to Austin. I'll treat you to a little whiskey, a little Shakespeare, and a whole lot of culture." He held up the ten dollar bill he had just won.

Jackson looked at Carter with skepticism on his face. "You're going to buy us tickets with my money?"

"My money," Carter replied. He slipped his pocket watch out of the vest pocket and checked the time. "We have just enough time to make a report to the local sheriff, send a telegraph down to Austin, and grab some dinner." The prospect of seeing theater made his pulse quicken. As a former actor, he cherished the theater and made all efforts to see as much as he could when he wasn't acting as a railroad detective.

A particularly attractive woman strolled near him. Her brunette hair was pulled up into a bun on the back of her head. The top of her dress was open, but a collar of delicate lace obscured most of her exposed flesh and tantalized Carter at the same time. She wore a brown full dress, snug at the waist and full along the legs. The shape of her made Carter start to think of other things.

He bounced on his heels and stood just a little bit straighter. He tipped his nonexistent hat to her. "Good afternoon, ma'am." He also offered her his best grin.

The woman looked him up and down, never breaking stride. She arched an eyebrow and sniffed. Within moments, she had passed him and kept walking down the street.

Shocked at the rebuff, Carter turned and caught Jackson's bemused expression. Carter took a look at himself and only then realized he was still in the "Seamus O'Grady" costume of ill-fitting and mismatched clothes.

"Actually, we'll need to make one additional stop. I have to change."

CARTER AND JACKSON had watched the performance of *Julius Caesar* the previous evening. During most of the performance, Carter regaled his partner with subtle criticisms of the cast, informing Jackson of how he, Carter, had once played Marcus Antony, and generally talked about himself most of the evening. Jackson had nodded in the right places, grunted affirmations, and allowed his verbose partner to hold court. That ended the moment they returned to their hotel whereupon Jackson eased into his room while Carter was still talking. He didn't slam the door, but the satisfying sound served to end Carter's running commentary.

After a breakfast, the two detectives boarded the train for Austin. Carter and Jackson sat in the middle rows of a passenger car. Their commanding officer, Colonel Jameson Moore, had offered to let the two detectives ride in first class or one of the railroad company's special cars, but they had opted to ride among the masses. It hadn't been Carter's preferred way of travel. Jackson had made the call, insisting that he and Carter shouldn't always live in luxury if they were to be good detectives. They had to feel what it was like for ordinary citizens to ride the great railroads of the country, see what they see, smell what they smell. It was the smell that got to Carter the quickest.

It was a surprisingly hot day in central Texas. The calendar read January, but winter had taken a respite from its cold, brutal nature. The mercury was nearing fifty degrees, still cool, but warm enough so that everyone who had boarded the train back in Waco had either shed their warm clothes or sweated through them. The stink of a train full of people permeated Carter's nostrils and curled his lip.

To deaden the fragrant odor, he had pulled out a thin cigarillo and put fire to it. He let the smoke trickle through his nose and out around his face. The smoke wafted up where it joined the other odors in the passenger car.

The car was a standard model. Most of the short, rectangular windows were open to let in the breeze. Bench seats were bolted to the floor. Each bench could seat two people, snug enough to barely leave any gap between passengers. If he were with a beautiful woman, Carter wouldn't have minded at all. He couldn't imagine sitting next to a perfect stranger, elbows rubbing with every jostle of the train.

Carter's eyes again swept to the blonde woman who sat one row ahead of him and across the aisle. She was petite, even under the petticoats she wore. The red dress hugged her form, accentuating her curves in all the right places. The long sleeves caressed her arms and made way, via frilly white lace, to her hands. The nails were painted red, her delicate fingers curled around a book. Carter couldn't read the title on the spine, so he focused his eyes more on the side of her face he could see.

Her skin was smooth and appeared soft, almost as if a Roman sculpturer had crafted her visage out of the whitest of marble. Her cheekbones were high, but swept down to her mouth. Her lips, also painted red, were closed as she read. The blonde hair, curly around the ears, was swept back and affixed by a barrette of coral. Her eyelashes blinked steadily, with the occasional narrowing as she read a passage more intently.

"Are you even listening to me?" The question came from Jackson. He sat next to the window. Unlike Carter who preferred to dress in the finest of clothes, Jackson was a rough and tumble man. A native New Yorker, Jackson found himself after his father had moved the family down to Texas. There, amid the real life cowboys and ranch hands, Jackson discovered he was made for the outdoor life. Where Carter was dressed in a black suit, gray vest, and black ribbon bowtie, Jackson wore what could only be charitably described as fancy range clothes. Dark brown, heavy pants under a blue cotton shirt, a thick leather jacket with enough scraps and scratches to indicate Jackson's active lifestyle, and a bandana tied around his neck. Tied to his right thigh was Jackson's holster, the nicest thing he ever wore. The smooth leather was well cared for as was the Colt .45 nestled inside.

"Yeah, I'm listening," Carter said into the air. "And no, I don't always get off kilter whenever a pretty lady is around." He tore his eyes away from the pretty blonde across the aisle and turned to Jackson. "Give me some examples."

Jackson smirked. "How long do you have?" He began naming names, ticking them off as he extended his fingers. "Joyce McLean. Isabelle Fernando. Susie Taggert. Macy Feathers."

At the sound of Macy Feathers, images flashed in Carter's mind. Good images that brought a smile to his face.

Jackson continued, but Carter didn't hear many of

them. His gaze landed again on the blonde. She turned her head just enough to get Carter in her peripheral vision. She half-smiled, clearly indicating she was eavesdropping. Carter's rakishly handsome face reddened.

"And then there is always Evelyn Paige."

The nice images in Carter's mind vanished in an instant. Other images flooded into his brain, some nice, some not so nice.

"Enough," he said, slicing his hand through the air. He took in the other passengers to see if they were listening. The older couple directly across the aisle feigned ignorance. The same was true for the woman and her little boy up toward the front of the car. Jackson had a loud voice. Chances were good everyone in the car had heard their discussion.

"Listen," Carter said, lowering his voice. "I prefer to help people. Is it my fault that ladies often need my help more than others?"

Jackson's reply was lost amid the thunderous boom of metal scraping on metal. The passenger car jerked violently to one side and then the other. Bags stored under the seats slid forward and sideways. Dust wafted from the floor and into the air. Women screamed and men grunted as they were thrown forward. Most, like Carter and Jackson slammed into the back of the bench seat in front of them. The metal frame was not a soft cushion for Carter's chest which impacted the structure heavily.

A creaking of wood indicated that part of the structure of the passenger car loosened. A second motion, opposite the first, sent many of the passengers who sat along the central aisle onto the floor. Carter almost landed on his face, but he was able to shove out a hand and halt his progress to the floor. Others were not so lucky. Many people landed on top of each other, causing even more panic and screams.

Amid the tumult, Carter noted the blonde woman had also fallen to the floor, but had landed where her feet had most recently been. The man who sat next to her was hunched down next to window. The book the blonde had been reading rested on the floor. He caught the title right before the book slid forward: Jane Austen's Pride and Prejudice.

Carter began to slide forward. His side caught on one of the seat legs bolted to the floor. He doubled over. Another man's shoes rammed into the back of Carter's head, now sticking out into the aisle. The detective cursed and moved his head to allow the man's shoe to pass by him.

Glancing up to Jackson, Carter noted his partner had braced himself against the back of the seat in from of them. But the gash on Jackson's forehead indicated that the taller detective hadn't got out of this crash unscathed.

Almost as an afterthought, the train finally skidded to a halt. Dust curled around the windows, snaking out shattered glass and going outside. The tinkle of glass sounded from the rear of the car. People cried, yelled, or moaned. They tried to right themselves and disentangle themselves from bags, arms, and legs.

Jackson got to his feet first. Turning, he bent and peered out of the window. "Derailments are either accidents or a prelude to an ambush." He spoke to the glass but also to Carter.

Carter heard the words, but his attention was focused on the blonde. He got his feet under him and stood, holding onto the seat in front of him for support. He stepped into the aisle, leaned down, and offered his hand to the pretty blonde. "Are you okay, miss?" Over his shoulder, he said to Jackson, "Let's hope it was just an accident."

The woman accepted Carter's proffered hand. Her fingers grasped his in a surprisingly tight grip. He felt her fingers dig into his palm. It was at once electric and sensual.

Despite the current tragedy, the blonde looked none the worse for wear. She hadn't bumped her head or been thrown into the aisle as Carter had been. The only sign that something had happened was her barrette. It sat askew. Some of her perfectly coiffed blonde hair had come undone. A strand fell around her face. The strand moved as she stood with Carter's help.

"Thank you, sir," she said. Her voice came out slightly creaky, as if she were trying to maintain her calm despite their situation. She smiled at him, her lips parting to reveal straight, even teeth. Her green eyes smiled at him as well.

Carter kept a grip on her fingers a bit longer than was truly necessary, but he didn't want to break the bond. "Are you hurt?"

Her smile broadened, creasing her perfect cheeks with delicate wrinkles. "I don't think so." With her other hand, she started to straighten her dress. "And it's not 'miss.' It's Jessica Reed. Thank you for helping me, mister...?"

The gunshot that came from outside the train silenced any response Carter would have uttered. It also put to rest any doubts the two detectives had regarding the nature of the derailment.

From Carter's side, Jackson moved forward. "Come on, Romeo. We've got company." His hand leapt to the holster, his hand finding the well-worn wooden handle of his .45. In a loud voice, he said, "Everyone stay down! We're railroad detectives. We'll take care of everything."

Carter's mind instantly came alive. But not before snaking his left hand into his jacket. From a shoulder holster, his withdrew his own pistol. It was silver plated, shiny, with an ivory handle. He winked at Jessica Reed as he released her hand. "The name's Calvin Carter. Time to go to work."

* * *

THE TWO DETECTIVES threaded their way to the rear door
of the passenger car. The gunshot had come from that direction. Each man knew the compliment of cars this particular
train: engine, tender, three passenger cars, four freight cars,
and a caboose. This particular passenger car was the first
in line.

The glass window of the rear door had shattered and
fallen into the car. Jackson's boots crunched the glass under
his heel. From outside came the sweet odor of dry grass
mixed with oil. He reached the door and put a hand to the
knob. He turned it, and the knob gave in. He looked back
to Carter. "Ready?"

The two men who had worked together for only a year,
had rapidly developed a bond, especially when it came to
their job. They complimented each other, often knowing
what the other would do. Carter and Jackson often found
themselves in situations like this, and had gotten out of
many scraps. It also meant they didn't need to formulate a
plan. They just knew what to do.

"Let's go," Carter replied.

Jackson opened the rear door. The two detectives gathered on the small landing between the first and second
passenger car. Through the small window, Carter noted that
the passengers in the second car were all starting to stand,
dust themselves off, and take stock of their belongings.
Some looked out the windows, trying to figure out where
the gunshots had emanated and what had caused the train
to derail.

Without a word to each other, Carter and Jackson took
a look around each side of the train car. Carter's trained
eyes took in the scene. The railroad tracks were mostly
straight, with only a slight curve enabling him to see only

the rear of the caboose. The rest of the cars bled into each other. Fifty yards away, a line of trees obscured the surrounding area. That must have been where the owlhoots had hidden themselves. Two men astride horses stood down where either the third or fourth freight car was positioned. Both men wore dark hats, dirty shirts, and range clothes. Bandanas were tied around their faces, but even if they were not, Carter couldn't have made out their faces. One man, in a shirt that used to be yellow, trained a rifle at the side of the freight car. The other, wearing a red shirt, had a pistol in his hand. He was the closer of the two. When Red Shirt turned his head to take in the rest of the train, Carter jerked his head back to avoid being seen.

"I've got two on the east side," Carter said. "One with a rifle, the other a pistol."

Jackson, with his back to the first passenger car, nodded. "Same here."

"They seem to be focused on one of the freight cars. Maybe third or fourth. Yours?"

"Yup." Jackson spat on the ground. The top half of his head was lighter than the bottom, evidence that he spent more time wearing a hat than not. His hat, however, was inside the passenger car, forgotten in the heat of events.

Carter peered forward, trying to see if he could take in what had caused the derailment. From around the side of the first passenger car, he noted Elmer Osgood, the lead engineer, had climbed down from the engine and was walking up to the front. He held his head in such a way that Carter assumed the older man had injured himself. The train man gesticulated wildly, yelling at someone still inside the engine. Osgood halted abruptly, dropping his hands to his sides. Then he raised them, as if surrendering. The next moment, another gunshot cracked in the air. Osgood jerked backward, then crumbled to the ground.

Jackson looked expectantly at Carter. "What was that?"

Carter gulped, grounding his teeth together. "Osgood just got shot." He bit off the words, spitting them out with venom.

Carter's father, Elliot, had been a train man his entire life. He had loved the sights, the smells, everything about trains, their engines, and the railroad. That love did not translate down to his second son, Calvin. The young boy was much more like his mother, Katarina, taken up with the world of arts and literature. In fact, Carter was busy acting in New Orleans when word reached him that his father had been murdered. Carter had returned to Texas and success-fully found his father's murderer and brought the man to justice. The railroad owner had liked Carter's abilities enough to offer him a job as a railroad detective. Carter had taken up the offer and found he had a penchant for being a good detective.

Elmer Osgood had been one of Elliot Carter's best friends. Both had served in the War Between the States, surviving the Red River Campaign together. Osgood had just always been around. Now, he was gone, in the blink of an eye.

Jackson brought Carter's mind back to the task at hand. "There's more back there," he said, indicating the freight cars. "Whatever they're after, it's there. I say we get closer and see what we can see."

Carter nodded. He stood and threw open the door to the second passenger car. Many eyes turned in their direc-tion at the sound of the opening door.

A parasol smashed into Carter's arm. "Ow!" he grunted and turned his attention to his assailant. It was an elderly woman. Her bonnet was askew and her grimacing face showed a few missing teeth. Her dress was plain and brown, much like the wrinkles on her face. She held the parasol with a grip that exposed all the bones of her hand.

"Get out of here you robber!" she croaked.

Carter yanked the parasol out of her grip and threw it back behind her. With a sweep of his hand, he opened his coat to reveal the shiny silver badge he wore on his vest. "We're not the robbers. We're the law."

The woman eyed the badge, then looked back up at Carter. "You don't look like a lawman."

"Looks can be deceiving."

A man with a bleeding gash on his forehead looked up at Carter. "What good are you two against four outlaws?"

Jackson threaded his way down the central aisle. Folks moved out of his way to let the lawman pass. "We're more than enough."

Carter threw one last petulant glare at the old crone and followed his partner. He looked at the people, the passengers under his jurisdiction now. They all gave him worried looks, hoping and willing he and Jackson to be successful. The pit of his stomach shared their concern, but he had long since figured out how to push fear deep inside himself and focus on the task at hand. Nevertheless, he flexed his hand around the grip of his pistol.

Jackson stood there, a sly smirk on his face. He indicated the front of the car. "See what I mean about you and women?" Without waiting for a reply, he opened the door. Each man repeated their reconnaissance to the rear of the train. Carter was able to see the wide open door of the third freight car. Inside, men were frantically moving around. The sound of smashing met his ears. He turned to Jackson.

"My two are still on horseback."

"Mine must be inside," Jackson muttered. "I see their horses but not them."

"I think they're going through the cargo."

"How do you want to play it?"

Carter grinned. "High and low?"

"Sure," Jackson replied, "but I get to go high this time." He pointed at his chest. "You remember what happened last time?"

Carter offered a wounded look. "Hey, how was I supposed to know the roof of the car was weakened and damaged by hail?"

"You've got eyes?"

"They were shooting at me!"

Jackson cocked his head to the rear of the train. "And they'll be shooting at us soon." He holstered his gun. "Help me up."

Carter slipped his pistol back into its holster and laced his fingers together. Jackson placed his thick-soled boot into Carter's hands and climbed up to the roof. Keeping low, Jackson stuck his head back over the edge. His .45 was again in his hand. "There's another rider. Behind the caboose. That's five total."

"Six in you count the guy who killed Osgood," Carter replied. He drew his pistol, letting some of the anger thread through his body. "I'll take the east. You get the west. Then one of us will have to deal with the fifth one. When we start throwing lead, the one up front will likely come calling." He squared his jaw. "I'll deal with him."

Jackson nodded.

"Oh, and stay low," Carter said. "I'd hate to ruin our surprise."

With another smirk, Jackson disappeared over the edge. Carter opened the door to the third passenger car. This time, he made sure his badge was clearly visible. He didn't need another distraction like the old crone.

At the rear of this car, the scared eyes of a young boy

met Carter's. "You think they'll come after us when they're done robbing the freight car?" the boy asked.

Carter gave him a reassuring smile. "No, son, they won't. Me and my partner will make sure of that." In a louder voice, but still quiet enough not to attract the attention of the ambushers, Carter said, "There's gonna be some shooting. I encourage everyone to get on the floor and wait for it to be over." Like dutiful children in school, most of the passengers complied and crouched or laid on the floor. The boy, however, made his way over to the window.

"I want to watch."

"That's not a good idea, son. Killing's not something that needs to be watched, even when it sometimes needs to be done." Gently, Carter reached over and eased the boy down to the floor and into his mother's arms. He smiled at her. She didn't smile back.

Outside, the two outlaws on the east side of the train kept their eyes peeled. In the robberies Carter had witnessed and others he had read about, two contingents were usually present. One typically focused on the freight while the other robbed the passengers. Here, the bandits only gave the passenger cars furtive glances. It was like they weren't even bothering with the valuables the passengers might possess.

That meant only one thing: whatever they were looking for in the freight car was worth more than all the passengers' loot.

Three short taps on the roof of the car indicated Jackson was in position. Carter's five ten frame couldn't reach the ceiling, so he tapped twice on the interior wall. All was ready. Per their well-rehearsed ideas about strategy, each man started a ten count.

Carter only got to seven before one of the bandits on Jackson's side exited the freight car carrying a large burlap bag. He slung it over the rear of his mount and set about tying it. The bandit's eyes swept upward and must have spied Jackson up on the roof.

"Hey! Lookit up there!" The bandit extended a finger, pointing to Jackson's position. The next moment, the bandit drew his gun, aimed, and fired at Jackson.

The gunshots surprised Carter but he reacted without thinking. He fired two quick shots at the robber on his side, the one wearing the shirt that used to be yellow. The first bullet smashed through the glass of the passenger car window. A startled cry from outside told Carter that one of his bullets found a home. His bullet thunked into the outlaw. The wounded owlhoot keeled over. His mount, a painted mare, must have been conditioned not to get spooked at gunfire. She stood almost perfectly still.

But Yellow Shirt's partner didn't. He reacted with almost preternatural precision. He brought up the Winchester rifle and threw hot lead back at Carter. The slugs slammed into the outside wall of the car, shattering windows and splintering wood. Carter had to duck and cover his face to avoid being sliced by shards of glass.

The bandit kept cocking his rifle and firing at the passenger car. The exterior wasn't too thick. Carter could trace the passage of the bullet holes from the bottom of the window down to the floor of the car…

…to where the young boy crouched with his mother.

Curling his lip in a snarl, Carter vowed the bullets would not reach the boy. He stood quick and fired through the broken window. He had good aim, better than many men in the west, but with the likelihood that that Rifle Man would alter his aim and shoot Carter, the railroad detective didn't aim for the shooter.

He aimed for the shooter's horse.

It was a bigger target after all. And even the most well-trained steed would react to being shot.

Carter's bullet pierced the animal's brown fur just in front of Rifle Man's leg. The small spout of blood stained the elegant fur and splashed onto Rifle Man's pants.

The horse bellowed in pain and stumbled away from the train. Rifle Man had to pull the reigns to avoid falling to the ground. The wounded animal reared up, turning at it did so away from the train. It was all Rifle Man could do to remain in the saddle.

Carter took the opportunity to rush outside. A quick glance to the west showed one bandit face down on the ground and another riding in circles to make Jackson's job of shooting him that much more difficult.

Trusting his partner to take care of his end of the business, Carter burst out the back door of the passenger car. He jumped to the ground between the two train cars and poked his head and pistol around the corner.

Bullets thwacked into the side of the first freight car inches from Carter's face. Splinters geysered in a plume of wood and Carter had to duck back. The next thing he knew, hot lead smacked into the ground at his feet. Reacting instantly, Carter leapt backwards. No platform existed between the last passenger car and the first freight car. None was needed. That meant when Carter landed, his back would fall full on the metal coupling. Knowing this, the detective executed a twist in midair that didn't quite have its full effect. His side landed on the couplings. The force sent shocking pain up and down his rib cage. He might have even cracked a rib.

But the bullets that had been intended for his feet went harmlessly into the dirt.

Wincing but determined to put an end to this robbery, Carter climbed onto the coupling. He faced a choice: go back into the passenger car to get a better look but put the people at risk or head to the west side and help Jackson get his man. He mulled over the possibilities as he opened the cylinder, spilled out the spent shells, and thumbed in fresh bullets.

Carter chose the latter.

Carter flattened himself along the side of the freight car and peered around the edge. The bandit was still riding in erratic patterns trying to avoid getting himself killed. Carter, a lefty, had the luxury of being able to keep his entire body protected while aiming for the horseman. He trained his pistol on the man, his line of sight preceding the man for a few more moments.

Carter fired. Above him, he heard Jackson fire as well. Their intended target yelled once then fell from his saddle. His gray horse, now free, turned and ran away.

"Tom!" Carter yelled. "What do you see on my side?"

Boot scooted on the roof of the car. "One dead?"

One? Carter thought. That wasn't right.

"That all?"

"Yup. I'm gonna check the rear." Within a second, Jackson's form leapt over the space between the cars. His footfalls grew fainter the closer he got to the rear.

Carter wasn't going to hunker down and miss all the action. Besides, he needed to see for himself if Rifle Man was still around. He jumped to the ground and peered around the edge of the freight car.

A bullet thwacked mere inches from his face. The splinters from the wood pricked the skin on Carter's cheek. He reared back, spinning in the space between the cars. He dove over the coupling and landed on the far side of the train. He tucked and rolled a few more feet, coming to rest on his haunches. He spun and faced the train. The rataplan of hooves were loud but gradually fading away.

That bullet had come from the front of the train. Carter closed his eyes in frustration. In all the chaos of the shoot-out, he and Jackson both had forgotten about the sixth man, the one who had put a bullet in the brain of Elmer Osgood.

Scrambling up the small rise, Carter made a different choice. Instead of hopping over the coupling, thereby exposing himself to even more gunfire, Carter opted to scoot under the train, allowing the thick steel wheel to act as a shield. He made his way under the train and gazed out to the east.

Near the tree line, the bushwhackers rode like lightening. Carter made a quick count. Seven riders charged away. One horse still carried the burlap bag across its empty saddle. Yellow Shirt's horse had found solace along the line of trees and didn't find the need to follow the rest. The man trailing the main group must have been the shooter from the front of the train. Carter made note of the man's horse — a gray with black hair around the hooves — and the man's shirt. It was a bright green under a brown vest. The man's hat had fallen off his head, but a cord kept it from falling. Wavy brown hair swirled in the wind. He wore his mustache and sideburns trimmed neatly.

"Cal!" Jackson yelled from the roof.

"Yeah?"

"We're alone!"

Carter sighed and closed his eyes. He felt his heart hammering inside his chest and breathed deeply to slow it. The passengers, having heard the all-clear signal, burst into applause and cheers and whoops of celebration. A moment later, Jackson climbed off the roof of the freight car and hopped to the ground. He angled his head to Carter who had scampered out from under the car.

"Let's go see what they were after."

Carter and Jackson, guns still in hand, cautiously walked around the west side of the train. The third freight car had its side doors wide open. Inside the car, crates and packages were strewn everywhere.

The two detectives climbed into the open car and looked around. Upon closer inspection, they noticed that wasn't entirely true. Various crates only appeared to be haphazardly cast aside, but in reality, they were all hastily piled to one side. In the area clear of crates, three longer crates of a particular shape sat in the center of the floor space.

"Those are coffins," Jackson breathed.

"And they're open," Carter said.

Each coffin had been stored inside a larger outer crate. All three outer crates had been ripped apart. It was clear to both men that the target of the ambush seemed to be the coffins.

"Why would someone want to steal a corpse?" Carter mused. "You think that was what was in that burlap bag?"

"Maybe something valuable on the body?" Jackson replied.

"More valuable than all the stuff the passengers carried?"

A nasty smell emanated from one of the coffins. It was a simple pine box, the kind any good carpenter could make in half a day. Jackson held his breath and opened it. He closed it almost immediately.

"Body."

Carter eased around to the second coffin. This one was more ornate than the first. He sniffed and frowned. This one didn't smell as bad as the other one. He opened the lid.

The interior was empty.

"Tom. Have a look."

The former New Yorker came to stand beside Carter. Jackson scratched his head. "Well, that's something."

"Check the third one."

Jackson climbed over the third coffin and opened it. "Same thing. Empty."

From the far end of the freight car, in the shadows, came a moan. Both detectives whiled, bringing their guns to bear. The coffin lid Carter had opened slammed shut.

"Hello?" Carter said. "Who's there?"

Another moan, then movement, and a grimace. A face appeared from the shadows. It was a man. His face unshaven and bedraggled. His clothes where disheveled and in need of a good laundry. Or cast into a fire. He held his head, wincing at his own touch. He looked up and saw the two detectives. His eyes widened in surprise. He raised his hands.

"Don't shoot me, please!" he cried. "I already told y'all what I know."

Carter and Jackson exchanged a glance. Narrowing his eyes, Carter said, "Why don't you tell us again."

CALVIN CARTER LOOKED down at the body of Elmer Osgood and gritted his teeth. The old man's face still showed surprise, the O of his mouth now rigid in death. The small dark hole in his forehead appeared clean, belying the damage at the back of his head. His blood had moistened the ground where his head now rested. Carter shook his head and tore his eyes away from the corpse.

With the excitement over, the passengers stood or sat on both sides of the derailed train. Most of the folks emerged from the derailment and violence with only scratches and growing bruises. One man happened to be standing when the train suddenly stopped. He had been thrown forward, his head smashing through one of the forward door. He now lay off to the side, bandages wrapped around his head. The large red stains on the cloth indicated how bad his injury was. The other passengers talked, laughed, and were already retelling the story of the ambush. Another train engineer tapped into the telegraph line next to the tracks and had alerted the station back in Waco, only twenty miles away, of the accident.

A doctor happened to be present as one of the passengers and he immediately began attending to the hurt passengers. Carter and Jackson told the sawbones to have a look at the freight car worker, who went by the name Adam Whitney, first so they could question him more thoroughly. The gibberish he spouted when Jackson grabbed a hold of him made both detectives question how scrambled the worker's brains actually were.

Carter trained his eyes to the tree line, the escape route of the ambushers. Often times, he and Jackson traveled with their horses, the better able to respond to changing situations like this one. But their previous job had been a short one, not requiring any horses. So he was stuck here, with the deep desire to chase after the owlhoots, especially the man in the green shirt, the one who had murdered Osgood.

Approaching footsteps brought Carter's mind back to the present. He looked and saw the young boy and his mother walking toward him. The boy's eyes were fixated on Osgood's corpse. A few steps behind her son, the young mother drew a shawl around her shoulders, trying to keep out the cold that didn't exist in the air.

Carter snapped his fingers at the boy. "Son, eyes up here." He repeated the snapping, finally getting the boy's attention. The boy's hair was tousled, giving the impression that he had just woken from a night's slumber in a soft bed. Around the corners of his eyes, streaks of dirt formed rough lines along his face, as if dirty fingers had tried to wipe away tears.

"You don't need to be seeing that," Carter said.

The boy gazed up at Carter, his eyes trailing over the silver badge on Carter's vest. "You were real brave, Mr. Detective." The boy's voice hadn't reached puberty so it still held the innocence of childhood.

Carter cracked a lopsided grin. "I wish I didn't have to be brave." He knelt, partly to get on the boy's level but mostly to block the sight of Osgood's body. "Do you know what I really want to do?" When the boy shook his head, Carter said, "I'm an actor. That's what I'm really good at. One of the best you'll ever see."

He looked up at the mother. "Do y'all ever get to a theater?"

With a demure expression, the young woman shook her head. "No, sir. We barely make it through the year on our farm. We don't have any extra money for things like that."

Inwardly, Carter castigated himself. His smile faltered. He knew that his actor's life was one of light frivolity. That was what he loved, what his mother promoted in him. Not like the hardscrabble life most people lived where even books were a luxury.

He tilted his head. "Of course."

"How many men have you killed?" the boy asked.

Carter opened and closed his mouth. He gave some thought as to how to answer the boy's question. "Son, what's your name?"

"Danny."

"Well, Danny, here's the thing. I'm a railroad detective. My job—when I'm not acting—is to bring lawbreakers to justice. Many times, justice might mean jail. Let's say if a man robbed a bank and just stole some money. He gets caught, he goes to jail. Other owlhoots kill other men. That's a different kind of justice. We don't just out and shoot someone like that. We have laws, a justice system. In cases like that, my job is to bring those bad guys in for trial. That's how it's supposed to work."

Carter inhaled deeply, letting the smell of the nearby grass calm him. "But in times like today, there's no time for niceties. Bad men do bad things. Take this old man behind us. No, don't look at him. He's already left this life and all that's left is a husk. Now, I knew this man. He was a friend of my father. So when those men ambushed this train and started shooting, my partner and I had to shoot back, defend ourselves and protect folks like you. What you think of as bravery is merely what we had to do to save lives and keep us among the living."

He sighed and patted the boy's shoulders. "Danny, I hope you never have to defend yourself like what you saw today. There's some bad people in this world, but there's more good than anything else. The good is what built that train and the tracks, made the clothes you wear, and writes the plays I act in. Always focus on the good, but be ready to defend justice when you have to."

Thomas Jackson edged toward them. In his hands was a burlap blanket. Atop his head, the detective now wore his customary dark brown hat, with a wide brim that curled around the edges.

"Is Whitney ready to talk?" Carter asked.

"Yeah." Jackson held up the blanket. "I brought this for Mr. Osgood."

Carter stood and pivoted, allowing Danny to watch as Jackson placed the blanket over Osgood's head and upper torso.

"You gonna get the man who did this, Mr. Detective?"

"The name's Calvin Carter, Danny," Carter said. "This is my partner, Thomas Jackson."

Danny inhaled sharply. "Like Stonewall Jackson?"

Jackson smiled. "Yeah, but I'm from New York."

"Don't hold that against him," Carter said, bringing a moment of lightness to the somber visage on the ground in front of him. "He's probably the best damn cowboy you'll ever meet."

Tipping his hat in acknowledgment, Jackson said, "We

should get over and talk with Whitney." He started moving
back to the train.

"Right," Carter said. "Take care, Danny. And listen to
your mother. Oh, and to answer your question, yeah, we'll
get the man who did this. I guarantee it."

* * *

ADAM WHITNEY SAT on the edge of the open freight car.
Now, in the clear light of day, Carter could see just how
scraggly the man was. Whitney had facial hair that grew in
patches, none of which connected with each other. His
beard and mustache, as they were, resembled nothing more
than tumbleweeds across his face. The bump on his head
poked through thinning hair and a receding hairline. A
black eye ringed his right side, and dried blood mixed in
with his beard.

The laborer's hands still shook as he gratefully accepted
a snip from the doctor's flask. Quickly, the doctor, an older
man with close cropped white hair wearing a black suit not
unlike Carter's, reached out and grasped the flashed before
it fell to the ground.

"Thanks, doc," Whitney said.

The old sawbones grunted. He turned to Carter and
Jackson. "I'll leave him to y'all. I got other folks to tend to."
With a slight nod and bow of his head, the doctor picked up
an old leather satchel, worn and creased with age and use,
and hurried off the other passengers.

Carter and Jackson stood on the ground and looked up
at Whitney. "You doing any better, Mr. Whitney?" Jackson
asked. The sweat from his neck had mixed with the dust in
the air and stained the collar which he had loosened.

Whitney nodded.

"Tell us again what happened," Carter said.

Whitney scowled. "I already tole you."

Reaching out to grasp a handhold, Carter hauled himself up into the freight car. He stood over Whitney who remained seated, his feet dangling over the edge. Jackson did likewise until both detectives loomed over the laborer.

"Tell us again," Carter said. He remained gentle but firm. "Sometimes the retelling brings out more details."

Whitney scrambled to his feet. He slipped on the dusty floor, fell to a knee, then stood again. He backed away a few paces. His face went from one detective to the other. "Why y'all asking me to go over it again. I got hurt, same as you."

"Details," Jackson intoned. "We need the details." He stood with his thumbs hooked into his gun belt. "We were up front. You got a front row seat to the ambush." He indicated the interior of the freight car. "And you can tell us what they did here."

Sighing, Whitney looked back into the car. "I ride back here when there's important cargo."

"Ain't that get hot?" Jackson asked.

"Sure does, especially in the summer. But it ain't bad in winter, especially seeing as it's as mild as it is. The vents up there, where the walls meet the roof bring in a good breeze. Mainly, I just lay back and snooze." He chuckled sardonically. "Normally it's one of the easiest jobs a train man can have."

"And you get locked in?" Carter asked.

"Yeah."

"What if there's a fire or some reason for you to escape? How do you get out?"

Whitney pointed to the ceiling. "That hatch. That's the escape route."

Carter and Jackson turned their heads and spied the hatch in the roof of the freight car. It was a small, man-sized opening on the far wall with a few iron rungs running under it along the interior wall. A padlock was still in place.

"You have the key?" Jackson asked.

Whitney fished a hand in his pocket and pulled out a large keyring. Brass and metal keys jangled in car as he shook them. "Right here."

"And you never opened the hatch during transit?" Jackson pressed.

"Not this time. In the summer, when it's hot as blazes, the man who rides back here will sometimes open the hatch and take in the fresh air. But not today."

Carter held out his hand. "Let me see those keys."

Whitney hesitated, then plopped them into Carter's open palm.

The keys were the standard mix. From his time on the railroad and riding the rails with his father, Carter could tell which key went to the engine, the caboose, and most of the freight cars. A few keys indicated they were padlock keys. Carter typically made a mental note of which compartments had padlocks on the exterior, but not this time. Much of the plating on most of the keys had been scraped away from constant use.

He motioned to Whitney's side. "You're not armed."

"No, sir."

"Any reason why not?"

Whitney shrugged. "Most of the time we don't get ambushed."

Jackson tried to stifle a laugh but failed. "Bushwhackers don't schedule an ambush. How are you supposed to defend whatever precious cargo you've got back here without any iron? At least a pistol."

Getting a little spine, Whitney spat. "Look, I don't make the rules. I just follow them."

Carter arched an eyebrow. "Were you told not to be armed? Surely you have your own weapon for protection."

"Sure, it's in my locker back in the caboose. I didn't figure I'd need it so I just left it in there."

Carter chewed on the inside of his lip. He changed tactics. "What's so valuable on this shipment?"

Whitney pointed across the interior. "I only was tole it was that crate over yonder."

The interior was piled almost halfway with wooden crates of various shapes and sizes. Off in the corner were bales of cotton. Where Whitney indicated sat the crate in question.

Carter walked over and examined the crate. It was big, but not as large as the coffin-shaped crates. The nails were still in place, and the lock remained secure and unopened. Pasted on the outside was a label. The addressee was listed as Derek Walker, San Antonio.

Frowning, Carter said, "So these bushwhackers derail the train, open this car, skip this valuable cargo—whatever it is—and proceed to steal corpses?" Carter's actor pedigree shone through as he pointed first to the empty coffins and then to the sealed crate. His voice rose a few notches, as if he were trying to reach the back seats of his imaginary theater. "And they didn't even attempt to break into this crate, the contents of which are so important that you got assigned to ride back here." He gave Jackson a quizzical look. "That doesn't make sense."

Jackson rolled his eyes in exasperation. Carter knew the look. It was when his partner had tired of Carter sliding into actor mode.

"Maybe they didn't know about that crate," Jackson said. Now it was his turn to be dramatic. "But they knew about the coffins." He pointed to them and turned to Whitney. "When did the coffins get loaded?"

Whitney's eye twitched. "Dallas."

"Were you riding back here then?"

"Nope."

"When did you start your shift back here?"

"Waco."

"How about this special crate? When did it get loaded?"

"Waco also." Whitney gulped. His feet started drawing lines in the dust on the floor.

"When you came on," Jackson finished.

Whitney nodded.

The two detective looked at each other. This situation didn't make any sense. Carter's brain began to tickle. He stifled a grin. This was a genuine mystery.

As an actor, he certainly found his forte. His mother had taught him well, even bringing in veteran actors to help train her son in the craft. Naturally, Carter had read all the classics, including Shakespeare, Sophocles, and Voltaire. But his reading had also widened to include fiction of all sorts. While he loved Charles Dickens, he had discovered a fondness for Edgar Allan Poe, specifically the detective stories featuring C. Auguste Dupin. Carter enjoyed a good mystery, and actively sought other works featuring any plot with a mystery. He lamented Dickens's death for the famous author would never have the chance to write the finale of his last novel, The Mystery of Edwin Drood. But Carter loved Wilkie Collins's The Moonstone and all of its twists and turns. By the time Carter's father had been murdered and Carter himself had tracked down the killer, the young man was ripe for a career change. The offer to be a railroad detective was too great, and Carter jumped at the chance.

Now, here, was a mystery with a curious set of circumstances.

From outside the car, the sound of footsteps brought

Carter out of his reverie. He and Jackson turned their attention to the person walking up to the freight car. It was Bartholomew Danvers, the co-engineer. His salt-and-pepper hair was disheveled and a thick patch of dried blood coated the side of his head and extended down to stain the collar of his white shirt. The brown pants and open vest matched, the brown shoes were scuffed from years of work. He looked up from the ground.

"Have you made any sense of what those bastards were after?" His voice came out as a growl.

Carter shook his head. "Not really. We're talking with Mr. Whitney here about what he experienced."

"Two of the coffins are now empty," Jackson said. He waved his hand over at the opened coffins. "Looks like the gang was after whatever was inside."

Danvers frowned. "Weren't there bodies inside?"

"Judging from the smell, or lack thereof," Carter said, glancing at Jackson for confirmation, "we're not sure."

Behind Danvers, a woman walked up. Carter's eyes moved to her, and he recognized her as Jessica Reed. The pretty woman had cleaned herself up and righted her hair. Where the other passengers looked out of sorts after the recent activity, Jessica Reed looked like she was ready to have a night on the town.

Accompanying her was the man with whom she was sitting. That he was tagging along meant they knew each other and were not, as Carter had suspected, complete strangers. He wore a gray suit and vest, and appeared almost as impeccable as Jessica. A silver chain of a pocket watch dangled from one of his vest pockets. He wore a derby hat, black with a silver ribbon. The only acknowledgement that the train had derailed was that his black tie was slightly askew.

Jessica looked up into the car and found Carter. She

smiled, but it was laced with grimness. "Is my father still there?"

Carter caught her full gaze. Her green eyes flashed into his. He momentarily got lost in them.

"Your father?" Jackson said, taking up the slack. He indicated Whitney. "He's right here."

Jessica took one look at Whitney and sniffed. "Not him. My father has passed on. I was taking his body back to San Antonio for a proper burial with his family." She patted the shoulder of her companion. "This is Timothy Walsh, my cousin. He's accompanying me."

Understanding finally lanced through Carter's thoughts. "Well, there's one corpse still here." He hooked a thumb back to the interior.

Jessica held up her hand, indicating she wanted to be helped up into the car. Carter all but rushed to the edge of the freight car. He gripped a handrail and leaned over the side. He took her hand, again marveling how firm were her muscles and how soft her skin. He hauled her up into the freight car. Idly, a certain part of Carter's mind wondered what other parts of Jessica Reed were firm and soft. The fragrant wash of lilac drifted into his nostrils from being close to her only accentuated those thoughts.

Jessica thanked him and scooted around some of the fallen craft and took in the coffin that still contains a corpse. Timothy Walsh climbed aboard without any assistance offered or needed. He tipped his hat to Carter, but the detective's eyes were following Jessica.

"No, that's not my father's coffin." Her tone was dismissive. "That one's too plain." She looked at the other two empty ones, with lids raised. "That's his."

Carter and Jackson came around to both side of the middle coffin. It was the most ornate of the three. It was crafted from strong wood, painted black. The interior appeared to be soft cotton, padded in the floor of the coffin and both sides. A pillow for the head was present, and frills around the edges of all fabric. On the lid was placed an ornate carved bouquet of flowers. These were painted in multiple colors.

"Are you sure?" Jackson asked. Carter noted his partner's skeptical tone with Jessica and wondered if it were Jackson doing his job or as a slight to Carter's clear infatuation with her.

"Absolutely. My father was a successful businessman. He passed away recently and we children wanted him brought back to San Antonio to rest in peace with the rest of his family." She broke out in a single sob.

Walsh reached out and grasped Jessica's shoulders. He pulled her close, allowing her head to rest on his shoulder. "You boys are detectives, right? Well, then you best not trouble my cousin and start detecting."

Carter scowled, showing his displeasure to Jackson. Carter didn't mind taking orders from his superior, Jameson Moore, but despised it from others. Nevertheless, Walsh was correct. Carter waited a few moments to maintain the appearance that he wasn't immediately jumping to Walsh's command.

Bending down, Carter examined the exterior of the ornate coffin. Other than the carved set of flowers, it looked like a coffin lid, albeit one made of expensive wood. He reached over and opened the lid. It squeaked a little.

Inside more evidence that a rich person commissioned this particular coffin. The fabric was even finer upon closer inspection. It was satin, not cotton. The pillow was the curious thing. The indention of where the head had recently laid was not as deep. A few hairs were scattered over the pillow. Now that both detectives had more time to examine the coffin, they both noticed something at nearly the same time.

Jackson voiced it first. "The shape here doesn't appear to be that of a man." He used his finger to trace the outline along the sheet and cushion. "You'd think there'd be an impression of a body inside."

Carter nodded. To Jessica, he said, "When did you father die?"

Walsh answered for her. "Three weeks ago. It took…"

Jessica pushed away from him gently and smiled. "It's okay, Timothy. They're just doing their job." She inhaled and sighed. "It took us nearly a week to get up to where father died. In that time, they had poor father in a simple pine box." Her words snarled out of her lips. "When I got there, I made sure to buy the best coffin around." She stood at the foot of the coffin, her hands clasped together.

Carter had known his fair share of prima donnas, but Jessica Reed was starting to edge her way up the list. He didn't mind in the least.

He ran his eyes along the inside of the coffin. He stopped when he got to the foot. "Take a look."

Jackson slid over and followed Carter's finger which now were pointing to where the corpse's feet and shoes would have been.

"Is that dirt?" Jackson asked.

"Appears so."

"You'd figure undertakers would make coffins as presentable as possible"

"Or at least the bodies." To Jessica, Carter said, "Did you have an undertaker dress your father?"

She nodded, saying nothing.

Jackson took over the inspection on the exterior side of the coffin lid. Carter let his eyes move over the underside. Like the coffin itself, the interior of the lid was lined with silk. The sheet, however, stopped where the upper chest and face of a corpse would be. At this point, it was merely bare wood. He stopped when his eyes landed on the spot where the corpse's face would have been.

"Tom, look."

Jackson came around and crouched next to Carter. He peered close, narrowing his eyes. "I'll be damned. Are those holes?"

"Think so." Carter stood and moved around to the open lid. He examined the carved wooden bouquet more closely. "This carving is raised up off the surface of the lid. It allows air to pass underneath it." He inhaled deeply and blew.

Jackson reacted almost immediately. "Hang on a minute. When you blew that air, it came directly in here." He positioned his hand right over the area. "Do it again."

Carter repeated his blowing.

"Damn straight," Jackson muttered. "The air came directly in here."

Raising his face over the lid, Carter stared at Jackson. "You know what this means, don't you?"

Jackson nodded.

"What?" Walsh said.

"What does it mean?" Jessica asked, fear filling her voice.

Carter stood. "This coffin has air holes."

Jessica frowned. "Why would my father need air holes?"

"He wouldn't. But someone else would."

"Who?"

"One of the men who ambushed this train," Jackson said.

Adam Whitney, who had remained silent during the entire examination of the coffin, suddenly cleared his throat.

Then he started coughing. "If y'all'll excuse me, I have to have a look after the other cars."

Jackson's strong arm shot out and clutched Whitney's shirt in a big fist. "Actually, we'd like to ask you a few more questions."

4

TO HIS CREDIT, Adam Whitney tried to put up a fight and escape. Carter didn't know why seeing as how there was nowhere to run. He stood back, a playful smile on his face. He was ready if somehow Whitney got in a good punch, but Carter highly doubted it.

The laborer swung at Jackson's arm, evidentially trying to dislodge it. Jackson was raised on a cattle farm. As a young man, it was rapidly clear he was strong, even stronger than some of the ranch hands his father employed. Even when the younger Jackson challenged the men at arm wrestling, the ranch hands would good-naturedly allow the son of the ranch owner to try and win. When Jackson did, most of the losers would hide their surprise and failure.

Jackson used his free arm to block Whitney's blow and clutched another handful of the freight man's clothes. With little effort, Jackson hauled him up off the floor. Whitney's feet dangled and strived to find purchase on anything. With a barely audible grunt, Jackson took a few steps over to where other crates were stacked and deposited Whitney, unceremoniously, on one of them. Walsh and Jessica watched the short event with surprise.

From the ground outside, Danvers clambered up the side of the freight car. The old man shook an accusing finger at Whitney. "Tell us what you did, dammit. Elmer's dead." His voice cracked when mentioning the dead engineer. "So help me if I find out if you had anything to do with it, I'll kill you myself!"

Whitney actually chuckled at that. "I'd like to see you try."

Jackson slapped Whitney hard across the face. The report sounded sharp in the freight car, but the crates deadened the sound. "I think you need to tell us what you haven't told us yet." Jackson brought his face lower, right in front of Whitney's. The detective's face, clean-shaven save for a neatly trimmed mustache, glistened with sweat.

"I already tole you what I know. I don't know anything more."

Carter glanced at Danvers. The old man was quivering with anger. Jessica and Walsh stood quietly, waiting to see how this all played out.

Replaying the conversion with Whitney in his head, Carter said, "You were quiet until we figured out there were breathing holes in the coffin. Breathing holes meant to keep someone alive in a coffin. Now, seeing as how a dead man has no need to breathe, I'm thinking that there was a man inside the coffin." He snapped his fingers and moved over to the open coffin. It still sat on the floor, but off to the side was the larger crate in which the coffin had been transported. "But each one of these coffins were also packed in a crate." He examined the crate that had held the fancy coffin. Sure enough, the slats were not close together. If there was truly a man inside the coffin, he would have enough air to breathe. Not much, but then again, maybe he didn't need much.

"But there's something else," Carter continued. His voice grew more confident with each passing word. He ran a finger along the edges of the crate. He stopped when he got to portions of the wood that were gouged and cracked. More gouges were along the edge of the crate lid. Each gouge corresponded to where a nail had sealed the crate.

Carter stood and rounded on Whitney. "This crate was still nailed shut. The clearance between the coffin lid and the sealed crate lid is pretty small. That meant someone had to open the crate in order to let out the man inside the coffin." He glanced at Jessica and gave her a rueful smile. "Seeing as how I highly doubt it was Miss Reed's father come back to life, that meant there was someone in that coffin"—now he turned to Whitney—"and that you let him out." The detective arched an eyebrow. "Am I right?"

Whitney flustered. His thick fingers worked at the creases in his pants. "I don't know what you're talking about. I..."

Jackson slapped the man across the face again. "Shut yer trap and tell us the truth."

"Look, detective," Whitney began, gingerly touching his reddening cheek, but Carter cut him off.

"Don't bother denying it." Carter pointed to the ceiling of the freight car, specifically the padlock on the extra hatch. "I know you have the key and could have let in any one of those bandits. But you could have also let someone out of the car and up through that hatch. When the train derailed, those bandits made a beeline to this freight car. Most of us up front got knocked to the ground. That left you plenty of time to climb up there and unlock the door."

Whitney stood. Jessica, Walsh, and Danvers backed

away a pace or two, fearing the cornered man might lash
out. Carter and Jackson stood their ground.

"You've got it all wrong," Whitney pleaded. "I didn't
open the hatch. Those sons of bitches came in the
side door."

Carter spun on his heel and sauntered over to the
freight car door. It was slid back on its rails. No evidence
presented itself of having been forced open. Carter held
onto a handrail and swung out into open space. He examined the exterior of the freight car door, then trained his
eyes to the ground.

"What are you looking for?" Jessica asked. She was the
closest to Carter's position and looked at the ground, trying
to figure out what Carter was looking for.

After another moment, Carter found it. He hopped to the
ground, bending his knees to absorb the small shock. He
scrambled down the small rise of the tracks and out into the
short grass just beyond. He reached down and plucked an
object from the ground. He spun and held it aloft for all to see.

It was a padlock. The same padlock that had been used
to seal the freight car door.

Carter returned to the car and climbed back inside.
Everyone inside, who had edged close to the door, made
room for him again. Jackson's hand rested firmly on Whitney's shoulder.

Presenting the padlock in front of Whitney's eyes,
Carter said, "Care to explain that?" He tossed it to Whitney. With quick reflexes, the laborer caught the lock and
fumbled around not to drop it.

"Explain what?"

"Look at it," Carter said. He stuck his thumbs in his vest
pockets and waited.

"I don't know what you mean," Whitney said.

Danvers snatched the lock from Whitney and looked it over. Turning it in his hands, the engineer came to a conclusion. "I don't see anything wrong with it."

"Precisely," Carter boomed. "Because it wasn't forced open. It was unlocked with a key. The owlhoots who ambushed this train had the key to this freight car already in their possession. When they came to collect what they wanted, they never had to force the lock at all."

All pairs of eyes turned to Whitney. The railroad man shrank under their collective gazes.

Jackson finally spoke up. "How'd you get the bump on your head? Was that to make it look good?"

Whitney perked up. "I was knocked out. Those bastards came in and roughed me up."

Jackson took the opportunity to slap the same area. Whitney howled in pain. Jessica flinched and bit her lip. Walsh and Danvers merely stared at the lying man.

"Guess he's telling the truth, Cal."

"Maybe," Carter said. He came to stand directly in front of Whitney. "But that still doesn't explain how our living corpse got out. Let's cut to the chase. How much?"

"How much what?" Whitney's expression was still screwed up in pain. After a moment, his expression softened when he realized where Carter was going.

"How much did you get paid to open that coffin and let out whomever was inside?"

Whitney's mouth opened then closed. "I don't know what you mean," he mumbled, not meeting the eyes of anyone around him.

Carter gestured to Jackson. "I can have my partner search you. He's not gentle."

Jackson moved closer to Whitney. The smaller man cowered in place.

"Fifty bucks! Okay, I got paid fifty bucks to open that coffin ten minutes after we left Waco."

"Show me," Jackson commanded.

Whitney shoved a hand into his pocket and produced a few folded bills. Jackson snatched them from Whitney's hand. "Hey! That's mine."

"Right," Jackson said. "Bribe money. We ought to let you keep it seeing as how you'll be out of a job."

"Damn right he is," Danvers said. Fury filled his voice. "Elmer was a friend of mine." He shot a finger at Carter. "He was even a friend of his father. And you had him killed!"

"I didn't know anyone was gonna get hurt," Whitney wailed.

"After a train derailment?" Carter asked. "What the hell did you expect to happen?"

Whitney had no answer. "We wasn't going that fast."

Carter merely huffed.

"It wasn't my fault," Whitney stammered. "They were gonna kill me otherwise."

"Then why pay you?" Carter asked.

"To keep my mouth shut."

"Who else knew?" Carter pressed. "You still have your keys. Either a copy was made or another man's keys are missing."

Whitney stayed silent. Jackson grabbed another handful of Whitney's shirt and made to slap him again.

"Skip Barton!" Whitney said. He held his hands up around his face. "Just don't hit me again."

"You should be so lucky," Jackson said, but released the laborer nevertheless. "Describe him."

"I dunno," Whitney muttered.

"I'll describe him," Danvers said. "Brown hair,

mustache, lean but strong as an ox. And his missing the little finger on his right hand."

"Thanks," Carter said. To Whitney, he said, "Did Barton get paid, too?"

Whitney nodded.

"Where is he now?"

"He stayed in Waco. I was going to meet up with him after the crash."

"Where?"

"Two Street."

Carter and Jackson both smiled. Two Street was Waco's all but illegal district where gambling and prostitution existed seemingly outside the law. The self-appointed Athens of Texas, replete with a university and numerous churches, somehow managed to have a district where prostitution thrived despite local laws to the contrary.

"It's been awhile since I've been there," Jackson said. "Time to return."

Jessica finally spoke up. "What about my father? Where is he?" Her voice took on a plaintive quality.

All eyes turned to Whitney. He held up his hands in defense, his eyes darting to Jackson. "Look, I don't know nothing about no dead guy. I was only asked to open the crate and help the man inside open the third crate."

"What was in the third crate?" Carter asked.

"That's the thing." Whitney grew pensive. "There wasn't anything in the crate. He got very, very upset, even accused me of taking it."

"Did he say what it was?" Jackson asked.

"No. But he pistol whipped me. That's how I got this bump."

A curious look came over her face. Then it creased into sorrow and tears. Walsh again hugged her close, giving the lawmen a sympathetic look. "Where's my father?" Jessica wailed.

Carter rested a hand on her sobbing shoulder. "We'll see if Skip Barton has those answers."

"And the ambushers, too," Jackson said. "They can't have got too far. I suspect we find Barton, we might find them, too."

"Why's that?" Whitney muttered.

He never heard the answer. A bullet zipped out from nowhere. It slammed into the side of Whitney's head. The force of the flying piece of lead knocked the laborer off the crate on which he was sitting. The velocity of the bullet drilled a hole through the man's right temple and blew brains, blood, and bone out the left. The unfortunate man was dead before his body landed on the floor.

Carter's mind didn't have a chance to register what his eyes saw before he heard the report from a rifle. Instinct, however, took over. He instantly crouched, spreading his legs for the lunge that would take him to safety. Or so he thought. There was Jessica to consider. A second after the slug ventilated Whitney, Carter leapt forward. His outstretched arms snagged Jessica's waist and hauled her to the floor somewhat unceremoniously. They both landed behind her father's coffin, safe for the moment. She exhaled a small huff when she landed, dazed but unhurt.

Timothy Walsh, on the other hand, remained standing. Carter couldn't see Jackson and assumed the other detective had dived behind the safety of the freight car door.

"Get down!" Carter yelled. His hand snaked inside his suit. When it emerged, the hand held his pistol.

Walsh didn't need to be told twice. He dove behind one of the other coffins. His landing sent up a cloud of dust the plumed around him and sullied his well-made suit.

"Tom?" Carter called. "You okay?"

"Yup," came the response. Jackson had already drawn his weapon. He stood just inside the door and peered around the edge. "Just waiting on another shot. How's Whitney?"

Carter didn't even have to look at the dead man to know the answer. "Gone." He scrambled to his feet, still keeping his body low and behind the open coffin. He glanced over at Jessica. "Are you okay?"

She offered him a weak smile. "It's not every day I get shot at. It's quite an experience. How do you cope with it?"

Carter cracked a smile and arched an eyebrow. "The company of a pretty woman, fine wine, and good food typically do the trick for me."

From Jackson came a sigh. "Unless the shooter has another round being prepped, chances are it's a one-shot gun. It's been more than enough time for him to reload." He moved across the opening as if to test the shooter. Nothing happened. He hopped to the ground. "Come on, Cal. Let's go see if we can flush this skunk out of the brush."

Tilting his head, Carter said, "It's best you stay down, Miss Reed. I wouldn't want you to get hurt and ruin our dinner."

"Dinner?" Jessica said, actually blushing. "Aren't you being a little presumptuous?"

"You tell me," Carter replied, then turned on his heel and followed his partner.

* * *

CARTER AND JACKSON hit the ground running. The gunshot surprised some of the milling passengers, but not all. Out of the corner of his eye, Carter noted that most of the people were more surprised at the ruckus the two detectives were making than the killing of Adam Whitney.

Together, they ran across the thirty yards of open field to the tree line. Both detectives welded their guns, but, as of yet, had nothing at which to aim, much less to shoot.

"Any idea as to where the sniper was?" Carter asked. He huffed alongside Jackson, his arms pistoning through the air.

"Not really," the taller detective replied. "When we hit the trees, let's split up. I'm still thinking it's a lone gunner or else there'd have been more shots."

And we'd be dead, Carter thought as he plunged into the line of trees. He slowed and got his bearings. Live oak trees with their gnarly bark dominated the area, but red oak and persimmon trees were scattered in the mix. On the ground, small shrubs made direct pursuit of the shooter impossible, and Carter weaved in and around them. Dead, brown leaves coated the ground, and Carter's boots rustled them, making a scratchy sound. He immediately halted. Jackson, he noted, had already stopped. Carter slowed his breathing, trying to listen for any clue as to the location or direction of the shooter.

He heard the rapidly disappearing sounds of hoof beats. The rataplan gradually faded away until, after a few moments, distance and foliage all but drowned out the sound of the escaping owlhoot.

Jackson came up to Carter. Irritatingly, Jackson seemed not to be winded. Both men were all but the same age, with Carter a year older than Jackson's twenty-five. Both men led an active lifestyle, but Jackson's time on his father's ranch conditioned him better for long sprints against enemies.

"See anything?" Carter asked.

"Just a color," Jackson replied. He still trained his eyes at the fleeing quarry. "Whoever it was wore a green shirt."

"Green shirt?" Carter's teeth ground together, his mouth forming a thin line. "Are you sure?"

"Pretty sure. You don't often see the color green riding a horse and being worn by a man that just killed our prime witness." He stopped and turned to Carter. "Why?"

"Because a man wearing a green shirt killed Elmer Osgood."

Jackson nodded. He and Carter had a relationship built on trust. Over all their cases, a few times, one man or the other had an ax to grind against someone. By silent consent, that man would be allowed to see their quarrel with the bandit or criminal to the end. Most of the time that ended up being jail. Other times, not so much.

"Then we'd best get to Waco as soon as possible," Jackson said. "I'm thinking we need to meet up with the Man in Green and see what he's got to say."

Carter remained silent.

5

A FEW HOURS after the excitement, other railroad men arrived from Waco in a single engine and tinder plus four passenger cars. Other engineers gathered around the derailed train, assessing the damage and arguing how best to right the train and get it back on track. Representatives of the railroad company, however, went out of their way to apologize to the passengers for the delay, assuring them that the blockage would be fixed with all due speed and that they'd get to their destinations as soon as humanly possible.

All Calvin Carter and Thomas Jackson cared about were the horses. After giving up the chase for the mysterious marksman, they had corralled the telegraph man to tap into the line and send another message. Specifically they asked for a couple of good horses be sent with the relief train. They knew from experience had they waited to return to Waco with the rest of the passengers, their quarry might be long gone.

And Skip Barton would be dead.

Now they stood looking at the two horses the railroad had provided. Carter deferred to Jackson and let his friend select his horse first. Jackson had the more discerning eye for all animals, a direct result of his formative years raised on a ranch. Both men considered it something of a lark that the real Texan knew horses only by color while the New York transplant knew more. Jackson took the gelding with steel dust gray fur. The beast sensed Jackson's authority and nearly came to him on her own. That left the roan for Carter. A good animal, the roan was brown and pawed gently on the ground while Carter adjusted the saddle.

They had already made arrangements to have their bags returned to the hotel they had recently vacated, the Claremont. Each man only carried a single carpetbag with him on assignments. Carter and Jackson had retrieved their bags and loaded fresh supplies into the pockets of their clothes. Fresh bullets for their guns, cheroots for Jackson and slimmer cigars for Carter. It was Carter, however, who took the time to apply more cologne. The pungent smell seemed out of place there in the country.

"Planning to meet someone?" Jackson grunted.

"You never know whom you'll meet," Carter replied. He looked at his partner. "You know, Tom, it wouldn't hurt if you cleaned up a bit, presented yourself in a more handsome manner. You never know what might happen."

Jackson stopped tightening the leather on the saddle. He shook his head. "Look, I'm perfectly fine meeting women. I don't have a problem."

"You don't have any women so, sure, you don't have a problem." Carter examined his Winchester, eyeing the barrel and verifying the derailment hadn't damaged the weapon. "Say, how long's it been since you've even sat with a woman and had a drink?"

Jackson grunted. Carter knew the answer. Their commanding officer deployed his detectives in a variety of manners. Some men worked alone while other worked as a team. Carter and Jackson were among the latter group. When asked why, Moore would get a glint in his eye and just assure the two younger detectives that their skills were best used in tandem. As a result, they spent a long time together, rarely taking any time off. So Carter knew exactly how long Jackson had gone without the comforts of a woman's company, and that included that special company that only a woman could offer.

Carter smiled and waved the small bottle in the air between them. "Want some?"

"No." Jackson slid his own Winchester in the saddle boot. He mounted the gelding, spinning the horse in a small circle to gauge her responsiveness. He looked down at Carter while he adjusted his hat. "Even though I may sigh and roll my eyes at you, you clearly have that special gift with the ladies. But I don't need your help in finding one. I'm not a charity case. I'm just more"—he paused, searching for the right word—"discerning."

Carter looped a boot in the stirrup and got on top of his horse. He performed the same technique as Jackson. With the horse and rider now familiar with each other, he stopped her movement. "I just enjoy finer things. It's how my mother raised me."

Jackson nodded once. "And this is how my father raised me." He offered his hand in a gentle prodding for Carter to go first. "Now let's go find Skip Barton."

Putting his heels to the horse's side, Carter led the way back to Waco.

* * *

CARTER AND JACKSON APPROACHED WACO, Texas, from the south. The town loomed in their sights for miles before they stepped foot inside the city limits. The mighty Brazos

River sliced the town in half. A good bustling town in the heart of Texas, Waco boasted of the state's first university, Baylor. It was also a hub for many travelers, both on the rails as well as horse and river traffic. It also included a few locales that residents, especially the more pious ones, wished were not included within the city.

The district didn't really have a name, but colloquially, it was dubbed The Reservation. It was a district, just south of the Brazos, where houses of ill repute and other dens of debauchery sat. The city fathers tried to pass laws outlawing the sin of prostitution, but none of them were enforced well. There was even talk of outright allowing the activities to happen, but have them be regulated.

It was to this area that Carter and Jackson headed.

During their ride back, the detectives had discussed where Skip Barton might hide out. It was Jackson who suggested the district, while it was Carter who figured the newly rich Barton might like to show off his wealth to anyone who might like a pinch of the money. That meant poker and women.

The two men, still astride their rented horses, ambled down Washington Avenue. On both sides, businesses, legal and illegal, plied their trades. Citizens walked and shopped, passed the time and said hello to each other. No one gave the two detectives more than a cursory glance, which was just fine by them. The closer they got to the Brazos, however, the type of person meandering on the street gradually changed. Gone were the nicely dressed women and handsome men. Here, men wore range clothes, beat up hats, and shuffled along the street, stumbling over clods of dirt. The smell of unwashed bodies mingled with the horse droppings, providing a pungent odor. Music blared from certain dance halls. Somewhere up the street, a small band played. From another saloon came the sound of a piano.

Surprisingly, Carter realized the instrument was actually in tune, a rare example in the west.

"How do you want to play it?" he asked Jackson.

The other detective steered his horse to a saloon. The words "Field House" were painted on the facade above the open door. Inside, men loudly played poker, the sounds of laughter, yelling, and cheering emerged. The sawdust on the floor dampened each footfall of a heavy workbook. Jackson dismounted and tied the reins to the hitching post. Carter did likewise.

"We could always split up," Jackson said. "Cover more ground. You really think he'll be freewheeling the money?"

"If you got a wad of bribe money, what would you do with it?"

"Invest in a cattle ranch." Carter barked a shot of laughter. Irritated, Jackson asked Carter the same question.

Visions entered Carter's mind: fancy houses, fancy women, fancy wines, fancy clothes. They swirled around, filling his mind's eye with all sorts of happiness. Gradually, however, those images faded. In their place was a stage, red curtains on either side, empty seats ready to be filled with an audience. He sighed.

"Invest in a theater."

Jackson nodded once, his victory complete.

Carter swept his gaze up and down the street. Dusk was in the air, the night coming on soon. More and more men crowded the streets, most of them likely to be ranch hands from nearby ranches or other day laborers coming into town to blow off some steam or spend lavishly on money they would lose come morning.

Off to the left and a block away, Carter caught sight of the Wheeler Saloon. One of the nicer venues of its kind in town, Carter had been inside its batwing doors more than once. "I'll take this side."

Jackson laughed. "Of course." He indicated the Field House. "This is more my speed anyway." He grew reflective for a moment. "You know, she doesn't know everything that goes on in this town."

Carter's mind was already thinking of the woman to whom Jackson referred. A warmness caressed the inside of his stomach. "I know, but she's a good first step. If there's some funny business going on in the district, she'll likely know about it."

Jackson pulled out his watch from his coat pocket. It was a dull brass, years since it was new. On the surface were scrapes and a few dents. He flipped open the turnip. "I got five after six. How long until we meet?"

Carter likewise pulled out his watch. It was silver plated, still shiny. It was one of the few things he owned that once belonged to his father. He cherished it and carried it with him everyone. He made sure his watch matched Jackson's. "Ten. Back here?"

"What if you need help?" Jackson said, smiling at the inside joke.

"What if you need help?" Carter replied. "I'll come running." With that, and a tip of his hat, Carter turned on his heel and crossed the street.

DESPITE THE PULL the Wheeler Saloon had on him, Carter was still a detective and certain steps were necessary. He stepped into all the establishments along his side of the street. Most looked just about the same as the next: some combination of a bar, poker tables, and dirty, sawdust-strewn floors. Right before Carter stepped into a certain saloon with the moniker of Lone Pine, he heard the distinct sound of flesh smacking into flesh. A moment later, a man, his arms pinwheeling in the air, vainly trying to catch his balance, stumbled backward out of the front door. His boot hit the top step, and gravity took over. He fell heavily on his back, the air whooshing out of his lungs.

In the doorway, a large hulk of a man filled the frame. With forearms as thick as Carter's thighs, the man flexed his fists, the corded muscles bunching up under his skin. He was clearly ready for the drunken fool to get off the ground and try again to make his way inside.

Being right next to the man, even Carter faltered under the menacing eyes of the bouncer. Carter tipped his hat and eased past the man-beast.

After a few more stops in other saloons, Carter finally found himself in front of his favorite place in Waco. The Wheeler Saloon was located on Washington Avenue, a long stone's throw from the Brazos to the north. The building was a two-story structure, but the upstairs wasn't the typical layout of many saloons. In many places in the west, the second floor of a saloon was often where the prostitutes would ply their trade. In Waco, city ordinances forbade such accommodations. To compensate and follow the letter of the law, those types of operations needed to be in an adjoining building. Thus, Wheeler Saloon was just that: a saloon.

Carter stood just outside the batwing doors. The Wheeler was nicer than other saloons along Washington or indeed in the entire district. White paint adorned all the wooden exterior. The windows that faced the street were cleaned daily. The floor on the interior wasn't coated with sawdust, instead by dark brown wood that still revealed all the scrapes of boots, but that only added to the allure. The lamps hanging from the ceiling were all cleaned as pristinely as the glass, even though smoke and the general fog that wafted through the establishment installed a faint patina of brown every evening. Even the scent of the Wheeler was unlike other saloons. To compensate for the odor of unwashed men, spilled beer, and tobacco, fresh flowers in pots were scattered throughout the saloon.

A woman ran that saloon, and that was why Carter liked it so much.

He pushed through the batwings and made his way inside. The sounds of a saloon filled his ears. Men catcalled and sang along with the piano man who sat at a bench and banged out the latest tunes. Carter smirked at the few missed notes. He was a decent pianist, a direct result of the years spent with a piano teacher in his youth. Again, it was a conflict between his parents, but, like most battles, his mother won. Not that his father didn't mind losing. Carter was the second son, and, with the burden of heritage having passed to his older brother, Carter was free to follow his own pursuits. That meant piano was in the realm of things he enjoyed and he followed it with a passion.

Off to the left hung a giant mirror. The name of the saloon was painted on its surface in gold. Directly in front of the wall was the bar. It was a large, ornately carved wooden structure in the shape of an L. The wood color matched the floor and that of the walls. Probably ten feet on the long side, it was crowded with men all jostling for their next drink.

As he had noted the other times had had stepped foot in the Wheeler, the clientele here was a bit more upscale than other places. Most of the men wore nicer clothes, many in suits. The men and women currently milling about, talking and enjoying themselves, may have hard lives on the farm or in the city, but they knew to clean up if they wanted to go to the Wheeler for the evening. Carter fit right in with this crowd.

He sidled up to the short side of the bar and waited.

Two bartenders moved back and forth, filling shouted orders from the patrons. One man Carter knew only a Phillip. A tall, beefy man with curly red hair on his head and forearms, Phillip was dressed in black pants, white shirt with rolled up sleeves to his elbows, and a black vest. A black bow tie was around his neck. Beads of sweat ringed his forehead, and he occasionally wiped his brow with one of his sleeves. Carter and Phillip had some good times together, with Phillip having helped Carter on a case.

Carter waited until the crowd around the bar thinned a bit, then signaled the bartender for a drink. At first, Phillip didn't notice him. Only after Carter ordered a whiskey did Phillip realize who his customer was.

"Calvin Carter," Phillip exclaimed in a booming voice. "What the hell brings you by?" He took the towel slung over his shoulder and wiped down the bar in front of Carter. He brought a clean glass from a compartment and placed it in front of Carter. Turning, Phillip reached over and picked up a bottle mostly filled with whiskey. It was not one Phillip and the other bartender were using to fill orders from other men. With an audible pop, Phillip removed the cork and filled Carter's glass with brown liquid. He replaced the cork and set the bottle on the bar.

"Good evening, Phillip," Carter said. He curled a hand around the glass and drank the whiskey in one gulp. The smooth alcohol tasted sweet and malty. It burned its way down his throat and warmed his stomach. Phillip made to fill the glass again but the detective waived him off. "Can't tonight. I'm working."

Phillip's eyes widened. "You're working a case? What is it this time? Thieves making off with money from a bank? Cattle rustlers? Those fat cats who own the railroad make you come and collect money from poor folks who can't pay their bills?" The last Phillip said with a certain sneer.

"No, no, nothing like that." Carter took Phillip's resentment in stride. Phillip had once owned land staked out by his grandfather. But he had trouble making ends meet. When the railroad men had decided to route the tracks through his land, Phillip jumped at the chance to get ahead in his life. The offer the company made to Phillip was less than generous, but he took it anyway. Only later, when comparing prices with other landowners who sold did Phillip learn he could have received more cash. When he voiced his displeasure to the railroad company, he had been told to back off by a few large, tough-looking men who reinforced their message with fists. Phillip backed off, but he had a permanent sour taste in his mouth regarding the railroad.

"You hear about the train derailment?" Carter asked. He watched Phillip's smile light up the bartender's face.

"Sure did. Best news I heard all day."

"You hear about Elmer Osgood?"

"No. The old geezer forget to pull a switch and made the train jump the track?"

Carter waited a beat. "He's dead. Murdered by the son of a bitch who derailed the train." He bit off the words with a certain amount of angriness that he hoped would translate.

Phillip's smile faded. "Sorry to hear that. He was a friend of your father's, right?"

Carter nodded. He swept his eyes over the crowd, taking in as many faces as he could. "I'm looking for the man who killed him. Tall, dark hair, wearing a green shirt and brown pants. I only saw him for a moment before he threw lead at me."

Phillip eased himself down to his elbows, leaning on the bar. "I've seen lots of men come through here tonight, even some wearing green shirts. I try and keep track of most of 'em, but I ain't as good as she wants me to be."

Carter grunted. "I know. So here's another man who may be easier to find. A fella by the name of Skip Barton. I haven't laid eyes on him, but he works for the railroad. Freight car man, so he's probably too disheveled to darken these doors, but he's missing a finger on his right hand. Little finger."

Recognition dawned across Phillip's face. He snapped his fingers. "That rings a bell." He turned and called to the other bartender who was trying to make up for Phillip having stopped serving customers. Nevertheless, Phillip waved the other man to come.

This bartender was shorter than Phillip's six feet by at least five inches. But what this man lacked in height he more than made up for in girth. Stocky would be too kind a word. The other bartender verged on fat. His belly was barely encased in the nearly identical uniform Phillip wore, but the man's gut protruded under the black vest to reveal a line of white shirt above the waist and below the vest. His sleeves weren't rolled up, but were actually a short sleeved shirt, likely the result of the fat arms that filled them. Heavy footfalls followed every step the man made.

He came and stood next to Phillip. "We got thirsty men over there. I ain't got time to just stand around and jaw with 'em."

Phillip said, "Randy, this here's Calvin Carter. He's a detective. Railroad man. Yeah, I know," Phillip said when a shocked look came across Randy's face. "But he's good. He's looking for an hombre without a little finger on his hand. The right? Yeah, the right. I told him I seen a guy like that. Didn't you?"

Randy's gaze turned to Carter. The detective got the impression Randy was sizing him up, almost as if he was deciding whether or not to talk. Carter put on an affable appearance and waited.

"Yeah, I think I saw him. He ain't around here no more. He left."

"Did you see what he was wearing?" Carter asked. "Can you describe him?"

"Why you want him?"

"Does it matter why?" Carter replied. "All you need to care about is that I want to talk with him in connection with the derailment that happened today."

Randy bristled at the insult. "Just wonderin' is all. Don't get in a fuss." He shrugged. "I dunno. Someone like that was in here earlier. Played some poker. Not sure how he did, but I heard him talking loudly. Saying he came into some money, wanted to buy the men at his table a round. Paid with a new bill. I almost didn't take it, but he slipped me another, told me it was just for me."

Carter cocked his head. "Really? You have that bill?" He held out his hand. "Can I take a look at it?"

The muscles in Randy's cheeks flexed. "Does it matter? It's just a five dollar bill."

Reaching a hand into his suit, Carter withdrew his wallet. He opened it and fished out his own five dollar bill. "Since it doesn't really matter, how about you and I trade fivers. The one that man gave you for this one?"

Randy hesitated, but then Phillip intervened. "Come on, Randy. It's an even trade. And I won't even demand a cut of your money."

With angry movements, Randy plunged his hand into his pocket. A wad of cash appeared in his hand. He flipped through the bills before landing on a crisp, new five dollar bill. He pulled it from the stack and threw it at Carter. The detective slid his five over to Randy, who took it, put it with the rest of his money, and shoved the money back into his pocket.

Carter examined the bill, turning it over in his hand. He even held it up to the lamp light. It indeed was crisp, almost as if it was cut and printed that very day. Something gnawed in the back of his brain, and he filed it away until he gathered more evidence.

Carter put the fiver in his wallet and stashed the wallet back in his suit coat. He put a gold eagle on the bar. "Thanks for the help. Y'all's outhouse still out back?"

Phillip hooked a thumb to the back door. "Sure is."

Carter rose and thanked both bartenders. Randy still gave him a stern look that was more wary than pleasant. Phillip had already turned back to the hollering customers. The detective threaded his way through the poker tables. He smiled at the ladies who were trying to convince some of the men that the best way to celebrate their winning poker hands was upstairs in a room. One man, lust in his eyes as he stared at the top of a brunette's dress that barely contained her ample breasts, rose and allowed himself to be led away. Carter kept a sharp eye out at the hands of each player. With such a distinctive trait as a four-fingered man, Carter assumed Skip Barton wouldn't be too difficult to find.

A short hallway led to a nicely painted door. Again, he admired Wheeler's for even keeping the way to the outhouse a classy appearance.

Carter turned the knob and opened the door. Outside, darkness and shadows hid most of the detail. In certain situations, Carter hated exiting a lighted room for if there were anyone in the dark wishing to ventilate him, the owlhoot would have the upper hand. Seeing as how no one was after him, Carter didn't think twice about stepping down the short flight of steps and down in the gloom.

He was wrong.

"Hold it right there, detective." The voice, deep and gravelly, belonged to a man he couldn't see. "And don't go for your gun. I got your dead to rights." All of the noise inside the saloon was drowned out by the distinctive click of a hammer being pulled back and ready to fire.

❦ 6 ❦

SLOWLY, Calvin Carter raised his hands, palms facing his unseen assailant. In situations like this, it was best to play it cool and see what might come from it. The gunman was talking with his mouth and not with his pistol. There was a chance he might get out of this alive.

"Close that door," the mysterious man said.

With the tip of his boot, Carter swung shut the door. Now, darkness enveloped him and his eyes adjusted. He stood in the short alley between the rear of the Wheeler Saloon and the other establishment. Up to the left were the back stairs that led to the adjoining building where the soiled doves plied their trade. Under the stairway was piled heaps of trash in barrels. Down the alley about halfway was the outhouse, the white paint of the wood showing like a ghost in the night. Between him and the outhouse stood a figure, silhouetted against the ghostly visage of the outhouse.

"Okay, friend," Carter said, "now what?"

The man stepped forward, keeping his gun level with

Carter's chest. "You're coming with me. You need to talk to someone."

Carter shrugged. "I'd be more than happy to talk here in the saloon. Hell, I'd even buy your boss a drink and let him beat me at cards. Why don't you run along and tell him that. I know the bartender. I'll get the top shelf whiskey for you."

The man's fist came out of nowhere and slammed into Carter's cheek. Lightening sparks of pain streaked across his vision. He spun from the impact and fell to the ground. His elbow pounded on the lowest step, and he landed awkwardly on the ground, on his left side, pinning his gun hand underneath his body.

Carter shook his head to clear his thinking and vision. He was just about to take his chances and swing his boot and hope to catch the man unawares when another person entered the alley. To proclaim his arrival, this new man cocked a Winchester rifle and brought it to his shoulder.

"I think it's time you left without any new holes in your body," the newcomer said.

Carter frowned in the night. That voice didn't sound like a man at all. In fact, it belonged to a woman.

His assailant paused. No doubt he was thinking the same thing Carter was. This was a woman. Sure, she had a rifle, but it was a woman. He was a man. This would be easy.

Carter squinted his eyes, trying to get a better image of the woman. She stood stock still, feet spread apart. The rifle appeared steady in her hands. The hat she wore obscured even the most cursory image of her face.

"I wouldn't do it," she said. Her voice was clear in the night. From inside, the muffled sounds of the saloon was punctuated with the sound of breaking glass, then an overturned table. It got Carter's attention. It also was the moment the gunman tried to turn and fire at the woman.

The single shot from the Winchester boomed in the darkness. Flame bloomed around the barrel, giving Carter an instant's image of the alley. The woman barely reacted to the recoil. The gunman was hit. He cried out once, a sharp piercing sound that died upon impact with the dirty ground. The sickening sound of flesh, blood, and bone slumping to the ground was one Carter had heard too many times in his life.

Footsteps sounded from inside the saloon. They rapidly approached the backdoor. In another moment, it swung open, sending bright light back into the alley.

"What happened?" Phillip asked.

With his back to the door, Carter couldn't see the bartender. Instead, his eyes were fixed on the woman who had just rescued him. Her light brown hair was combed straight. It caressed her shoulders and matched the color of her leather jacket. Under the jacket she wore a blue denim shirt, buttoned all to the top except the last button, leaving her collar open. Around her neck was a leather thong upon which hung what appeared to be a carved turquoise pendant. She wore corresponding leather pants, the same color as her jacket. The black boots were thick with mud splatters on them. Around her slim waist was slung a gun belt. On each hip was a holster, tied to each thigh. Silver pistols peeked out of the holsters.

Carter's eyes ran down her entire body and then back up to her face. Her chin was smooth with a slight cleft. The lips were full and still in a firm line, having been the outward sign of her concentration. Her cheek bones were high, her nose thin and petite. Her eyes were a dark brown, and they seemed to bore through Carter when the woman relaxed, lowered her rifle, and turned her attention to him.

"Nothing," the woman said. "Just a little disturbance." She shifted the rifle to her left hand and leaned down and offered Carter her right. "Just making sure the dandy didn't get himself shot."

Carter had to make an effort to close his mouth. He couldn't determine whether to take umbrage at being called a dandy or that this beautiful woman had just saved him bacon. He took the proffered hand. Her fingers were rough, almost like sandpaper. The muscles underneath were strong, however, and he found himself comparing the grips of this mysterious woman to that of Jessica Reed. The latter certainly had high marks for skin care, but this woman had the gun.

Standing, Carter brushed himself off. He adjusted his coat and tie, straightened his vest, and, after opening it and making sure no dirt was inside, replaced his pocket watch back into his vest pocket. He picked up his hat and placed it back on his head. He considered himself and the way he looked. It was the way he always looked. Dandy certainly seemed to fit.

"Thank you," he said. He offered her his hand again. "Calvin Carter."

The woman brushed past him and climbed the stairs. "I know who you are," she said over her shoulder. "Mrs. Wheeler sent me to make sure you were unharmed. My job's done. Let's get inside so you can tell me why you're so damn important." Phillip, who had stood mutely in the doorway, pressed himself smaller as the woman eased beside him and walked inside.

Carter dropped his hand back to his side. He offered her back a wide grin. "Mrs. Wheeler and I go back a ways," he called after her. She had already disappeared back in the saloon. He turned to Phillip. "Who is that?" His voice was a mixture of awe and reverence.

Phillip beamed. "That's Mrs. Wheeler's secret weapon. Her name is Celeste Korbel."

"Celeste," Carter said, letting the name roll over his tongue. He kept muttering the name as he climbed the steps and went back into the saloon.

* * *

"Calvin, darling, I hope you are well."

The voice belonged to Viola Wheeler, widow and owner of the Wheeler Saloon. Her husband, Brett, had established the saloon years ago, but a bullet put a premature end to his life. With nothing else in the world other than the saloon, Viola made the unorthodox decision to keep the saloon in operation. A few changes were implemented, the place was spruced up, and after word got out, a different, higher-class of clientele starting frequenting the Wheeler over other saloons. Naturally, other saloon owners didn't take kindly to Viola's new style of establishment. It took business from them. Rougher men were gently or none too gently encouraged to spend their money elsewhere. When things got ugly, those hard cases would be shown the door, the front steps, or even the dirty street.

A certain number of saloon owners banded together to try and show Viola just how business was run in this part of Waco. They rounded up some men from out of town and hatched a plan to take down the Wheeler and its owner. Those outlaws tried. They failed. It turned out local law enforcement enjoyed having a place like the Wheeler in town. It brought in more money. Folks traveling to and from anywhere in Texas would likely stop by the Wheeler just to see if its reputation was earned. Most of the time, these travelers left impressed. Word got out. More folks came to the Wheeler. They brought their money, and everyone was happy.

Especially Viola Wheeler. The saloon owner was now in her early fifties, but she still looked as glamorous as a woman a score and a half younger. Now, as she sat in one of her special chairs particularly placed throughout the interior of her saloon, Carter thought she looked like a queen. Viola's dark brown hair was long, one of her more prized qualities. Tonight, it was curled and wrapped up in a style reminiscent of the photos of Queen Victoria, coral barrettes positioned expertly to keep her curls perfectly coiffed. The extravagant gown was purple and gold, the long sleeves tapering down to dainty hands, the neckline plunging low enough to give a whiff of what lie underneath, but no more. A choker of black lace was around her neck, at the center an ivory charm upon which was carved the profile of her late husband. The skin on her face was smooth and shone brightly under the lamp light. The only sign of her age were the delicate wrinkles at the corners of her eyes and mouth. Thin wrinkles around her mouth was proof that she imbibed in cigarettes more often than she should have. Her blue eyes dazzled up at Carter as he approached.

She held her hand out, palm down, and Carter again had the impression of Viola Wheeler being a queen. Of her own establishment, that was beyond question. He took her one hand in both of his and shook it warmly. He also bent low and kissed her knuckles. The smell of lavender lotion filled his nostrils.

Still holding her hand, Carter looked up in Viola's eyes. "You look as lovely as ever, Miss Viola. How do you keep yourself looking so young?"

Viola was polite enough to blink in false modesty. "Oh, Calvin, you know this place keeps me occupied. As to keeping myself young, well, I think you know the answer to that." She took her hand from his and reached up behind her shoulder and caressed the arm of the man standing beside the chair.

Carter had noticed the gentleman when he approached Viola's throne. The other man was at least ten or fifteen years younger than Viola. He was tall, broad shoulders, with thickly muscled arms that barely fit in the black suit he wore. The silk tie seemed to stretch and strain around his thick neck, and the man kept moving his head in such a manner that Carter got the impression the man didn't always care for wearing ties. The chiseled jaw line was sharp, and a well-groomed mustache and goatee surrounded his strong mouth. The forehead was pronounced with a hard ridge line, accentuated with dark eyebrows. The green eyes seemed to be the only soft part of this, Viola's man.

"Calvin, this is Nicholas," Viola purred.

Carter extended his hand. Nicholas the Giant looked at the proffered hand for a moment, then back up at Carter.

"Nicholas," Viola said, "I already told you Calvin's okay. He understands me. Shake his hand, now."

Nicholas slowly put out his hand and clasped Carter's. The detective expected the hard squeeze, but not to this extent. He gripped hard. Nicholas gripped harder. Carter hoped the strain didn't show on his face.

"Pleased to meet you," Carter said, affecting an affable tone. "How long have you been around?"

That question brought a final hand clamp from Nicholas before the giant released his grip.

"Don't be so boorish, Calvin," Viola said. She pouted her lips and shook her head, giving the impression of a mother chastising a young boy. "Nicholas has been with me just under half a year. He's worked out wonderfully." A curl of her mouth and an arched eyebrow told Carter all he needed to know. "But enough of this talk, pull up a chair and tell me why my girl had to save your ass."

Throughout the entire meeting and introduction, Celeste Korbel had stood off to the side. Her rough leather jacket and pants looked out of place in a fine establishment such as the Wheeler Saloon. So, too, did the Winchester, which she held, barrel up, inside her folded arms. Carter had noticed, however, in the brighter light, just how attractive Celeste truly was, and he wondered what she would look like when she cleaned up and dressed for the occasion.

With Viola's gentle mocking of Carter's situation, Celeste grunted. She made no move to get Carter a chair, so Carter had to walk over to a poker table with only three men and take the fourth chair. He looked around and saw no signs of the overturned table and broken glass he heard from outside. Viola was quite the cleaner upper when things got nasty. She wanted to present the best face possible, and that included cleaning up messes with quick efficiency.

With Carter situated to her right just like a royal court, Viola said, "I hear you're asking after a man without a little finger on his right hand." She leaned over her elbow on the arms of the chair. "Why?"

Viola Wheeler was not only the owner and proprietor of the Wheeler Saloon and all the reputation that it entailed. She also had her finger on the pulse of what happened in and around Waco. In the times Carter had visited the saloon and got to know Viola, he had seen sheriffs, marshals, and even Texas Rangers waltz in and ask Viola for help. There was no shame in going to one of the best sources of information in the city. It was one of the reasons Carter had suggested to Jackson he take his side of the street. Carter had history with Viola and he fully expected her to help him.

"You heard about the derailment south of town?" Carter asked.

"I have. Dreadful. Simply dreadful."

"Well, this man we're looking for, he…"

"We?" Viola interrupted. "Who else is with you?"

"My partner, Thomas Jackson. You've met him before. Tall, ruggedly handsome, more cowboy than me." Carter offered a disarming grin. "But not as refined."

Recollection hit Viola and she laughed at a memory. Nicholas the Giant remained mute and unmoving.

"Yes, I remember him. How is he?"

"Fine. No doubt he's rustling up some answers to our questions, but I came to the best source of information in town." He inclined his head to Viola. The owner returned the nod before Carter continued.

"The man we're looking for is Skip Barton. He and another man, Adam Whitney, took bribes to…" Carter stopped, finally realizing how odd the scenario was. He cocked his head, searching for the right words to say, then ending up with the straight up truth. "Well, as best as we can tell, they were paid to hide a man in a coffin, load that coffin on the train, let the man out at a certain time, and help him escape when the train derailed."

Nicholas the Giant's eyes actually moved to stare at Carter. Celeste shifted her feet, giving Carter more of her attention. Even Viola was momentarily silenced.

"Is that all?" Viola said.

"No." Carter's voice grew grave. "Some bandits attacked the train. They made off with this mystery man and something else tied up in a burlap bag. Tom and I took two of them out, but not before one of the train engineers was murdered." He paused. "He was a friend of my father's."

Viola nodded sagely. "I understand." Her eyes went distant, drawing on some old memory. "When you meet this man, what do you want to know?"

"Who paid him? Who was the man in the coffin? And what was in that burlap sack? From what Whitney told us, this mystery man was very upset at finding one of the other coffins on the train empty."

"Then press this Whitney for more information." This came from Celeste. Her matter-of-fact tone indicated that she had some experience with that."

Carter looked up at her. "We can't. The owlhoots shot him before we could question him fully."

She raised her eyebrows, curiosity finally taking over.

Viola waved her hand, motioning for Nicholas to grant her his ear. She whispered something Carter couldn't make out over the din of the saloon. With a curt nod, Nicholas again resumed his position next to Viola.

"Calvin, darling, I think I may be able to help you." She left the silence between them pregnant with anticipation.

Carter saw it and sat up straighter. "What is your price?"

Viola smirked. "A piece of the action."

"What action?"

"The action that'll help me here in town."

Carter opened his palms. "Officially, I can't comment on an ongoing investigation."

"And unofficially?"

"Unofficially, I'm all ears."

Viola opened her mouth, revealing straight, white teeth. "I'm so happy you see things the way they are here. Now, what I'm about to tell you has only one condition."

"Name it," Carter said, eager to move forward with this investigation. Inwardly, he praised himself for coming straight to Viola Wheeler.

"I need you to help me find the son of a bitch who stole my money."

❧ 7 ❧

CARTER SAT IN HIS CHAIR, inside the Wheeler Saloon, amid the cacophony of voices, cheers, jeers, boot scraping and chair scrapings, and couldn't find his voice. He cleared his throat.

"I'm sorry, what? Someone stole your money? From here?"

Some of the frivolity left Viola Wheeler's face. "Not from here. From the bank up here in town. Fleming's Lone Star Bank." Carter's face must have betrayed his thoughts. "Yes, Calvin, dear, I use banks. When you deal with as much cash flow as I do, it's not always safe to keep the money here. So I keep it in a few other places. The bank actually does its job well, except when its been robbed." She spat out those last words in a snarl.

Carter leaned back in his chair. He glanced up at Celeste who still stood. She regarded him with eyes he couldn't read. Even Nicholas the Giant's countenance was something bordering on noncommittal. He returned his attention to Viola. "I don't understand. Why do you need someone like me? What about the sheriff? Hell, what about the Texas Rangers?"

Waco, Texas, was the home base of the famed Texas Rangers. Formed in 1823 by the father of Texas, Stephen F. Austin, the Rangers were the law enforcement group when few existed in the colony of Texas. Over the years, through the Republic years, statehood, Confederacy, and back to statehood, the Rangers' reputation grew.

Viola waved her hand, dismissing his comments. "They're doing what they can, but here's the thing: they've got no one to chase."

Carter reached into his jacket and withdrew a thin cigar. He placed it in his mouth, running his tongue over the end, tasting the sharp bite of the tobacco. With another hand, he brought out a match and lit it with his thumbnail. He put the fire to the cigar, inhaling deeply, the smoke filling his lungs, calming him. He looked for someplace to place the spent match. Feeling Viola's gaze on him, waiting to see if the detective would drop the match on the floor, Carter smirked and place the match in a coat pocket. "So the only way you'll tell me what I need to find Barton is to help you with this bank robbery?"

Viola maintained her steady gaze. "Yes."

"You know, I could just keep doing detective work. Sooner or later, I'd find him anyway. Men like him don't stay hidden forever."

"You could," Viola said, "but then don't you want to do me a favor? Maybe make up for the last time?"

Carter's mind went back to the last time. He grinned, enjoying the memory. "Okay, I think you'd better tell me more."

"That's my boy." She signaled Nicholas. "Please have Phillip bring us all drinks. You know my favorite. Calvin will have whiskey. Celeste?"

Celeste still stood, but her fidgeting gave Carter the impression she was most at home when she was in action. "Whiskey's fine by me." She left and, a moment later, she returned with an empty chair. In a gruff manner, she all but threw the chair into place. It scraped across the floor, nearly tumbling over onto Viola. Celeste managed to grab it before it hit her boss. She turned the chair and sat in it, her Winchester leaning up against her knee.

If Viola noticed, she said nothing.

Nicholas returned with the drinks. Viola's drink of choice was red wine. The rest of them, including Nicholas, enjoyed whiskey. Carter sipped his drink and wasn't surprised to discover it was the top shelf.

"Okay," he said, "tell me."

Celeste held up her hand. "Hold on." Her voice was laced with irritation. "Why him? What makes him so damn important?"

Before Viola could respond, Carter jumped at the chance. "Well, I've dealt with few bank robbers seeing as how I'm a railroad detective, but I've read reports. Hell, I've even talked with thieves in prison. I call it research. I like to learn about my adversaries as much as I can. Patterns develop, patterns that can be used for other cases. There was one time when I singlehandedly stopped an entire group of outlaws. They were so surprised that I was already at the train depot that I got the jump on them. My partner and I arrested them all." He shrugged. "Well, we arrested all but two. Those men," he paused for effect, "didn't need any irons."

He glanced over at Celeste. There was a fury in her eyes, an impatience that bordered on contempt. He cocked a corner of his mouth up. "Besides, if I'm reading your boss correctly, and despite my chagrin she is offering to deal with me only in exchange for helping you, I have one asset you or any of the lawmen here in town don't possess."

"And what's that?" Celeste said, her tone mocking.

"No one knows I'm here. Sure, they may figure out I'm here for the derailment, but I can certainly poke around, see what folks are saying. Did you know my other profession is an actor? I can impersonate anyone and infiltrate anyplace." He hefted his glass and drained the rest of the whiskey. While keeping his gaze locked on Celeste's deep brown eyes, Carter said to Viola, "Tell me why you think I'm uniquely qualified to help you."

Viola actually applauded Carter's little speech. "That's the Calvin Carter I know. Bravo. You really ought to do more on stage. You've really got a gift."

"I still do," Carter replied. He turned his attention back to Viola, but not before raking his eyes across all of Celeste. Here in the bright light of the saloon lamps, and despite her rugged clothes, Carter could see the beauty of the woman. He wondered about her story and how she came to be in the employ of Viola Wheeler. "But now, your money."

"Yes, yes, down to business. A large majority of the cash I make I deposit downtown. It's the Long Star Bank, just over the river. I know the owner. His name is James Fleming. He's a good man, but a penny pincher. He rarely spends frivolously, except on his house and his wife. She spends more of his money than he ever does. Anyway, he's quite thorough when it comes to his business. He prides himself on being one the best bankers in town. He socializes with all the rich people in town, of which I am one." She batted her eyes demurely.

"Naturally," Carter said. "Tell me, how well do you know him? Does he ever make his way down here?" He winked.

Viola gave a noncommittal answer. "From time to time,

everyone in town comes here, even if they don't want to be seen here." She drank off some of her wine, letting Carter draw his own conclusions before she continued.

"It was just this morning when James got to the bank. It's his routine, so I've been told, to check all the doors before unlocking the front door. His son, a tall young man who is also named James, although he's a junior, accompanies him. Both father and son carry a gun. For protection. James opened the front door and made his way to the safe, there in the center of the lobby. It's huge, one of the new ones out of Chicago. It's a centerpiece of the lobby. James likes to show off the bank's wealth, including my money. There's even a large glass window in the bank so that anyone passing by can revel in the cash inside the safe."

"James opened the safe this morning and swung open the large door. As his son tells it, the cry of anguish his father uttered at seeing the shelves of the safe empty was a sound not of this earth. The elder James actually fainted and knocked his head on one of the desks. Poor man needed stitches to close up the gash. Be that as it may, the younger James rushed to get the doctor and tell the sheriff about the theft."

"What did the sheriff find?"

"Nothing. Not a damned thing. Nothing of any value was left inside the safe. He checked the doors and locks. He found a few scrapes on the back door and he thinks someone picked the lock overnight and stole everything."

Carter held up a finger. "That means the robber not only picked the lock of the bank's door, but also the safe?"

"You catch on quick, Calvin, dear."

Carter smirked. "Always. So why haven't there been any posses or arrests?"

Viola held up here hands in resignation. "Who the hell are they gonna arrest? It's like a ghost robbed the bank and

stole my money." The ferocity in her voice was one Carter
had experienced only a few times.

"Where is the sheriff on his investigation?"

"That's the thing. He doesn't know where to start looking. Sure, he and his deputies rousted some of the boarding
houses in the bad part of town. Stormed the Amos stables
down near the railroad station. Caused quite a ruckus. But
there ain't been nothing to find. It was like my money just
vanished."

Carter chewed on his inner lip, thinking. He and
Jackson were on the way back to Austin to get their next
case. The two detectives took the derailment as license to
make it their next case. They had been so fixated on finding
Skip Barton, especially after Adam Whitney was killed, that
neither of them had bothered to telegraph their
commanding officer, Jameson Moore, to let him know what
they were doing. Carter had been through more than a few
situations where it was better to ask forgiveness than
permission. He had silently made the pledge not to telegraph Moore at least until the next day. The derailment
itself was enough to delay the trains down to Austin
anyway. Why not look into the situation and maybe find the
culprits. Carter thought to it as preemptive thinking. Moore
might see it differently.

Now, this other situation came to his attention. Carter
knew he and Jackson could find Barton. Of that, he had no
doubt. But if Green Shirt was after Barton, then Carter and
Jackson had to get to Barton first, make him talk, maybe
even put him in protective custody, anything to ensure he
lived long enough to identify Green Shirt. Jackson
preferred investigations that were of their own accord,
following leads the two detectives found themselves. Carter
could see things in another light. He disliked the word

"shortcut" but that seemed to be the situation here. If there was any way he could find Barton quicker, he'd take it.

"Okay, I'll take a look, see what I can uncover."

Celeste let out a bark of a laugh. "So predictable."

Carter shrugged. "What? I'm doing your boss a favor."

"Calvin, dear, thank you. I have your word, now. Don't I? You won't leave Waco without helping me?" She held out her hand.

Carter took it in his, sealing the deal. "You have my word."

"Good." To Celeste, she said, "Show him."

With a smirk that would look precious on the Cheshire cat, Celeste tapped Carter's shoulder. She half turned him, her strength surprising him. She pointed.

He followed her line of sight. She indicated a man over near the front windows. His back was to the window. He was grinning from ear to ear, a lit cigarette dangling from his lips. A derby hat hung precariously on the back of his head. The dirty blonde hair curled underneath, revealing a receding hairline. The face was full of curling sideburns that linked to the mustache. The man laughed as he threw some more chips into the center of the table. Even from this distance, Carter could make out only four fingers on the man's right hand.

He sighed. He turned to Viola. If Celeste's grin was that of the Cheshire cat, then Viola's was the cat's mother.

They had swindled him.

"Skip Barton," Celeste said. "Get to work."

8

CALVIN CARTER GAVE Celeste another full look. He was now the closest he had been the entire evening. Her grin revealed white teeth behind lips that, now upon closer inspection, were fuller than he had realized. Naturally, he began to wonder what it would be like to kiss those lips. Somehow, his face must have given away his thoughts, because those lips ceased grinning and curled in to a snarl.

"What's the great detective gonna do now?" Celeste muttered. Her eyes now reflected the fierceness in her voice.

Despite his wandering mind, Carter already had an idea. He winked at her. "Beat him."

"What?" Celeste said. "You can't do that in here."

"Watch me."

Carter stood, patting her shoulder. It was his first time to touch her voluntarily. Under the thick leather of her jacket, he felt a strong shoulder blade and muscles. She jerked her body out from under his touch. Part of his mind found him undressing her. The other part was back to business.

He took in more of Skip Barton's surroundings. Numerous poker tables lined that half of the saloon. Every player was a man, more or less dressed up for the evening. Some tables only had players wearing suits, others had shucked their jackets and hung them over the backs of chairs. Smoke from smoldering cigars and cigarettes, either in ashtray or between lips, wafted up to the ceiling, collecting in a gray fog. Loud voices punctuated the room. The piano player banged an in-tune piano. Carter recognized the song. It was a popular, rousing tune from the previous year.

Carter walked over to the table where Barton was playing. He kept his focus on his quarry, but also noted the three other men at the table. The two he could see seemed like men of roughly equal station to Barton. Both were in shirt sleeves, rolled up to the elbow. The shirts likely had been washed within a few days or so, for they still showed signs of being pressed. Ties were loosened, and wide-brimmed hats shoved back on their heads. The man to Barton's left was smaller, almost meek looking. The closer Carter got, the more he realized that man was older, maybe north of fifty. Gray hair dotted both his beard and head. The man to Barton's right was about the same age as Barton, somewhere around thirty. Thick, beefy, and with sunburns on his forearms but not the top of his forehead told Carter this man worked outside, no matter how well he cleaned up.

The man whose back was to Carter proved more difficult to read. The man's shoulders appeared strong under a brown jacket. The man's hat obscured his face, even from a profile. Carter glanced at the pristine glass window and caught sight of this other player in the reflection. The glass, while fine, still offered only a wavy impression of this fourth player, but something familiar about the man's face triggered a memory. Nevertheless, Carter kept moving forward.

Now, he took note of the winnings in front of each man. The old man had only a few red chips stacked neatly in a stack. The sunburned man had more than triple the old man's, while Barton had the most of all. With another few steps, Carter made out the chips of the man whose back was to him. That man had a stack nearly as much as Barton. He saw a way into the game.

He reached in his jacket and pulled out his wallet. Doing a little quick math, he calculated the amount the old man had. Carter withdrew enough money to cover the chips and doubled it. He put his wallet back in his pocket. Then he put on his most gregarious smile.

"Well, now, old timer, it looks like you could use a little rescuing. Why don't you let me buy you out while you still have chips enough to pay for some drinks? Plus a little extra." He extended the folded bills between his fingers, waving them in the air to get the old man's attention.

At the word "old timer," the old man's attention jerked up from the game and to Carter. His eyes were red rimmed and bulging. Honestly, he looked scared. His shaking hand seemed barely to hold the cards. He took a look at the money Carter was offering, then back at his hand.

"Why don't you just fold and walk away," Carter persisted. "You'll end up walking away with a profit."

Barton and the sunburned man each finally reacted to Carter's proposition. "You can't do that," the sunburned man said. "It's an honest game in here."

"I aim to keep it honest," Carter replied coolly. "I'll take his chips and continue." He indicated the rest of the room. "Besides, most every table is full up and I'm itching to play. I want to see just how good I am, and I figured I'd help someone along the way."

"Can you pay?" Sunburned Man said.

"Does it look like I can pay?"

Barton cleared his throat. His cheek twitched. His eyes darted to the fourth man who hadn't moved an inch upon Carter's approach. Hesitantly, Barton grabbed his glass and brought it to his lips. He was surprised to find it empty. Looking at the glass like he had never seen such a thing before, he raised it over his head and called to the bar. "More whiskey over here."

"What do you say, old timer?" Carter said. "Want to still have some money when you go to bed tonight. You can even tell your wife you won. She wouldn't be the wiser and she might even reward you in the special way only wives can." He winked.

The old man snatched the money from Carter's hand. He threw his cards face down on the table and stood abruptly, the chair scraping across the wooden floor. He was about Carter's height, but maybe only half his weight. His clothes hung on his body, showing the man even more frail than Carter had assumed. When the man spoke, his breath reeked of whiskey and cigars.

"You got a wicked sense of timing, young man. I was on a streak of bad hands. But I think my luck just came in. Have at it," he said, indicating the chair. "They're wickedly good players, but this one," he pointed at the fourth man, "this one is really good." He cackled, and his laugh turned into a cough. He hacked, spat on the floor, and walked to the bar, laughing all the way.

Carter had already forgotten the old timer by the time the detective had angled the vacated chair. He nodded to Barton, and then to Sunburned Man. "My name's Calvin Carter. Mind if I sit it."

Sunburned Man huffed once. "You bought it. It's all yours. My name's Sidney."

Barton was momentarily distracted by the approach of Philip the bartender. He carried a tray upon which were four glasses, each filled with whiskey. He replaced all the empty glasses, then left. Barton took his new glass and emptied the contents in a single gulp. Only after that did he say his name to Carter.

The detective sat and finally had a chance to get a peek at the fourth man. His stomach did a flip when he saw who the other man was.

Thomas Jackson.

HIS PARTNER GAVE Carter a level stare that, to the other two men at the table probably came off as healthy wariness for a new opponent. But Carter knew his partner's looks so he knew the emotions behind Jackson's calm facade.

Jackson was going to kill him. Or, rather, chap his hide when this little excursion was over.

It took a moment for Carter to compose himself. He angled his head at Jackson. "Sir. And you are?"

"Jackson," Jackson said. He said it without much emotion. "And what do you do?" Again, his voice spoke volumes.

"I'm just traveling through town," Carter said. He pulled out another cigar and lit it with a Lucifer. "I'm an actor down in Austin."

"Actor," Jackson said with a combination of derision and skepticism. "So you're not worth much are you?" He said the words to Barton and Sidney. Jackson laughed and the other two men joined him.

"You'd be surprised what an actor can do. In fact, there was one time, down in Galveston, when I gave such a fine performance of Shakespeare's Henry the Fifth that the papers said I should make my way up to New York."

"Why didn't you go?" Jackson said, sarcasm dripping from his voice.

Carter shrugged. "I dunno. I've heard not much good comes from New York." Without missing a beat, he went on. "What's the game," he said to Barton.

"Five card draw. Ante's a dollar." He chuckled. "You only have seven. We'll see how long you last."

Carter shrugged. "You never know."

The deal from Sidney. He shuffled the cards and dealt five to each man. Carter picked his up and fanned them out. Not great, but a pair of sevens looked back at him. The rest were trash.

"So," he said to Sidney, "what kind of work do you do?"

"Rancher. Own quite a few acres out west of here. Big enough to let me come into town and win some extra cash."

"Nice, nice," Carter said. He thought about asking Jackson just to see what the other man would come up with. In many of their cases, Carter drew on his acting chops often. He could weave a tale so convincing that his mark would have no choice but to believe him. Jackson, on the other hand, wasn't so adept at subterfuge. He was a good detective, believed in following leads wherever they led, even shaking down some folks who needed answered jarred loose, but "play acting" as Jackson dubbed Carter's penchant for drama, was not his thing. In the times in which it had been necessary, Jackson was competent, but not as gifted as Carter.

So Carter turned his attention to Barton. "How about you, Mr. Barton. What's your calling?"

Barton sniffed, then rubbed his cheek. Carter didn't know the other man's tells, so either he had a great hand of poker or he didn't want to answer. "Railroad."

"Oh, railroads," Carter said. "That's some fine work. You know, I've traveled over a lot of this country by rail and I've been in some simply wonderful train cars. The efficiency and professionalism of the men who work on the railroad is second to none, as far as I can tell. I've often wondered what it would be like to work for the railroad companies." He was laying it on thick, but Carter had the sense of a man like Barton who would willingly take a bribe. The detective didn't know if Barton had knowingly helped in the derailment or if it was merely another scheme. "What part do you do?"

Jackson sighed. "Ain't it time to open the bidding? Skip, what's your bid?"

That brought Barton back to the game. He actually shook his head, and tossed in two chips.

Carter took Jackson's interruption in stride. "Forgive me, but I just love knowing how other men do their work. Funny thing, no one really asks me the same thing."

"That's cause no one really cares how an actor works," Jackson grumbled.

Carter had to hand it to Jackson: he was selling it like a pro. "You don't have to denigrate other men's professions. We each have our role to play on this great earth." He picked up two of his remaining chips and toss them on the pile. "What do you do?"

Jackson didn't meet his gaze. "Cattle puncher." He threw two chips into the middle of the table. "I'm sort of between jobs."

"Well," Carter said, "maybe Mr. Sidney can give you a job. I bet he'd like to relax a little knowing someone of your caliber is looking after his horses. Ain't that right, Mr. Sidney?"

Sidney put in his chips. "Got all the work I can handle.

Don't got room for more." To Barton, he said, "How many?"

Barton raked his eyes over his cards, calculating the odds. He pulled out some and laid them face down on the polished wooden table. "Two." Sidney slid two new cards off the top of the deck.

"Holy cow, Mr. Barton," Carter said, "you must be holding some great cards. I'm actually taking three." He laid down his cards and received threw new ones. He was rewarded with a pair of deuces. Two of a kind, seven high. "What kind of work do you do for the railroad? Engineer? Oh, did you hear the dreadful news about that train derailment? Horrible. I hope no one was hurt. Do you have to go down there and help?"

Barton grunted. "Naw."

"But you work for the railroad. Don't y'all help when something like that happens?" Carter dragged on his cigar and blew a smoke ring up to the ceiling.

"Naw," Barton repeated. "I'm more in shipping and receiving. Look, I'm here to stop thinking about work. Let's just play and drink."

"Here, here," Jackson said. "Enough of that kind of talk, you dandy." He put emphasis on the word "enough" that Carter got the message. Idly, Carter wondered how Jackson had found his way here. "I'm only taking one," Jackson said. He kept his face neutral and he discarded, then accepted a new card.

"One card," Carter said. "This doesn't look good for me."

"If you don't stop yer yammering," Jackson declared, "it sure will be."

Carter winked at Barton and Sidney. "Guess I'll shut my mouth." He stayed quiet long enough for Sidney to announce he, too, was taking three.

He also remained mute while Barton looked over his cards and made his bet. With a clear dare in his voice, Barton put in five chips. "I bet five."

Five was all Carter had. He had tried to draw Barton out for a conversation, but the railroad man was having none of it. The detective played for time, acting like a nervous wreck. He scanned the room. Viola Wheeler and Nicholas the Giant had drifted away into the crowd. Celeste Korbel, however, leaned on pillar, unnoticed by most of the folks in the saloon. She watched Carter's little act with clear contempt on her face.

Carter inhaled once, then stacked his five chips. Together, he slid them to the center of the table. "I'm in."

"That's all you have," Barton blurted.

"It is. But that's okay. I'll be winning this hand anyway."

Barton's mouth dropped open. "You that confident."

"Very much so," Carter said. "No matter what, I've got what I came for."

"What's that?" Sidney asked. He, too, was shocked at Carter's brazen bet of all the chips.

Carter shrugged. "'Fortune brings in some boats that are not steered.' The bard wrote that. I'm just transposing my vehicle to a train. My train's coming in."

Barton shook his head, clearly flummoxed at Carter's words. Jackson merely grunted again. "Don't mind him. He'll be out of the game in a minute." He put in five chips. Then, after a glance at Carter, he slid in three more. "And I raise."

A certain part of Carter was stung by Jackson's move. They rarely competed against each other. Instead, their relationship consisted of a mutual admiration. They complimented each other, Jackson's more skilled ability to ride horses and shoot versus Carter's quick thinking ability and the knack for knowing which way to play a certain scheme.

Every now and then, however, Jackson would one-up
Carter. Perhaps this night was one of those times.

But he never found out. Out on the street, through the
window, movement caught Carter's attention. He turned
and squinted, trying to get a good look at what caught his
eye. Horses were tied to the hitching posts, the beasts
pawing softly at the ground or drinking from the trough.
The light from inside only penetrated the darkness so far.
The other lights from other establishments didn't reach the
front of the Wheeler Saloon. So Calvin Carter never got a
good glimpse of the man whose boots comped on the boardwalk. He certainly never heard the click of the hammer. But
he and everyone else in the saloon clearly heard the
gunshots.

9

THE SHOTS BOOMED in the night. In the darkness outside, flames bloomed from the gun barrel of a man standing in the street. The fire lit up the night in three bursts of sunrise.

The first bullet shattered the glass in the large window directly behind Skip Barton. Shards of falling glass blew inward, cascading down on Barton and the players closest to him, Carter and Sidney. Tinkling of a hundred pieces of broken glass sounded in the moments between gunshots as the glass fell to the floor, on to the table, and on the window sill.

The second bullet thunked into Barton's back. The force threw him forward onto the table. His cards flew onto the pile of chips. His body moved the table and he seemed to be lifted bodily off the chair for a split second.

Carter heard the impact, even as he was diving to the floor and away from the broken glass. He landed hard on his left shoulder, his boots kicking around the table legs and amid the broken glass. Sidney was nowhere near as fast. He sat rooted in place, shock playing across his face as pieces of glass cut his face and hands. Thomas Jackson, on the other hand, also reacted instantly. He stood, his chair pushing into another player at another table. His hand went to his side and his Colt all but jumped into his hand. He brought the weapon to bear by the time the second shot found its home.

The third shot sounded. This time, the gunman hadn't accounted for Barton's body not being in its previous position. That bullet skimmed over its intended target. From behind Carter's field of vision, he heard the startled cry of another saloon patron being struck by the bullet. By now, the screams of the ladies in the room and the cries of the men reached Carter's ears. Shocked as some of the men were, others were already drawing their guns with the aim of returning fire.

As fast as those men were, they were not trained as well as Thomas Jackson or Calvin Carter. Jackson stood in place, his Colt leveled at the open maw of the window. Even with the bloom of flame from the shooter's gun, Jackson wasn't able to get a perfect bead on the man outside. Didn't matter. Jackson thumbed the hammer of his gun and threw lead into the darkness.

Carter pivoted on his back, not even realizing he was crunching glass under his body. His hand plunged into his suit jacket and found his Colt in the shoulder holster. He brought it out by the time Jackson started firing. Staying on the ground so as to avoid any unnecessary ventilation, Carter angled his shots just slightly above the rim of the broken window. He pulled the trigger again and again.

"Shit!" came the voice of a man outside. The firing stopped.

Jackson continued firing, laying down bullets he hoped would find their intended target. Whether or not the intended target of the assassination was Skip Barton, nevertheless, the man was injured and likely dying. Carter stopped shooting. Instead, he reached around the table and grabbed a handful of Barton's shirt. With all his strength, Carter pulled the injured man down to the floor. Barton slid off the edge of the table, first his left arm, then his lolling head, and finally body flopped to the floor. His head clonked on the floor and remained still.

Carter jammed two fingers into Barton's neck. The pulse he found was weak and inconsistent.

"Damn," he muttered.

"I hit him," Jackson called out.

In a flash, Carter made his decision. He got his feet under him, crouching just underneath the window sill. "Get a doctor," he yelled just before he sprang up and leapt through the window.

The assassin's bullets hadn't removed all the detritus from the window. Carter still had to shield his face with outstretched elbows. The broken wood and glass ripped new holes in his jacket, but at the moment, he didn't notice nor care. His trajectory took him through the window, landing on his feet just behind the hitching posts. Falling glass followed him, skittering along the wooden planks of the front of the saloon. He opened his eyes, trying to get a bead on the shooter's position.

New gunfire erupted not from inside the saloon but from a position off to Carter's left. Bullets pinged off the boardwalk, making their inevitable way to the detective. No time to think. Carter dove away from the bullets, rolling over once, and slamming into the water trough. Water sloshed over the sides, dampening his pants and legs. With his gun up by his face, he turned to return fire.

Jackson was already doing so. He had altered his aim to account for the newcomer, who, accounting for the location of the blasts, seemed to be on horseback. But then the shooting ceased. With a muttered curse from

Jackson, Carter assumed he had run out of fresh bullets. The transplanted New Yorker could reload with astonishing speed, but that meant precious few seconds would be wasted. A second later, his ears still ringing from the reports, Carter heard the sound of hoof beats on the dirty street.

"He down?" the shooter on horseback said.

"Think so," came the voice of another man.

"Make sure," the first man's voice said.

"No, wait!" said a third man. He must have been the original shooter since his voice came from the street, directly behind the horses who now were spooked enough to be straining at their reins.

Fresh gunfire erupted, but it was all aimed at the original shooter. A cry of anguish filled Carter's ears and the slugs of lead ventilated the original shooter. One of the mounted owlhoots threw a few more bullets in Carter's direction. It was all he could do to curl into a ball and hope the horses tied to the rail and the water trough were enough to protect him. The next thing Carter knew, the men on horseback whistled at their mounts, and they turned to flee into the night.

"Not so fast," Carter muttered.

He stood, figuring if they were riding away, they wouldn't be shooting. By now, men and women from the other saloons including the Wheeler had begun poking their heads out of doors and windows. Shouts of surprise sounded, but no one dared shoot back at the gunmen.

Carter grabbed the reigns of the nearest horse. He couldn't make out the color, but it was dark. The startled beast's eyes were wide with fear, but a quick word from Carter calmed him. He leapt over the trough, landed on his feet, and backed the horse away from the post. Reigns in hand, Carter's boot found the stirrup and he slid up on the horse. He put his heels into the flanks of the horse and set off in pursuit of the assassins.

* * *

THE GUNMEN on horseback had a good block head start. They had made a beeline up Washington Avenue, heading north. Carter knew Waco pretty well, having stayed in the town often on his cases. With its location in central Texas, the town was often the main rail stop as people headed up to Dallas or Fort Worth or down to Austin and San Antonio. The Wheeler Saloon was located on the corner of Washington and Fifth Street. The owlhoots were heading north to the giant roadblock in their way: the Brazos River. Only one bridge existed over the mighty river. A suspension bridge, completed in 1871, spanned the nearly five hundred feet across. It was large enough to allow both cattle, stagecoaches, and pedestrians at the same time. Before they got to the bridge, the assassins were mostly contained. If they crossed the bridge, he would likely lose them.

Ahead of him, Carter spied the two riders. They were putting their horses to the test, slapping their flanks, hunkered down and riding low. Their silhouettes dated in and out of the street lights that lined Washington Avenue the closer the street got to the river. Carter still couldn't make out any distinguishing features other than dark clothes. A part of him hoped he'd catch up to them and one of them would be wearing a green shirt.

His borrowed horse was up to the task of pursuit, but he was not closing the distance. They still outpaced him by half a block. Carter certainly didn't want to start shooting for fear of hitting a bystander. He was a good shot, but even someone like Thomas Jackson had trouble hitting a target while riding at full gallop atop a horse. Still, with his horse not gaining any on the fleeing suspects, Carter had to do something.

He counted in his head the number of shots he had fired. Three. That left three more bullets in the gun. He didn't know how many he'd need when he finally caught up with them, but that number wouldn't matter if they got away.

Still gripping the leather reigns, Carter raised his gun. The bounding horse swayed his arm up and down. It was nearly impossible to get a good bead on either of the fleeing men. But even if the mere fact that Carter was shooting at them would make them pause a second, he might be able to reach one of them. He told himself he'd use only two bullets, leaving a final bullet in the cylinder.

Carter tried his best to time his arm movements with squeezing the trigger. The first shot sailed harmlessly over the heads of his intended targets. The only way they'd have known he was shooting at them was if they heard the report of his gun over the sounds of the pounding of theirs horses' hooves. Gritting his teeth, Carter took aim a second time. He felt how his arm was moving, getting the rhythm of the motion up and down. He tensed his muscles, slowing down the motion. He even counted off in his head, like a drill instructor, practicing when he'd pull the trigger. When Carter's finger squeezed off the second bullet, his efforts had a different result.

The horse of the man on the left whinnied. It stumbled a step and slowed. The rider dug his heels into the horse's flanks, yelling at the wounded animal. The hind left leg started to limp. The galloping speed drastically decreased. The horse couldn't rear up with fear and pain for that would have put more pressure on the wounded leg. Instead, the hurt horse started favoring the left, angling out of the middle of the street and toward one the buildings.

By now, Carter was rapidly closing the distance. For a split second, he debated with himself if he should slow and reload. He shook it off. Better to just get to the assassin and then he'd deal with whatever came his way.

The wounded horse had had enough of its rider yelling at it and jamming spurs into its side. The beast all but stopped on a dime, lowering its head and neck to balance itself. The rider was caught unawares. He slammed into the horse's lowered neck, flipping forward. One boot left the stirrup. He went flailing over the horse's shoulders, his arms outstretched, hoping to find anything that could stop his momentum. He found only air. With the one boot still firmly shoved in the stirrup, the helpless man pinwheeled to the ground, landing in a heap in the mud. The yelp of pain was Carter's reward for his constant effort.

Whether or not the other rider knew his partner's plight or not didn't matter to Carter in the least. He neared the downed man. This was a moment where Jackson's time on a cattle ranch would have come in handy. All the other detective would have had to do was lasso this varmint. Carter was far from a true cowboy. Besides, his borrowed horse didn't have any rope. Carter would have to do this the old-fashioned way.

Carter let his horse bear down on the fallen man. The owlhoot was likely injured but still conscious. He looked up at the approaching horse, its hooves beating the ground right near him. Instead of drawing his gun and shooting, the frightened man threw up his arms to block the impact that never came.

Seeing his advantage, Carter steered the horse away from the assassin. He reigned in, slowing his horse, but not by much. He got his right boot out of the stirrup and swung his leg around. He rode, standing in one stirrup for about ten yards before he leapt from the running horse. He landed on his feet and kept running, gradually slowing himself to a halt. His borrowed mount slowed as well now that Carter was off his back. The detective still had his gun and its single bullet. The outlaw didn't know that. All he knew when he moved his arms away from his face was that Calvin Carter was staring at him down the barrel of his Colt.

Amid heaving breaths as his chest pulled fresh air into his lungs, Carter said, "Don't move an inch or I'll ventilate you." His grin was without humor.

In the light spilling out from a nearby saloon and dance house, Carter noted the man's features. He hadn't seen a razor in days. Whiskers coated his cheeks and neck. Dirt had mixed with the man's sweat, giving him grooves of mud streaking over his skin. The clothes, Carter noted, were all black without a trace of green anywhere. The man's fingers were stubby, the nails all bitten down to mere nubs. The man's hat had been crushed under his body. He winced at some unseen injury.

"I ain't movin'," he called out. The pain in his voice verifying he was wounded. "I think my leg's broke."

"Then you won't be running away."

Now that the excitement was over, crowds began spilling out into the streets. The chase had gone nearly four blocks, so the noise of the shooting and the hooves got everyone's attention. So there were quite a few folks in range when more gunfire erupted.

❧ 10 ❧

CARTER LOOKED AROUND, trying to find the source of the new shooting. Men and women all ducked, screamed, and started to scattered back to shelter. The thinning of the crowd in the street gradually revealed the other owlhoot on horseback. He had figured out his partner was downed and had turned around. Now, he was charging forward, gun raised.

Another bloom of fire blossomed from the man's gun. Carter dove to the ground, right next to his fallen opponent. He heard the soft chuff as the slug of lead thudded into the dirt.

A thought charged through Carter's mind. The first assassin, the one who had opened fire on Barton, had been injured. His partners wasted little time in deciding he was too much of a liability before killing him. If the other man on horseback had turned around and was coming this direction that meant the injured man now lying next to Carter was in for the same fate.

But Carter had only one bullet left in his gun. He certainly had no time to reach back to his belt, get fresh bullets, and thumb them into his gun. This mounted assassin would put many more holes in him long before that. Even one extra hole would be more than enough.

Then there was the injured man. He, too, cowered the closer his partner got to him. He knew the score. He knew what to expect. For all Carter knew, this man next to him was the very one who had already shot the third assassin.

All these thoughts went through Carter's head in a matter of seconds. He sure as hell wasn't going to go down without a fight, and he still had one bullet remaining. If he died today, he would die with empty shells.

He rolled on his back and brought his left hand and his Colt to bear. The approaching rider either didn't notice or didn't care. He let loose another bullet. The rider must have been a much better shot than Carter because that bullet found a home in the injured man. He let out a yelp and doubled over, rolling on his side and putting himself in a fetal position.

That move also freed up his holster and gun which had been wedged underneath the man's body and the ground. Carter wasted no time. His right hand shot out, grasped the other gun, and pulled it from the holster. The other man's gun was heavier than Carter's Colt, but he didn't have to aim well. Just aim in that direction. His left hand would still be the primary shot.

Carter squeezed the trigger of the gun in his right hand. It roared and bucked. With it being heavier, the recoil also was greater than he expected. Nevertheless, he kept pulling the trigger. The gun fired two additional rounds before clicking on dead metal. The rider, heedless of the bullets being sent his way, was now less than ten yards away. His outstretched arm showed the gun glinting in the nearby lamps.

Not even bothering to cast aside the spent gun, Carter

aimed and fired with his Colt. Another report sounded almost simultaneously. Carter's ears registered the dual sounds, but only after realizing the other shot came not from the rider's gun, but from somewhere else. The rider grunted as at least two slugs found a new home in his flesh. He fell backward, lolled off the rear of the saddle, then flopped on the ground. He didn't move.

Carter sighed with relief. Whomever had also fired at the rider was at least friendly. He cast aside the borrowed gun and holstered his own. He didn't throw a glance over his shoulder at the mysterious Good Samaritan with a gun. He rolled the first man over. His cries of agony piercing the night.

"I'm gut shot," he squealed. He lifted his hands. They were dark with his blood.

"We'll get a doctor," Carter muttered. He sat up straighter and raised his voice. "Someone get a doctor!"

"If he's gut shot," a voice said from behind him, "then he ain't long for this world." The voice was one he recognized.

Carter turned and gazed up at Celeste Korbel. The woman loomed over him, the lamps of a nearby saloon silhouetting her, casting her face in shadow. But he saw her steady hand and the gun still gripped by her powerful fingers.

"I had him," Carter said. "I was the one who shot him. I didn't need your help."

Celeste let out a sarcastic laugh. "You're a southpaw. You're aim ain't nearly as good as mine. Besides, you stole my horse." She whistled a particular melody. The horse which had carried Carter in his pursuit against the assassins gently walked back to Celeste. The beast nuzzled her hand. "Like I said, being gut shot means he ain't long for this world."

The man on the ground screamed again. "I need water,"

he said, his voice growing ever more feeble with the passing seconds.

Carter returned his attention to the man. "Who are you? Why did you shoot Skip Barton?"

"Make sure he didn't...talk," the man said. Even in the ambient light from the surrounding buildings, his face was pale and ashen.

"Why?" Carter repeated. "For God's sake, man, clear your conscious and die peacefully." He shook the man and slapped his face.

The man coughed. Blood bubbled up from his throat and seeped out between his teeth. "I got paid for my silence, too. I gave my word. I can die knowing I kept it."

People had surrounded Carter and the dying man. Celeste stood with her horse. She had holstered her gun and waited. Mumbles from the crowd started to get louder as then quieted as the man's screams went from piercing to whimpering. He was still a man, a dying man, and no matter what he did, he was owed respect.

A few more moments passed and the man stopped moving, crying, and breathing. Carter checked his pulse. Nothing.

"Dammit!" the detective exclaimed. He shoved the corpse away from him and got to his feet. He brushed himself off, righted his jacket, and straightened his tie. He bent down and retrieved his hat, setting it atop his head. With one last look at the man, Carter sighed and turned.

The fist came out of nowhere. It connected with his jaw. He saw stars and nearly lost his balance. He shook his head, trying to clear the cobwebs from his brain. Then he got a gander at whom had thrown the punch.

Celeste Korbel.

"That's for stealing my horse."

Carter squinted, still wincing from the pain of the

punch. Celeste clearly had strength underneath all the
rough exterior. He put a hand to his jaw and verified it still
worked. That was when she hit him again on the other side.

"What the hell was that for?" Carter protested.

"For getting my boss's saloon shot up." She sniffed.

Carter screwed up his face, still smarting from both
punches. "Anything else you're sore about?" He held up his
hands in mock protest.

Turning, Celeste mounted her horse. She looked down
at Carter. "Nice job getting the information from Skip
Barton. I wonder if he's dead already or if your partner—
that was your partner, wasn't he?—got any good information out of him. I thought Miss Viola said you were a good
detective."

"I am," Carter said, standing a little straighter.

"Haven't shown it yet." With that, Celeste rode off back
in the direction of the Wheeler Saloon.

Carter looked around, locking eyes with many of the
bystanders. They looked at him with an odd mixture of
surprise, wariness, and outright curiosity. He smiled, tipped
his hat to a particularly lovely woman, and started following
Celeste Korbel.

SURPRISINGLY, the pianist at the Wheeler Saloon was again pounding the ivories by the time Carter returned to where all the excitement had started. The window was a gaping hole and would remain so throughout the evening, but inside, the party was again in full-swing. Men were already surrounding tables, cards in their hands and drinks on the tables. The laughter of ladies mingled with men's voices as they played, talked, and compared notes about what had happened and what it could mean. Carter pretty much assumed that most of them probably told their friends how much better they could have conducted themselves had they been in the position Carter and Jackson had been.

Skip Barton's body wasn't where Carter had last seen it, although the blood stain was. The stain was large, and Carter suspected Viola Wheeler was going to have a conniption fit figuring out how to get the stain out of the carpet. Perhaps sawdust floors were the way to go, but, then again, men didn't often get back shot at the Wheeler.

The body had been transported across the street to a doctor's office. He had been among the rousers in the saloon and, from what Jackson related, had jumped at helping Barton as soon as the detective let everyone know who he was, who Barton was, and why the dying man was so important. Four men, including Jackson, had taken one of Barton's four appendages and carried him across the street. The doctor lit the lamps and told them where to put body. None of the men had even bothered to look at the dead man lying in the street.

The examination room was small and cramped. Along one wall was a cabinet with glass door. Inside the doors were bottles and other instruments of the medical profession. On the opposite wall hung a print of a lake somewhere in the west. The center of the room was dominated by a wooden table. The legs were of crude wood, but the top was smooth and polished. Barton's body was laid out on top of it. One arm dangled over the side. The man's shirt had been ripped open and left bunched on each side of the body. Barely perceptibly, Barton's chest rose and fell.

After Jackson related to Carter all that he had missed, he said, "How about you? I hear you let one die and another one get the drop on you before a woman took care of things for you." In a voice resembling a stage whisper, Jackson concluded with, "And it wouldn't be the first time."

"I'll have you know," Carter began, "that I didn't need any help. I was perfectly able to take care of things. Besides, I shot first. She fired second. My bullet hit the guy and knocked him off his horse. End of story."

Jackson sucked air between his teeth. "That ain't how she told it." He wore a half amused grin on his face.

"Then she's lying."

Jackson stepped back, revealing the person across the room was none other than Celeste. "Wanna tell her that?"

Carter, momentarily surprised, felt his face flush. He inclined his head. "I hit him," he insisted.

"So did I," she said. "And I got him first."

The doctor, whom Jackson had said was named Teague, cleared his throat. "If we can get back to the matter at hand," he said, chiding everyone in the room. Besides Carter, Jackson, and Celeste, the three other men who had helped hung around, waiting to be the first ones to know the end result. The doctor was a man likely in his forties. His brown hair was still thick and showed few traces of gray. The close-cropped beard was of equal luster. He wore a tan suit with a blue vest underneath. Carter idly wondered if the good doctor knew some of Barton's blood had cast a streak across the pants.

"My apologies, doctor," Carter said. "What can you tell us?"

"This man's alive, but only by the grace of God. The bullet is wedged somewhere in his upper chest. I found the entrance wound but not the exit. A little probing didn't yield the slug. Likely the bullet hit a bone and ricocheted deeper into the body. The bubbling around his mouth indicates that blood is in the lungs." He glanced at the clock on the wall. "Chances are good he won't make it until morning."

Every man and Celeste took the news in silence. Carter broke it. "Did you ask him anything?"

Jackson's retort was blurted out of him. "Sure did, right after those gunmen started making new holes in the wall and Barton. No, Cal, I didn't. The man never regain consciousness."

Carter nodded, acknowledging the stupidity of his question. "Any clues on his person?"

"Haven't checked yet. The doctor's been trying to save him." He moved to stand next to the table. "But I will now." Jackson shoved his hands into Barton's pants pockets. All the contents he retrieved he placed on one of the side tables.

He repeated the process for Barton's jacket, both inside and out. The end result was an odd assortment of things a man carried but seemed rather useless when the owner was dead: a folding knife, a small notebook with a piece of twine holding it closed, a few coins, tobacco in a small sack, and folding papers. The real prize was the large yellowed envelope. It was thick and Carter pretty much assumed what lay inside. Jackson picked up the envelope and opened it. Inside, fresh greenbacks of multiple denominations were neatly stacked.

"Jehoshaphat," one of the men breathed. "How much you figger's in there?" He wet his lips, awed at seeing so much money in one place.

Jackson fanned the bills. "Not sure. Two hundred, maybe more." He turned to the men. "It was bribe money, so don't go telling everyone Barton was rich. He wasn't. He was just guilty. This here's blood money, connected to the derailment. Now, why don't y'all git outta here and let us do our jobs."

The men hesitated, the shuffled out the one door and into the main room and then the front door. Jackson eyed Celeste. "That includes you, too."

Celeste shook her head. "Ain't leaving. This man was shot in Viola's saloon. I'm part of the folks who keep the peace there. So if you're gonna talk jurisdiction, then I got it in spades."

Carter again reflected on Celeste's use of big words. He was highly educated himself, his mother insisting that her second son, who didn't have the burden of heritage and lineage, be free to learn as much as he wanted. Turned out, that was quite a bit. But his reading of Celeste kept being proved wrong. He would have to probe her, find out her backstory, perhaps over dinner.

"She's right," Carter said. When Jackson glared at him,

Carter continued. "She's local. She likely knows more than we do about the town. We could use her."

"Use me?" Her voice dripped with incredulity. She leaned off the wall and rounded on the two railroad detectives. She pointed her finger at Carter then Jackson. "I don't get used. And I'm not asking. Miss Viola has had her reputation tarnished by this incident. She'll want to have a hand in its resolution."

"Fine," Jackson grumbled.

"Fine," Carter said. He meant what he had said, but wondered if Celeste would be more hindrance than help. An idea struck him. "Do you know the other guy, the one still in the street?"

Celeste shrugged. "Haven't had a chance to see him."

Carter motioned for her to lead him out of the room. "Then let's go have a look, shall we?" When she cocked an eyebrow at Carter's gentlemanly gesture, he sighed. "Okay, I'll lead."

* * *

THE BODY of the original assassin still lay on the ground when Carter, Jackson, and Celeste looked down on it. None of the bystanders, who had thinned out considerably, wanted anything to do with it. Down the street, other crowds had gathered around the location of the other two shootings. From what Carter could make out, citizens were taking care to move those men.

The corpse was on its side. The blue pants and black shirt didn't match, but seeing as how it was a nighttime shooting, perhaps those were the man's darkest pieces of clothing. The dead man still gripped his gun. The dirt underneath him was stained dark with his blood.

Jackson took his boot and rolled the man over on his

back. In the light that flooded out of the Wheeler, all three
stared at the shooter. He was young, probably not more
than thirty. His face was clean-shaven. His skin was taunt
over his cheekbones, which had the effect of curling his
upper lips higher on his teeth. Something had happened to
the man's right ear since the lob was gone. The closer
Carter peered at it, the more he realized the wound was a
direct line, almost like a knife had been used to slice away
the lobe. Whether it was punishment or not, Carter had no
way of knowing.

He spied Celeste as she looked at the dead man. She
gave no indication that the sight repelled her. Her countenance was matter-of-fact, like this kind of thing happened
every day. Judging by how well she used her gun, Carter
reckoned there was much more to Celeste Korbel than she
let on, especially after she had shoehorned herself into this
investigation.

"Recognize him?" Carter asked.

Celeste chewed on her lower lip. The sight was one
Carter found quite appealing. "Yeah. Ty Merrick. He's the
youngest of an old rancher, lives outside of town. All the
other Merrick offspring turned out good. Ty didn't. Fell in
with some hardcases, steered him wrong. Nothing the elder
Merrick could do turned young Ty around." She indicated
the young man with her chin. "Now look at 'em."

"Wonder if those other two you took down were part of
the gang?" Jackson said. He put special emphasis on the
word 'you' just to get Carter's ire up.

"Let's go find out," Celeste said. She set off at a brisk
pace. The two railroad detectives quickly matched her pace,
Carter on her right and Jackson her left.

Carter let a minute of awkward silence go by before
starting up his conversation. "So, Celeste, how would you
characterize your relationship with Viola Wheeler?"

Her eyes staying focused on the road ahead, Celeste said, "Employer, employee."

Frowning, Carter said, "That I could guess."

"Good for you, detective," she muttered.

"I think what my partner is trying to say," Jackson said, chuckling to himself, "is how did you come to be employed at her…well, I'm not even sure what word to use? You ain't a bodyguard, you can't really be her own sheriff." He paused, giving her a sidelong look. "Or are you?"

Celeste let a dozen more paces pass before replying. "Viola's Sheriff. I kinda like the sound of that. Rings true. I'm what you call the secret weapon. Well, less so now than before. You see, you've got men like Nicholas who certainly look intimidating. It helps Miss Viola maintain a sense of order inside her business. One look at Nicholas or the others and no man would dare to cross Miss Viola."

"Me, on the other hand," she continued, "I'm something different. I'm what you might call an experiment. Miss Viola likes power, but sometimes she likes to use soft power, power no one sees coming. That's where I come in. Say there's a man who comes in, causes a ruckus, maybe gets accused of cheating, maybe doesn't want to pony up and pay his tab. Other people see him being disrespectful to Miss Viola, but she wants a certain air of mystery surrounding her. Others will see this man leave the saloon and they all expect one of her strongmen to handle it. But none of them leave. Next thing anybody knows, this certain disrespectful man returns to the saloon. He may be bloody, he may not be. But one thing all see is the disrespectful man apologizing to Miss Viola. He makes amends and she either tells him never to come back or forgives him with the caveat he never transgress again." She finished her tale. "I'm the strongman no one expects."

Carter's eyebrows rose and kept rising the more Celeste

spoke. In his peripheral vision, he studied her. Nothing she said seemed a lie or a tall tale. She was genuinely sincere in her place on this earth.

His mind also went back to Viola Wheeler. Her deceased husband certainly hadn't operated the saloon in this manner. What changed?

"Then let's hope we don't bring disfavor on Miss Viola Wheeler," Carter said.

"You already have."

The crowd around the second shooting site had thinned. The bodies of both dead men had been dragged to the side of the street, directly in front of a blacksmith's shop. The boarded up doors indicated he was home for the evening or else didn't want anything to do with the activities on his doorstep. A few people stared at the corpses. One in particular caught Carter's attention.

"Sheriff Briscoe," Carter said, breaking the ice. "How are you?"

Sheriff Harlan Briscoe looked up at the newcomers and scowled. He was broad-shouldered with thick arms that tapered down to massive fists that extended past his long-sleeved white shirt. The leather vest he wore bore the star of his office. The shirt was unbutton at the collar and tufts of black hair dotted his chest. He was slim in the waist, and his pants were tailored. His gun belt was well oiled and both holsters were tied to each of his thighs. The boots were of the same color as his gun belt. The similarly colored hat sat low on his head.

"Calvin Carter," the sheriff intoned, "I thought you left my town."

"I did," Carter said making his way around the two dead bodies to stand next to the sheriff. "But the derailment sent us back."

"Howdy, Thomas," Briscoe said to Jackson. The detective tipped his hat to the local lawman who turned and cast a keen eye on Celeste. "What brings you here?" His voice had lost some of its joviality.

"Always good to see you, too, Sheriff," Celeste said. She remained standing in the street, at the foot of both corpses. "They were part of the group that shot up Miss Viola's saloon. I suspect you've heard about that. Ty Merrick's lying dead in the street up yonder. We came to see who these two were."

Briscoe sighed. "Declan O'Brien and Larry Kirk." He gestured to each man in turn. The man Carter recognized as the one beside whom he had fallen was O'Brien. "What the hell were they doing?"

Jackson cleared his throat. "They were busy killing the only man who knew about the derailment from today."

"I heard about that. You think these two are involved?"

"Yup," Jackson replied. "They done shot Skip Barton. He was one of two men we suspect took bribes to look the other way when some crates were loaded onto the train. Just after the train jumped the tracks, a group of bandits ambushed us. They focused on one of the freight cars. There were some coffins inside. They opened the coffins and got what was inside it. By the time Cal and I got back there, they had made off with...well, we're not entirely sure. But it's certainly was at least a man."

"And something in a burlap sack," Carter chimed in. "And I can tell by the look on your face you're not believing what we said. But it's true. Barton's partner, a fella by the name of Adam Whitney, told us he and Barton were paid to open the coffins a few minutes after the train pulled out of Waco. Whitney did, and he said a living man was inside one of the crates. The coffin even had air holes. Whomever was inside took off with the owlhoots who attacked the train. We didn't get a good look at any of them, but they also carried off a burlap sack. That seemed to be what was in one of the other coffins."

Carter fell silent for a moment. "There's another thing. You remember Elmer Osgood?"

"I got to know him over the years," Briscoe said.

"One of the bastards shot him," Carter said. He bit off the words. "Man in a green shirt. The same man who likely took a sniper rifle to Adam Whitney and killed him, too." He pointed back up the street. "Barton was our only lead."

Briscoe pursed his lips, considering something he wasn't sharing. Coming to a conclusion, he nodded to himself. "O'Brien, Kirk, and Merrick all ran as part of Jeff Taggart's gang. They rarely did anything other than raise a little hell here in town so I could never nab them for anything. But I heard stories. Most of 'em I just chalked up to wayward souls looking for kinship with fellow wayward souls. But Taggart might know something." He spat on the ground. "But robbing trains..." His voice trailed off. "That seems too big for them."

"Know where we can find him?" Celeste said.

"We?" Briscoe blurted. He looked from Jackson then to Carter. "You working with her?"

"No," Carter corrected, "she's working with us. There's a distention."

"That," Jackson said, "and since the shooting started at the Wheeler Saloon, Miss Viola seemed to think she's entitled to part of the investigation."

Briscoe spat again. He itched the back of his neck. His shoulders rose and he stretched out his muscles. Some of his bones snapped and cracked. Skepticism still ran full sway over the lawman's face. He hooked his thumbs inside his gun belt.

"Well, I don't necessarily see it that way. If anybody should tag along, it ought to be me or one of my deputies.

But seeing as it's a train matter, y'all will likely to tell me to butt out." He wagged a finger between both detectives. "Just like y'all did before."

It was Carter's turn to screw up his face. "We had our orders, Sheriff."

"But it is my town," Briscoe replied with some force behind his voice. "I say what goes on here."

Carter waited, the awkward silence becoming more pregnant by the second.

"But seeing as y'all would defy me anyway and just yer own damn thing, I might as well point y'all in the right direction." He turned and angled a hand toward the river. "Last I heard, the Taggart Gang was staying in a ramshackled old cotton gin north of the Brazos. Probably why they were heading this way. You can't miss it."

Jackson tipped his hat. "Much obliged, Sheriff." He started to move up the street. Celeste had already turned as soon as she heard the hotel name.

Briscoe again pointed his finger at Carter and Jackson. "And I don't want you boys shooting up my town like y'all did last time, you hear?"

Carter only grinned. "Who were we to know those men had a Gatling gun? Thanks."

Briscoe put a hand on Carter's arm. "Y'all do what y'all gonna do, but I wouldn't trust her. She's part of Viola Wheeler's little cadre. There's a lot of shit that goes on here that I can't prove, but I'd bet she's behind. Watch yourself."

With a serious face, Carter said, "We will."

☙ 12 ❧

FULL DARK COVERED THE REGION. The distant sounds from Waco echoed faintly in the night. The damp ground gave off a moldy, earthen odor that permeated the air. The humidity was thicker than normal, and overhead, swift moving clouds partially obscured the fading half crescent moon.

The abandoned cotton gin Sheriff Briscoe pointed out was less than a mile north of the Brazos. That gin had been the primary one for the city, but the arrival of the railroad changed the topography of civilization. The tracks had been laid out in a pattern dictated by the company, and this old gin wasn't part of that plan. The owners went bankrupt and shuttered the old structure. Central Texas heat, wind, rain, and snow had done their work on the dilapidated building.

Shaped as an L, the old cotton gin consisted of the main warehouse, two stories tall. Open windows that once housed glass now let in all the elements. One of the windows was still shuttered closed. Abutting on the south side was the shorter, covered area where carriages used to unload the raw cotton from the fields. Immediately next to the unloading dock, at a right angle to the larger structure, was a storage area. In the darkness, Carter couldn't make out if the storage area had three walls or if they had all fallen.

The dark hulk of the gin was in a mostly open area. A few trees dotted the landscape, but by and large, if the three of them were going to approach the gin, they would be exposed.

"See any movement?" Carter asked. One of the few things Carter admitted Jackson was better at was night vision. Somehow, the years out on the range had honed the New Yorker's eyes.

"Nah." Jackson stood next to an oak tree, the denuded branches wafting gentle in the breeze. "But I smell something. Maybe they're in there, cooking."

A few paces away, their horses breathed heavily, softly pawing the ground. After Sheriff Briscoe and directed them up here, Jackson and Carter had woken the old geezer who ran the nearest livery. Turned out that the horses they had rented to fix their previous case were still available. Carter and Jackson were happy, because those horses had proven their mettle when the bullets started flying. The old man, shrunken by age but still vital in his disposition, wasn't as pleased. Despite being harangued constantly as he took their money, the livery owner actually smiled when the two detectives had informed him that they were going after the folks who derailed the train.

"Be sure ya hurt 'em," the old man said. His name was Foster, but Carter kept thinking of him as just the old coot.

"That's not what we do," Carter had said. "We only want to ask them questions."

"We will," Jackson had said immediately afterwards. He had winked at the old man and led Carter out into the livery.

To her credit, Celeste had waited for them. She already had her horse. While the two detectives went to fetch their new mounts, Celeste had gone back to the Wheeler Saloon, presumably to let Viola know the plans. By the time Carter and Jackson had led their horses out of the livery and mounted up, Celeste was there, waiting. In the light given off from the livery man's lantern, her countenance appeared enigmatic.

"We're ready," Carter had said. He knew the way. Any passenger riding the train and coming into Waco from the north could see the abandoned gin from the comfort of a passenger car, but Carter had felt the need to let Celeste lead. He wanted to see what she would do, and if Briscoe's warning about her held any currency.

True to her word, she had led them straight to the gin, halting about fifty yards from the south entrance of the gin. Now, she stood patiently by the horses. When Jackson made him comment about them cooking, she pulled her Winchester from the saddle holster. "I say we just go up there and start asking questions."

"I don't wanna get shot," Carter said. "Maybe they have a lookout?"

Celeste considered the statement. "Last I heard, Taggart's gang had about five, six men. If we took out three of them, they're down by half. There's three of us and three of them. That's even odds." She looked Carter up and down in the moonlight. "Well, mostly even, Mr. Dandy."

Carter was about to take umbrage when Jackson interrupted. "Not now, Cal. You can deal with your wounded ego later. Right now," he said, pulling his pistol from its holster, "let's go talk." He moved from behind the oak and started crouching up to the gin. Celeste brushed past him, intentionally brushing his shoulder a little too hard. His gumption up, Carter started to protest, but then reminded himself of where they were and what they were doing. He snatched his gun from its holster and followed.

* * *

THE TRIO APPROACHED the gin from the south. Directly in front of them was the loading station and the storage area. From that angle, those parts of the gin obscured all doorways and windows. It was effectively a blind spot.

The closer they came to the building, the more detail came into view. The storage area's roof was held aloft only by four support poles. All four walls had crashed inward sometime in the past. Only a thin wall of wood blocked their view of the main unloading door, a large hanging wooden door that appeared to slide open. Over on the left of the building sat a small pasture where the horses that used to pull the carriages full of raw cotton would have rested. Three horses, unsaddled, now meandered in the area, their heads bent low to the ground, lipping at the sparse grass. The odor that Jackson had first noticed grew stronger. Bacon and biscuits.

Faint light flickered through one of the upper windows. It seemed Taggart and his boys felt comfortable enough to have built quite a decent fire on which to cook. They heard the sizzling sound of the bacon frying in a pan. Carter's stomach lurched at the tantalizing aroma, reminding him that he hadn't eaten since a quick bite at the hotel upon arriving back in Waco after the derailment. In a distracted moment, he pictured himself at a nice table, all cleaned and washed, with Celeste sitting across from him. In his mind's eye, she wore a dark blue gown with a low neckline that revealed the kind of breasts Carter imagined her to have. He smiled at the thought, but failed to notice Jackson and Celeste had halted. Carter ran right up onto her.

She shoved him backward. "Get off," she muttered.

He maintained his balance, holding his hands up as his way of apologizing.

"Listen," Jackson whispered, "we're going to split up. Celeste, you take the west, I'll come in from the south through the main doors there. Carter, you circle around to the east and make sure them varmints don't try and sneak away on foot."

Celeste didn't bat an eye. Mutely, she moved away and got into her position.

"Chatty girl," Jackson said. "Think we can trust her, given what you told me?"

Carter's shoulders raised and lowered in the darkness. "Not sure. But for now, I think yes. How are you going in?"

"Loudly."

Nodding once, Carter broke away from Jackson's position. He angled around the unloading area and came around on the east side. He passed a first-floor window, still paned in glass. Pausing in his steps, Carter squinted and peered through the windows. Sure enough, three men all sat on old wooden barrels. Each of them held plates and ate their bacon and biscuits with their fingers. They all wore range clothes that needed a good laundering. At their feet was the fire, ringed with rocks. A metal grate was laid over the rocks and the frying pan and a coffee pot sat atop the grate, over the fire. Carter was about to keep moving when a shadow moved into the gin. It wasn't from any of the three outlaws.

There was a fourth person inside.

Carter looked to his left. He couldn't see the pasture so he had no direct line of sight with Celeste to warn her. He also couldn't make out Jackson's position. Using the internal counting in his head — was he up to forty or fifty? — he assumed his partner was nearing that sliding door. No matter how smoothly the door may still operate, now Carter realized Jackson may have trouble opening the door. Unless he found the regular door. Maybe so. Still, Carter crept closer to the window, making sure to stay out of the light spilling out from the campfire inside.

The shadow moved again. Whoever it was stood opposite the campfire from Taggart and his fellows. The gang was talking to the newcomer. Well, mostly listening. Carter couldn't make out any words. Glancing down to the ground to verify nothing untoward was in his path, Carter neared the window. He changed his angle and brought the fourth man in view.

His back was to the window, but Carter noted the man's wavy brown hair. He also took stock of the man's vest. It, too, was brown as well as the pants. Around one shoulder was slung a bag. Whatever was inside weighed the fabric down. The man's hand was inside the bag. The hand was moving, almost like he was retrieving something from inside. These details Carter's brain registered on a subconscious level. The one thing Carter noticed right away was the color of the man's shirt.

It was a bright green. The same color green as the sniper from the train derailment and ambush. The murderer of Elmer Osgood.

All at once, Carter steeled himself for a fight. He gripped his Colt tighter. He didn't fear violence or fighting. It was part of the job for a railroad detective. Most of the times, he did it as a matter of course. This time, however, he was going to enjoy it.

Green Shirt raised his voice. The few words Carter caught were, "...y'all failed in the simplest way possible. And we can't have that." Green Shirt brought his hand out of the bag. He held a glass bottle. Liquid sloshed around inside. He held it aloft as if presenting it to the Taggart gang.

One of the gang actually laughed. "That the whiskey you promised us?"

"Not exactly," Green Shirt replied. He threw the bottle down at the fire. The glass smashed on one of the rocks, sending the fluid into the fire. Instead of extinguishing the flames as Carter had expected, the fire was fed. A great flash filled the interior of the cotton gin. Carter's eyes, accustomed to the dimness outside, was momentarily blinded. But not before he saw the liquid flames lance up and splash onto the three remaining members of the Taggart gang.

Carter mashed his eyes closed, turning away from the brightness. As such, he only heard the screams of the men as fire washed over their bodies. The high-pitched squeals filled Carter's ears and a part of him felt sorry for them. He returned his gaze back to the window, blinking rapidly, trying to clear the ghosting vision in front of his eyes. Between blinks, he saw what happened next.

Green Shirt didn't stop and let the fire burn his victims. He had drawn his gun and fired. Three short blasts. They came in quick succession, each shot aimed at a different man. In turn, Taggart and his two friends, who had stood and vainly tried to douse the flames over their clothes and bodies, were felled by Green Shirt's bullets. Their bodies spun away, landing in old, dry hay and grass that someone had brought into the cotton gin. The cries of pain ceased like they never even happened.

Carter didn't wait another second. He brought his gun up, leveling it at the window. "Tom! Go!" he yelled at his partner. He pulled the trigger. The first bullet smashed the window to pieces, shards falling to the ground. They caught the light from the fire and dazzled Carter's vision again.

Inside, Green Shirt responded with amazing rapidity. He turned and fired twice at the window. His aim was deadly accurate, and Carter had to slam himself on the ground to avoid being ventilated.

To Carter's left, he heard Jackson's reply. A single shot from Jackson's gun was intended to give him enough cover and surprise to get the sliding door open. Whether it would have worked or not with an adversary unlike Green Shirt would never been known. All Carter knew was that he heard a unique sound. His mind registered it as the sound of a glass container being thrown, the fingernails of Green Shirt raking across the outside of the glass. The next thing Carter heard was another gunshot and the smashing of glass. The detective didn't need to guess what had just happened, for all at once, orange fire erupted over near the sliding door.

Jackson yelled a curse. His body was silhouetted against the rising fire. He was patting his arm which, to Carter's shock, was on fire.

By Carter's count, Green Shirt had fired six times. Unless he had another gun, he would have to reload. Carter stood and pressed his body up against the side of the gin. He peered around the edge of the broken window, trying to catch sight of Green Shirt.

Two bullets slammed into the window siding. Splinters blossomed from the wall and Carter spun away to avoid being blinded. So much for that question. Green Shirt clearly had another gun.

In his approach along the east side of the gin, Carter hadn't seen any horse in waiting. That meant Green Shirt's only avenue of escape was to the north. Crouching low, Carter scurried under the window and avoided any more flying lead. He raced the fifty-foot long side of the gin's wall, his feet pounding in the damp ground. More shouts from the loading bay. Jackson must have been calling Celeste for help or telling Carter to get the bastard. Carter needed no encouragement. He only needed speed.

He rounded the north edge of the warehouse and what he saw seemed like it was Hades itself. A bottle was arcing through the air in his direction. Liquid filled the bottle nearly halfway to the top. A cloth was shoved inside with part of the cloth hanging out of the bottle.

And the cloth was on fire.

A SINGLE GUNSHOT rang through the night. For a split second, Carter thought he would be hit. Instead, the lead bullet shattered the falling bottle, igniting the flammable liquid and cascading liquid fire down upon the edge of the gin, the ground, and Calvin Carter's body.

He dove, outstretching his arms to block some of the falling fire. He was successful in avoiding most of the liquid, but not all. A good amount landed on his left arm and an additional amount on his leg. He wore a long-sleeved shirt under his jacket, made of good, sturdy wool, so Carter didn't immediately feel the searing heat, but his leg was another matter. The hot liquid soaked through almost instantly, bringing with it intense heat and pain.

Carter screamed in alarm as well as pain. His ears registered his scream and picked up something else. The sound of laughter and the rataplan of horses' hooves. Green Shirt. But there was no time for Carter to care about that other man. He was on fire.

He landed on the damp ground and kept rolling. He rolled back and forth, dousing the fire on his leg as fast as possible. He dug his leg deep into the ground, letting it smother the flames with, he hoped, no permanent damage to his leg.

His jacket was another matter. In the effect to kill the flames on his leg, Carter had angled himself upright. That gave the fire on his wool jacket a few more seconds to soak in. His nose detected the distinct odor of burning hair. He cursed again. Finally, he got up on his knees, his leg still smarting from its ordeal, and ripped off his jacket. His gun he had long since dropped in favor of survival. Flames licked close to this face and he turned away to avoid any burns on his face.

The jacket off, Carter balled it up, inside out, dousing the flames. In a fit of desperate rage, he threw the jacket away. He lay there, on his hands and knees, heaving great gulps of air into his lungs, head down, and hair messed and hanging down over his eyes. The ground never looked so good. He stared at the dirt that had saved his life, only realizing, after a moment, that the reason he could see the ground was because the gin was going up in flames.

Carter turned and looked at what the contents of the bottle that landed on the gin was doing. The dry wood sucked up the flaming liquid, igniting it along the way. The fire rapidly spread up the wall. The cross breeze was gently sucking the fire into the larger warehouse of the gin.

In the fire light, Carter looked around and found his gun. He scrambled in the dirt for it. He grasped it with muddy hands and brought it up, looking down the barrel at the area on the north side of the gin. He so wanted to find Green Shirt and put a bullet in him. Forget asking questions. Forget the larger case. Just a bullet in the other man's brain. That would be enough.

Carter found no trace of Green Shirt.

Voices sounded from the other side. After a moment, he realized the voices were calling his name.

"Over here!" Carter yelled. He holstered his gun. He walked over to his jacket and snatched it from the ground. Unfolding it, he looked at it in the light of the fire. Holes were burned through the fabric. Only then did Carter think to look at his arm and shirt. More holes there, and now the wincing pain rushed to his brain. He cursed, this time at the top of his lungs.

Other parts of his brain—the detective part—now took over. They had come up here looking for clues to why the Taggart gang had shot Skip Barton. The lawmen had killed three of the members, and now, Green Shirt had killed the rest. The only reason for Green Shirt to come up here and kill them was to keep them from talking. Well, if they can't talk, then maybe something else can.

Carter shoved his arms back into his jacket. Some of the fabric ripped, but he didn't care. He was going to need some additional protection against the fire for what he was about to do.

Jackson and Celeste, both holding their weapons, ran around the corner of the gin. Their faces showed surprise when they saw Carter walking to the open door.

"What the hell are you doing?" Jackson yelled.

"Investigating in hell."

CARTER STEPPED through the door and into the gin warehouse. The wall to his left was engulfed in flames. The sliding door where Green Shirt had thrown his firewater at Jackson was also afire, but not as much as this near wall. Down the middle of the empty warehouse, various pillars stood like shadowed sentries, holding up the second story

and roof. The large central area was big enough for a
wagon to traverse through. It was down this central area
Carter ran to the bodies of the Taggart gang.

Upon arrival at the gang's campfire, Carter realized he
had caught a break. The firewater Green Shirt had thrown
their way had fueled the campfire, but had run most of the
way opposite where the dead men now lay. Those flames
had eaten away at some of the support pillars near this side
of the warehouse, but they were still holding. The hay that
had rapidly caught fire was all burned up, leaving only
parts of the damp ground. A few wooden slats that served
at the floor was smoldering but not yet fully engulfed.

Carter halted at the corpses. Each man's face had a new
black hole somewhere on the surface. One man now
possessed a nice, clean hole in the forehead. He must have
been the first. The other two, who had been in the throes of
agony with the fire—just as Carter had been—had bullet
holes at odd angles. Only half a cheek remained on one
while the third man had no jaw. In its place was a gaping
maw of dark blood and brains.

Avoiding the gruesome visage as much as possible,
Carter started shoving his hands into the pockets of the
three dead men. Whatever was inside them, he grasped and
then put into his own pockets. There would be time later to
assess what he had found. At this point, time was not on
his side.

The high roof of the warehouse also gave Carter an
additional precious few seconds. All the smoke was rising
up, to the second story, and then snaking out into the night.
Little smoke wafted around on the ground level. But the
heat was rising. Gentle creaks of old wood eroding under
the unrelenting fire told him that smoke was not his biggest
threat. Collapse of the structure proved a greater problem
than anything else.

He moved to the second man and repeated his search. Something sharp pricked his finger. He winced, muttered yet another curse, and continued. The last man also wore a jacket so he had extra pockets to pillage. Carter tore through the man's jacket pockets and shoved everything he found inside his own jacket pockets. A certain part of his brain registered the feel of shapes to their actual identity. A folding knife. Tobacco papers. Coins. This jacketed man had a wad of something that resembled paper inside his pocket. It didn't take a genius to figure that was money. In Carter's experience, gang leaders accepted payment for their services and distributed the winnings to the other members of his group. This was likely Taggart.

Finished with Taggart's jacket, Carter had to angle the body up to get into the gang leader's pants pockets. The heat was rising. A sharp crack sounded and Carter looked up to find the source. One of the pillars had broken off. The wood visibly sagged under the weight of the second story landing. More creaks filled his ears. The crackling of the fire was sounding louder by the second.

Carter determined he had enough. He tried to pull his hand out of Taggart's pocket. It wouldn't budge. Carter yanked harder, but to no avail. Another pillar cracked. Only then, after a quick glance up to the flaming wall and back down to the corpse did Carter realize that Taggart's body had sagged against his hand. Whatever Carter held in his fist was preventing him from pulling out his hand. Not knowing what it was and, at the moment, not caring, Carter released the object and withdrew his hand. He paused only a second, allowing his brain to think about the shape his fingers had caressed. He mulled it over, and he arrived at nothing, at least nothing he could come up with in the midst of the inferno.

He heard more shouts. Carter looked around for the

source. Jackson and Celeste were standing just outside some windows on the western wall of the gin, the side that was not on fire. Jackson was gesturing wildly for Carter to escape with his life. Even Celeste, cool and composed up until now, was waving for Carter to get out of there.

Turning back to Taggart, Carter noticed the man wore a knife on his belt. Carter unsheathed the blade and, adjusting his grip, brought the knife down along Taggart's pants pocket. The sharp blade easily sliced through the fabric. Carter ripped the pocket the rest of the way and opened it to reveal what was his hand had found.

Another pillar broke. The wood from the second story groaned under the weight. Sharp cracks filled Carter's ears. It was now or never.

He grabbed the object in Taggart's pocket, stood, and started running to the west. He tossed aside the knife along the way. In all his life, Carter didn't think he had run as fast as he did that night as the flaming cotton gin started to crumble. No door was built on the west side, only windows. Surprisingly, some still had panes of glass in them, some didn't. He made a beeline to the one where Jackson stood. Thankfully, this window was free of anything other than freedom.

With a mighty leap, Carter jumped and dove head first through the window. He sailed cleanly through the window. His effort was so successful that his momentum carried him well past the gin itself. He landed and curled into himself, allowing his body to roll away from the burning structure. He came to rest near the pasture fence. He sat there a moment, breathing deeply, letting his body adjust to the fact no more terror threatened it. Jackson and Celeste ran up to him. Jackson knelt down at his side, staring expectantly in Carter's face.

"Are you okay?" his partner asked. Worried tension filled his voice.

Carter nodded, not yet ready to speak. After a moment, he said, "Yeah."

That was when Jackson slapped Carter across the face. "What the hell were you thinking? You could have gotten yourself killed."

"Clues, my friend," Carter said. He smiled despite the sharp pang across his cheek. "I was being a detective."

"You were being a bastard," Celeste said. She regarded him from down her nose. "But a brave bastard. And a damn nice piece of running. Maybe Miss Viola was right about you."

Carter stood, brushing off his clothes, and adjusting his ruined jacket. "What's that?"

"That you're a bulldog. When you get a hold of something, you never let go."

Beaming, Carter said, "Why, Miss Celeste, I do believe you just paid me a compliment. That would be a first."

"A likely last," she replied. Nevertheless, Carter saw something different in her eyes. They stood looking at each other for a few awkward seconds.

Jackson cleared his throat. "So, what did you find?"

"We'll have to get back to our hotel and have a look, but the last thing I got was this."

He opened his palm. In the light of the burning gin, now pluming up into the night, a small pouch was visible. It was tan cotton with a drawstring. The pouch was heavy in Carter's hand. It also jingled. With his other hand, he worked the end of the bag open and spilled the contents onto his palm.

Gold double eagle coins dazzled in the firelight.

❧ 14 ❧

BY THE TIME Carter and Jackson returned to the McLelland Hotel, both men were dog tired. It had been a long
day, and it had started, ironically, in the same building.
The McLelland was a four-story structure that curved
around the northwest corner or Fourth and Austin Streets.
The corner drug store was boarded up for the night as
were most other nearby establishments. Half a block away,
the McLelland Opera House was also shuttered for the
night, the evening's performance of William Shakespeare's
Julius Caesar having concluded. Carter and Jackson
caught the performance two nights ago, and Carter had
made the acquaintance of some of the cast members. He
made it a point to always watch some theater while on his
assignments. It kept the fires burning for the craft of
acting.

Some saloons still operated, and their boisterous revelry
could still be heard floating through the night air, but
Carter paid it no mind. He had very few things on his mind
at the moment: a chance to clean up after his tumble in the
dirt, assess the extent of his wounds under the bright lights

of his hotel room, have a few fingers worth of whiskey, and climb into bed.

Naturally, the inferno that was the old cotton gin got the attention of the folks south of the Brazos. Folks stopped their activities and rode out, wanting to get a front row view. Others, like the fire brigade, rousted themselves and made the dash across the bridge. One look at the raging fire told them they would be needed only to contain the fire. When Sheriff Briscoe, riding a nice paint whose coat shone in the flickering firelight, found Carter, the local lawman had a grim countenance on his face.

Carter shrugged and said, "It wasn't me." He then went on to describe the man he knew only as Green Shirt. When he was done, Briscoe sighed and watched the gin burn.

"There's close to ten thousand souls in this town, and I'm nowhere near knowing all of them. Throw in the passersby and it's a damn near impossible job to know everything I need to know. Sometimes, I consider it a miracle that my deputies and I keep the peace as well as we do." He spat on the ground and watched the people watch the fire. "But I'll ask around. Maybe one of my deputies can help y'all." He turned and looked straight into Carter's eyes. "Tomorrow. Why don't y'all head back to wherever y'all staying before you burn down a building that's really important?"

With the dismissal, Carter, Jackson, and Celeste all mounted their horses and rode back to town. The three of them had remained quiet, letting the murmur of the crowd and crackling fire hold sway. By mutual decree, Jackson and Carter decided not to tell Sheriff Briscoe or any of his deputies about what Carter had pillaged from the pockets of the Taggart gang. Before the main bulk of the crowd had arrived, Carter and Jackson examined the treasure Carter had taken off the corpses. They had hoped to find something more, but most of the objects were the detritus men typically carried. Nothing other than the gold double eagles stood out.

Now, standing in front of the McLelland, Carter arched his back. A few bones cracked and relief washed over him. "Ah, that's more like it. I'll be glad to just lay my head down and get some shut eye."

Jackson, always more at home on a horse, nonetheless stretched his neck and shoulders. He sighed. "I'm with you."

Carter craned his head around Jackson to get a look at Celeste. The woman hadn't spoken much on their ride back to town. His eyes traveled up and down the exterior of the McLelland Hotel. A few lights shone through some of the windows, but nearly all of them were dark.

Pulling the reigns of his horse, Carter guided the beast in front of Jackson and came to a stop next to Celeste. His horse faced opposite hers so that he was face-to-face with her. He pointedly ignored the look Jackson was giving him.

"So, um," Carter began, "I guess thank you is in order."

In the ambient light and under the shadows of her hat, Celeste regarded him. Her eyes were difficult to make out. "For what?" He voice had a quality to it Carter hadn't heard before. It took him a moment to put a word to it. Soft. Up until that moment, he had only imagined if anything on Celeste Korbel was soft.

Through a broad grin, Carter said, "For saving my bacon earlier tonight."

"Really?" The soft voice continued. "So you finally came around and saw the truth."

Carter sniffed. He hated admitting he was wrong, but this was his way of thanking her. And possibly seeing what might happen next. "I guess you could say that. Now, I could have got him. Pretty sure I actually did. I'm a good shot, damn it. Even for a southpaw. I'd like the chance to prove it to you sometime."

Celeste angled her face, bringing more of it into the nearby light. A ghost of a grin marked her face. Again, Carter wondered just what kind of life Celeste lived. From what he gathered from her behavior tonight, she was an excellent shooter. If her story about keeping things in line at the Wheeler Saloon was something other than a tall tale, then she could hold her own in a fight. But Sheriff Briscoe knew something about her, too. Despite what he said about knowing the habits of ten thousand people, he seemed to know Celeste's. And he warned Carter about her. Nevertheless, back at the cotton gin, as the three of them watched the structure burn, Carter and cast not a few sidelong glances her way. Interestingly, he had also realized she had thrown a few his way, too.

"What's the plan?" she said.

"Well," Carter shrugged, "I've got a bottle of good brandy upstairs. I'm sure I could scrounge up a couple of glasses from somewhere. Maybe we could…"

"No," she interrupted, lancing away some of her softness, "about tomorrow. What's the next move?"

The sound Jackson made was his attempt at stifling a laugh. It came out as a humorous grunt.

Carter sat up straighter in the saddle. "Right. Well, I figure we could, um, what, Tom, start with breakfast, and, see what the day brings us. Yesterday"—he paused, remembering just how much they had done since sun up—"um, today, we ate here at the McLelland's dining room. Care to join us?"

She thought a moment, she shook her head once. "No. I'll be here, bright and early and make sure y'all don't leave me behind. Evening, gentlemen." With a nod to Jackson, who tipped his hat in response, Celeste Korbel turned her horse and angled it down the street.

Carter watched her go, wondering.

"That was good, Romeo," Jackson said. "Remind me to take notes the next time you try and woo a woman. I want to know how the great Calvin Carter can get any woman to faint under his handsome stare."

Thinking a moment, Carter said, "I could write a book."

* * *

THE INTERIOR of the hotel was quiet and dark. The desk clerk had greeted them at the front door after the two detectives had taken care of their horses at the horse shed around the corner. The act of caring for a horse was ingrained in Jackson's blood and soul. Carter knew enough before he met Jackson, but the former cattle puncher had instructed the former actor in the intricacies of horsemanship. Carter had taken to the care of every animal he used in the service of his job. He found the horses responded well under his caring hands. And seeing to the horse that night had calmed him and made him forget about Celeste.

Almost.

The desk clerk had given each detective a small lantern to enable the two of them to see down the darkened hallways and not stumble around, waking other guests. Carter tried to climb the stairs lightly, so as to soften every footfall. This was when his training as an actor, who often had to dampen his footfalls on stage, came in handy. This was one of the things the former actor had imparted on the former cattle puncher who, when the two had met, clomped around like a bull in a China cabinet. Jackson had learned, and now both men tiptoed up to the fourth floor and angled themselves down the hall. They barely made a sound.

Their rooms were at the end of the hall. They each had their own room, and both rooms had windows that overlooked the street. Their commanding officer, Jameson Moore, taught every young detective to stay in rooms with a good overlook of any surrounding streets whenever possible. That way, Moore told them, they'd get a chance to see if any varmints were coming up to ventilate them. The McLelland Hotel had an enviable layout, with the corner of the building looking down on either 4th or Austin Street. Carter's room faced south to 4th while Jackson's looked down on Austin.

Jackson led the way down the hallway. No light shone under any closed door save one. Idly, Carter wondered who would be awake at this hour, but thought nothing of it, even as he passed that door. Jackson was putting his key into the lock of his room when the person in the only lighted room turned the knob.

All at once, Carter's senses went on alert. A hundred scenarios flooded his mind, the key one being that Green Shirt or one of the men who ambushed the train earlier that day had found out where he and Jackson stayed for the night. This was the moment, Carter thought, where he'd be shot in the hallway of a fancy hotel. He was having none of that.

Shielding Jackson from the person in the room, Carter drew his gun and brought it to bear. He crouched into a fighting stance and also lofted the small lantern so as to give as much light as possible to the hallway without the light shining directly in his eyes. He waited as the light from the person's hotel room spilled into the hallway. A silhouette was framed in that light, and the shape of it was decidedly female.

A woman entered the hallway. She wore a red dress with long sleeves, white lace tracing around her hands.

Something triggered in Carter's mind. He had seen this dress before. The woman turned, and in the half light, Carter noted the woman was a blonde with high cheek-bones. The hair had been let down and it now draped over her shoulders and down to her chest. It took him a moment to place her and bring her name to his lips.

"Jessica Reed?" Carter asked.

She smiled, blinking her eyes at the light from Carter's lantern. "I'd thought you might forget."

Carter still held his gun, realized it, the stashed it back into its holster. Behind him, Jackson finished turning the lock and opened his door. He made no move to go into his room.

"What are you doing here?" Carter asked.

Jessica shrugged. "Well, I needed a place to stay since the train was derailed. I heard they've almost got it fixed. Might still be a day or two. And since the two of y'all were going to find my father"—her voice cracked slightly—"I figured I might as well be close at hand when y'all find him."

Jackson said, "How'd you know where we'd be?"

Jessica angled her head and took note of Jackson behind Carter. "I overheard you telling the train men to carry your bags back here. Y'all just finished a case, and y'all were coming back here. By the time I got back to town, I asked around and found this hotel. It's nice. I asked the desk clerk where y'all's rooms were and got this one." She gestured in her open door.

"What about your companion, Mr. Walsh?" Carter said.

"Oh, he's a few doors down. The one you passed when y'all topped the stairs." She clasped her hands together at her stomach and searched for the correct words. "I've been waiting for you all night. I heard you when you got in the hallway."

Inwardly, Carter cursed. He thought he and Jackson were exceptionally quiet this time.

"Well?" Jessica asked.

"Well what?" Carter replied.

"Well, what have you discovered? I heard all the commotion a few streets over. Was that your doing?"

Carter relaxed a bit. He sighed once and took a step toward her. "It was."

"I hope you weren't hurt?"

Thinking back to when he found himself lying on the ground, an owlhoot aiming at him, and Celeste likely being the one to shoot the varmint, Carter said, "Only my pride."

Jessica looked at the sleeve of Carter's jacket. The white of his shirt peeked through the holes in the jacket. A look of concern crossed her face. "What happened here?"

"Got burned," Carter said. "It's worse than it looks, believe me."

"I smelled the smoke. I was told it was from across the river. Did you have anything to do with that?"

"You could say that." A thought occurred to him. "How did you know about the fire?"

"Timothy told me. I was so tired from the wagon ride back here that I went to bed and read my book. He was restless so he went out tonight. He saw some of the, um, shootings y'all were in tonight. He also saw the fire, although he didn't cross the river. He told me when he came back and went to his room."

Jessica closed the gap between them and came to stand in front of Carter. She brought with her the sweet scent of perfume. It wafted up through his nose and melted something inside of him. She reached out and poked her fingers through the holes in his jacket. She ran the fabric under her fingers. "This is fine material. I'm so sorry this happened to you, and all to find out what happened to my father's body."

She looked up at him and Carter noted she still wore the red lipstick from earlier in the day. Or, rather, had reapplied it.

A lump formed in his throat. "Would you care to join me for some brandy? I could, um, fill you in on what we've discovered so far."

She smiled. "I'd like that. Just let me close my door." She turned and walked back to her room. She darted inside. A moment later, he heard the sound of glass tinking on each other.

With a sly smirk on his face, Carter turned to Jackson. The other man's expression was one of wonderment and sarcasm.

"I told you," Carter said in a low voice, "I could write a book."

❧ 15 ❧

No sooner had Carter opened his door than Jessica Reed reemerged from her room. Thomas Jackson had already let himself into his own room and shut the door to give Carter his privacy. Jessica closed her door but didn't lock it. In one hand, he held two small glass. The closer she got to Carter, who stood at attention waiting for her to proceed him into his room, the more he noted the twinkle in her eye and the mischievous grin on her face. His heart beat faster, especially as she whipped her hair around, giving him another aroma he could love.

Even he arched an eyebrow as he shut the door. He twisted the key in the lock, not caring that the deadbolt clanged into place. He spun the key on the keyring a couple of times before placing it on the bedside table.

The room wasn't too large. The bed dominated the center of the room. The brass bars were polished to a shiny luster and reflected the light being given off by the lantern Carter carried. The bed spread and pillows were neatly made, but he wondered if they had been changed since that morning. Next to the bed was the bedside table with an oil lamp and matchbox for late-night emergencies. On the other side of the bed was a wing-backed chair that sat in front of the one window that overlooked 4th Street. The window was partially raised to allow fresh air to swirl and banish the stale mustiness of the room. The only other piece of furniture was a small dresser consisting of three drawers with a wash basin and pitcher on top. A mirror allowed guests to make sure their clothes were all perfect before going out for the night.

"You're room seems a bit larger than mine," Jessica said. She ran her fingers over the top of the dresser.

"It's one of the corner rooms," Carter said. He walked to the bedside table and lit the oil lamp, extinguishing the lantern he had been carrying. "The boss insists all detectives have a room overlooking the streets so no owlhoots who might wish us harm can get the drop on us. The McLelland is great because most of the time, we work with a partner and this room and the next gives us views of both streets."

Jessica set the glasses down on the dresser. "Where's your cognac?"

Carter walked over to a corner of the room and plucked his carpetbag from the far side of the bed. He plopped it on the bed, opened it, and rummaged along the edge. The bottle he withdrew was rectangular with a cork firmly wedged in the neck. He presented the bottle to her as a wine steward presented wine, label out.

"Camus Cognac. I'm not familiar with that brand."

"They're an outfit out of France. I was given a case of it by a friend who enjoyed a play was in." He popped the cork and wafted it under her nose. "How's that smell?"

"Wonderful." Her voice had gotten lower, more sultry. She turned and retrieved the glasses. "I'd love to taste it while you fill me in on what you've discovered so far."

The grin that etched across Carter's face betrayed his

thoughts. He poured cognac in both glasses then recorked the bottle. He put it back in the bag and set the bag on the floor. They stood at the foot of the bed.

"I'm sorry the hotel didn't furnish the room with two chairs," Carter murmured.

Jessica rolled her eyes to the bed. "Well, one of us can sit in the chair and the other on the bed." Without waiting, she turned, again flipping her hair, and lowered herself on the bed. She still sat straight up with perfect posture. Whomever her tutor was in whatever finishing school Jessica Reed attended, the woman deserved high marks.

Carter made a show of coming around the bed to sit in the chair but quickly abandoned it. There was only one reason Jessica Reed was in his room and any pretense went out the door as soon as Carter locked it. He sat next to her, his weight lowering the area between them. She partially slid closer to him, as he expected. He kept his back straight, matching her style. He held out his drink. "To the French, who know how to make great cognac."

She clinked her glass to his. "To the French." She sipped her cognac, never breaking eye contact with him. He watched as her lips puckered and drew the liquid into her mouth. The warmness of the cognac didn't hold a candle to other warmness now flowing through him.

"What do you think?" he asked after he had downed half the cognac.

"Lovely. The smoothness is something to behold. So, you're a railroad detective yet you carry around imported cognac. That seems"—she searched for the word —"unique."

Carter offered her a lopsided grin. "There's a lot of things unique about me. For one, I used to be an actor."

His statement was met with raised eyebrows. "An actor? How in the world did you end up as a detective?"

Carter looked away from her, thinking about his father and his father's murder. As sure as he was of Jessica's intentions in that moment, he wasn't sure if telling that story at this moment was the best idea. "It's a long story," he finally said, bringing his eyes back to hers. In the light of the oil lamp, her green eyes practically glowed. "Maybe some other time. But we're here to talk about your father."

At that, Jessica lowered her eyes and stared into her glass. She swirled the liquid around, watching the alcohol glaze the inside of the glass. "I'd rather not talk about it either."

"Hey," Carter said, boldly reaching out and putting a finger under her chin. He gently pulled her face up and met his stare. "I tell you what? Why don't we drink to our fathers and then forget them, at least for tonight?" He held up his glass, prompting her.

A small sniff of a laugh escaped her, but she reciprocated. "To our fathers." Another clink then they both drained the liquid.

"Would you like more?" Carter asked.

She inhaled deeply, bringing her breasts up and down. The low-cut top of her dress stretched ever so slightly, revealing perhaps an inch more of her cleavage. She held out her empty glass. "I think you know what I want, Detective Carter." She arched her own eyebrow.

Carter didn't need to think twice. Gently, he took her glass from her and placed both on the dresser. He turned back, gazing at her, the soft light of the lamp washing over her face. "I could be coy and ask if you want me to give you a report on the case, but I figure we're beyond that." He came back to the bed and sat.

"I would consider that cruel," she murmured. She parted her lips and ran her tongue over them.

Carter's heart beat just a little faster. "Then we'll table that discussion for another time."

He leaned closer to her, shifting his weight again, and sliding her closer to him. The final few inches between their hips vanished and she was up beside him. He felt her warmth simmer through his entire left side, wherever their bodies connected. He wrapped his left arm around her and brought her toward him. Their lips met. They were soft and he tasted the cognac just inside of them. A moment later, her tongue snaked into his mouth, searching for his, no longer tentative. He replied in kind. The heat between intensified and he crushed her tighter in his embrace. Jessica willingly folded herself into his arms, bringing her hand up and running her fingers through his hair. The soft touch of her fingertips and nails sent shivers of gooseflesh down the nape of his neck and over his arms.

He smiled at the feeling, breaking the kiss.

Jessica pulled back, her eyes beseeching him. "What's wrong?"

"Nothing," Carter replied, "nothing at all. I'm just looking at your beauty."

He ran his finger over her jawline and up to her ear, where he curled his fingers around the lobe. His fingers then turned and wandered down her neck. She arched herself, giving him more leeway to go where he wanted. He traced the line of her dress to her shoulder and gently tested how tight the garment was on her. Tight enough.

Her fingers left his face, her touch like a searing fire wherever she touched him. She unbuttoned the top few buttons surreptitiously hidden under a flap on the front of her dress. With that done, the pressure on the top of her dress loosened.

"Try it now," she purred.

Carter snaked his thumb under the hem of her dress at

the shoulder. The fabric gave way. He slid the top of the dress over her shoulder. The skin there shone in the lamp light.

"Much better," he said. He bent and placed his lips on her shoulder. She moaned in response. "Very much better."

* * *

FOR BEING in a crowded hotel in the middle of the night, their lovemaking was surprisingly quiet. Perhaps each one knew their surroundings and acted accordingly. Even the bed seemed to acquiesce and absorb their movements with quietness.

Afterward, they lay together, each staring up at the ceiling. Jessica lay on her side, her entire body pressed up against him, her warmth still sending comforting feelings all through him. Carter's arm was around her, his fingers idly caressing her back. He watched the lamp light dance on the ceiling and felt happy.

"You forgot something," Jessica said. She ran her fingers through the hairs on his chest.

"What's that?"

"Your report. You were supposed to tell me what you've discovered about my father."

Some of the contentment that had washed over Carter dissipated. He had been with his share of women. He willingly gave himself to each and every one of them. But they all seemed to be part of whatever assignment had been given him. A part of him longed to find the one. Other parts of him enjoy the search.

His fingers rested on her backbone and he traced the bones of her spine, using them to count off the items he knew.

"Unfortunately, not a lot. The men who derailed and

ambushed the train got away. There was one man who was wearing a green shirt. That bastard"—he paused, looking down at her—"pardon my French, shot and killed the engineer whom you saw. He also killed that freight worker, Adam Whitney. Damn near killed us, too."

She hugged him closer. "I remember. I don't think I've ever been that frightened before."

He leaned over and kissed the top of her head. "I can't imagine it would happen again, at least with you." His arm was long enough that he had almost her entire back in range. He ran his fingers up and down her spine and continued.

"We got back here to town. Skip Barton was in town and we needed to find him. Tom and I found him, each in our own way, at the Wheeler Saloon. But before we could ask him any direct questions, those owlhoots from the Taggart gang shot him. He's still alive, but barely."

"Think he'll regain consciousness, maybe tell his side of things?" When she talked, he felt her lips on his chest.

"The doc doesn't think so."

"So how'd y'all get up to the cotton gin?"

"The sheriff recognized the dead men we shot up as members of the Taggart gang. Said the rest of them stayed up in the old gin."

"Why didn't y'all just arrest them?"

Carter shrugged. "They hadn't done anything yet. All Tom and I wanted to do was ask them some questions."

"Like what?"

"Like who hired them?"

Jessica turned and looked up at him. "What do you mean?"

He looked down at her. He put his free arm behind his head to support himself. "We've been through town before, but even I know the type of gang Taggart ran. He's small time. Banks, stagecoaches. He and his boys were content to live off the crumbs they got. As much as they cultivated an image, they never killed anyone. So it makes little sense that these small time crooks go from robbing stagecoaches to derailing a train."

She shrugged. "Maybe they got tired of their station in life. Perhaps they just wanted to try something new."

He shook his head. "It still doesn't add up. And then add this to the mix. The three of us went up to the cotton gin and…"

"Three?"

"Yeah. Tom, me, and this…"—he paused, searching for the right word to describe Celeste Korbel—"agent from the Wheeler Saloon. Her name is Celeste. The owner of the saloon, a madam named Viola Wheeler, took umbrage that all the shooting destroyed part of her business, so she told Celeste to help us out."

"Is she as pretty as me?"

The question was like a trap ready to spring. Carter's mind flashed to the moments he and Celeste stood in front of the conflagration, the bright fire giving him an unfettered look at the other woman's face. Celeste was older than Jessica Reed, her eyes wiser. Celeste had seen things Jessica hadn't, and that seemed to Carter to have a certain romantic quality. Celeste Korbel had hard edges where Jessica was all soft curves.

"Not at all," he said behind a smile.

She tapped his lips with her finger. "Good answer. So what about the cotton gin. Did you find those men you were after?"

Carter nodded. "We did. But the man in the green shirt was already there."

"He was?"

"Yeah. He got there ahead of us." He grew silent,

wondering how gruesome he should be in the description of what happened next. Jessica Reed seemed young in some respects, but quite mature in others. "He killed the three remaining members of the gang before we could ask them who hired them. But that's okay. We know. We may not know who the man in the green shirt is, but his killing of the Taggart gang proved he hired them. It's only a matter of time before we uncover the rock he's hiding under."

Jessica moved one of her legs to encompass his. "You seem confident."

"We are. I was able to search the bodies of those outlaws before the gin came down."

"You did? While it was still on fire?" Her voice sounded astonished.

His fingers ran all the way down her back, stopping just at the cleft of her backside. "I did. I'll admit, it was a little tense at the time, but the reward was worth it."

"What did you find?"

"A clue. Gold double eagle coins."

She frowned. "How is that a clue?"

Carter told her about the bank robbery and how well it was executed. "Tom and I are going there tomorrow, talk to the bank manager, see what we can see."

Jessica extricated the arm that was underneath Carter's body, brought it up, and rested her head on it. "How do you do it?"

Carter raised his eyebrows. "Do what?"

"Detective work. How do you deal with people shooting at you all the time?"

He pursed his lips, thinking. "It's never easy, but it's part of the job. You never get used to it, but over time, you learn to stifle your fear and do what needs to be done. In some ways, it's a little like acting. Stage fright is a real thing. Every actor has it, or should. It gives you the edge to perform to the best of your ability. Without it, an actor grows stale and boring. If there's anything an actor doesn't want to be, it's boring."

He inhaled deeply and sighed. "Acting under pressure, courage under fire, they are somewhere in the same arena. When the bullets start to fly, instinct takes over. You just perform."

Jessica smiled knowingly. "You performed well tonight." The fingers of her free hand traced the contours of his chest. "I know I'm not officially your client, but I want to thank you for giving me such a full report." She brought her leg up and pressed herself closer to him.

Her fingers sent cool shivers over Carter's body. "My pleasure," he said. He watched as her fingers traveled farther down his body. "I hope my report satisfied you."

"It did, but I'm going to need you to repeat it all, word for word."

16

THE NEXT MORNING, Carter's eyes caught sight of the McLelland Opera House through the dining room windows as he walked around the tables and came to sit at the table where Thomas Jackson was. One of the best features of the McLelland Hotel was its proximity to the opera house. A few memories of his time as an actor flashed through his mind. In front of his partner were the remains of his breakfast. The aroma of frying bacon, cooking eggs, and baking biscuits filled the room. The other guests all huddled around their own tables, happily eating and talking with one another. The sun had just risen over the horizon and bright light filled the room.

Carter registered the smirk on Jackson's face. "Did you sleep well?"

Jackson shook his head with exaggerated sarcasm. "Better than you. Sleeping wise, that is." He took a sip of his coffee. "You'll be happy to know I was so damn tired I didn't even hear you give her your report."

Winking, Carter said, "Turns out, I had to repeat it."

A waitress arrived and brought Carter coffee in a fancy

ceramic cup and saucer. He ordered his breakfast and
waited for her to leave. Jackson stared over his coffee cup
at Carter. "What?"

"I don't know how you do it," Jackson said. "I mean,
I'm clearly more handsome that you, but you always seem
to find the affections of a lady wherever we go."

Carter shrugged. "Well, I'll argue which one of us is
handsomer—you'd lose—but it's probably the way I carry
myself." He waved his hand out in front of him like a magi-
cian just before a trick. He had changed into his only other
suit, a light khaki-colored three piece suit. His white shirt
was crisp and the red tie cinched all the way to the neck. "I
just clean up better. And I radiant charm."

"That's not all you radiate." He looked up and his eyes
raked across the dining room. "Well, speak of the devil."

Carter turned and laid his eyes on Jessica Reed. She
and Timothy Walsh were threading their way over to
Carter's table. Her smile beamed larger when they found
Carter's. She wore a green dress, cut in a similar style as
yesterday's red dress. Carter noted the small flap underneath of which were likely the buttons that would allow him
to disrobe her again. In his mind's eye, he was doing that
right now.

Timothy Walsh wore a stern visage on his face. Dressed
in a black suit, gray pants, and gray vest, Walsh appeared
haggard. Bags hung under his eyes and he came across as
much older than even yesterday. Carter guessed the man's
age as a few years older than Jessica. Walsh followed in
Jessica's wake as she came to stand next to Carter and
Jackson.

"Good morning," she said, first to Carter and then to
Jackson. Both men rose from their chairs.

Jackson inclined his head to her. "Miss Reed. Mister
Walsh. Did you sleep well last night?"

Jessica blushed and moved her head demurely. "I did. Thank you for asking. May we join you?"

Moving first, Jackson shifted from his position, taking his empty plates and coffee cup with him, and allowed Jessica to have his place. She graciously obliged. That left Walsh seated next to Carter. The three men sat. Within moments, the waitress arrived with coffee for Jessica and Walsh, who ordered their breakfasts.

"Jessica tells me y'all have a clue," Walsh began. "Something about gold coins?"

Jackson arched an eyebrow in Carter's direction but said nothing.

"Yes," Carter said. "We're going to stop by the bank."

"Why the bank?" Jessica asked. Her tone was innocent but Carter suspected all at the table, even Walsh, knew of her visit to Carter's room last night.

"A couple nights ago…" Carter began before Jackson cut him off.

"The gold coins we found on Taggart's body," Jackson said, putting some authority in his voice. "We'd like one of the bankers here in town—a man with close ties to the railroad—to have a look at them, maybe help us determine where they might have come from. If we can narrow down our search, we'll be closer to finding Carter's mystery man in the green shirt."

Carter smiled. He had caught the hint. "Right. The man in the green shirt not only killed one of the railroad's engineers, but also killed the remaining members of the Taggart gang. And he may have paid them with the coins." He jostled his pocket, letting the muffled sounds of the gold coins signal their presence.

"What would that mean?" Walsh asked. He accepted the coffee cup from the waitress. He scooped a spoonful of sugar into the beverage and slowly stirred the drink.

"We don't know," Jackson cut in before Carter could say anything more. "That's why we're going." He edged his foot over to Carter's and nudged his partner to shut the hell up. "We have a few other leads we'll be following as well. How about y'all?"

Jessica sipped the hot coffee from the white porcelain cup. She left a red lipstick stain on the rim. "We can't very well leave without my father. I hope you haven't forgotten him."

"We haven't," Carter said. "Don't you fret about that."

The waitress arrived with a large tray. She delivered plates of food to Carter, Jessica, and Walsh. Carter's stomach lurched at the heavenly aroma of eggs, bacon, grits, and half an orange. A pat of butter sat in the middle of the grits, melting before his eyes. Eagerly, he grabbed his fork and broke the yolks and allowed the custard-like liquid to mingle in with his grits. He took a mouthful of eggs in his mouth and toyed with the idea of immediately ordering more.

Talk of the case ceased and Carter realized he didn't know much about Jessica other than a few, more intimate things. "I live in San Antonio," she said. "We both do." She indicated Walsh. "Father was a wealthy man and that enabled me to have a life of leisure."

"What about you, Mr. Walsh?" Jackson said. With him being the only one without any food, he was free to sip coffee and watch his table companions.

Walsh dabbed the corners of his mouth with a napkin. "I live in San Antonio as well. I work, or rather, I worked for Mr. Reed before his passing. I was a secretary for his business. He operated a textile company, shipping various materials all across Texas and the western territories."

"Interesting work?" Jackson said.

"Very. It has enabled me to travel far and wide, seeing this great land of ours."

Jackson wagged a finger between Jessica and Walsh. "And y'all are, what? Engaged?"

"Oh heavens no," Jessica said, rather abruptly. "Timothy is merely my traveling companion. He didn't want me to make this terrible journey by myself."

Carter noted Walsh's face when Jessica spoke. The other man's face was a mask, a stilted smile plastered on it. If he didn't know any better, Carter might've thought Jessica's words hurt him. Maybe there wasn't anything going on between them now, but Timothy Walsh certainly wanted more.

The sound of jangling spurs interrupted his thoughts. They seemed rather out of place in a fine establishment like this. He looked over to the front door to spy the source.

Celeste Korbel had entered the hotel dining room. Not surprisingly, she wore an outfit so similar to the one she wore the previous evening that Carter couldn't help wondering if the clothes were the same. The tan pants showed no signs of last night's activities. They hugged her hips and legs in such a way as to accentuate her curves. He imagined it was to better enable her to draw one of her two pistols from their holsters, but Carter didn't care. The vision of her standing there, thumbs hooked in her gun belt, captivated him. His eyes traveled north on her body and he realized her shirt was a different color—now, it was blue. He now envisioned a wardrobe in her room consisting of the exact same clothes of tan pants and leather jackets and shirts of various hues. He watched as she scanned the room. Seeing him and Jackson, she sauntered over to their table.

Upon seeing her, Carter had stopped his fork halfway to his mouth. In his peripheral vision, he noted Jessica saw his movements stop and followed his gaze to Celeste. He also noted a few of the other diners took in the sight of Celeste as she made her way to their table.

In the clear light of day, Carter had the best view of her to date. She had cleaned up some. Her face was smooth without a trace of dirt. Her lips had no lipstick, but their color was a natural, deep brown. It was the same kind of brown repeated in her eyes. Those eyes now showed amusement as she came to stand next to their table. She nodded at Carter and Jackson, then took in Jessica and Walsh, who had to turn and see at whom everyone at the table was staring.

"Morning," she said.

Carter angled his head ever so slightly, enabling him to catch a whiff of her. The scent was clean and nice.

"You might want to eat that before those grits get too cold," Celeste said. She motioned with her chin to the fork hanging suspended in Carter's hand.

"Oh, right," he said. He shoved the food in his mouth and quickly swallowed the hot grain. "Let me introduce Jessica Reed and Timothy Walsh. They're the ones from the train. It is Miss Reed's father who, um, went missing." Celeste nodded to each newcomer.

"And who is this?" Jessica said. Her tone had gone decidedly chilly.

"This is Celeste Korbel," Carter said, completing the introductions. "She is, um, helping us with the case. She had a local connection with what happened last night. She works for the owner of the Wheeler Saloon that got shot up last night."

Celeste grabbed a chair from the next table. She positioned it between Carter and Walsh and sat. "I've seen the damage now in the light." She shook her head. "I've got a message from Miss Viola to you, Carter. Next time, use the door."

Shrugging, Carter said, "I can do that, as long as people don't shoot at me."

She chuckled. "Then again, maybe you have a thing for windows, seeing as how you leapt out of the gin through one." She turned to Jessica. "Do you know what he did last night?"

Jessica pursed her lips, curling the edges of her lips up ever so slightly. "I do. I heard the whole story. Twice, in fact. He's good at what he does. Very brave."

Carter merely sat there. His gaze was fixed on the far wall and the painting that hung there. Walsh busied himself with the last bit of eggs on his plate. Jessica seemed to have forgotten her food.

"I think you're being a little too generous," Carter finally said. He spoke the words in such a way that a listener might draw different conclusions as to which woman he was talking.

"I'm ready," Celeste announced. "What's our next step?"

Jackson, who had sat quietly watching Carter squirm under the scrutiny of both women, cut in. "Cal's gonna finish eating, pay his bill, and then we'll start the day." He turned to Jessica. "If we find out anything, where will you be?"

Without her eyes leaving Carter's, she said, "Around. We can't very well leave without father. So until you find out what happened, we'll just be around."

"Good," Jackson said, rising. "We'll be in touch."

To Carter's right, Celeste stood as well. "I'll be out front waiting for you boys." She turned and again sauntered out of the dining room. The leather jacket didn't reach farther past her waist and he watch her backside as she moved away.

The clink of a fork hitting porcelain brought him back to his senses. Jessica had all but thrown her fork down. All too abruptly, Carter stood, scooting the chair backward, nearly toppling it.

"Right," he said, turning to face Jessica again. Her eyes narrowed with jealousy. He gave her one of his patented grins, the type of grin that had assuaged women in the past. "We'll be in touch." He turned and led Jackson out of the dining room.

The last he saw of Jessica Reed, he got the distinct impression she hadn't been assuaged.

17

As officers of the law, Carter and Jackson had the ability to walk into any bank and obtain assistance from the bank manager in any case. Very few times in their assignments had they met with local resistance. But with a case like this one, Carter and Jackson decided to call on a man they knew and who had ties to the railroad.

Thaddeus Ewing owned a bank that bore the name of Waco Regional Bank. That location was at the corner of Third and Austin Streets, a block north from the McLelland Hotel. The three lawmen—for that's what Carter had come to think of Celeste because what else was she?— forwent riding on their horses in favor of walking.

As the people of Waco moved about their lives, Carter got the distinct impression they were also abuzz with the events of the previous night. Groups of men stood in clusters, all craning their necks to read the newspaper held by a man in their center. Carriages and wagon squeaked as they were wheeled up and down Austin Street, horses blowing every so often. Clods of dirt and dung littered the two lanes of traffic along the road, and passersby darted around the lawmen, intent on their daily activities and needed to get by the slow walking trio.

They passed a cigar shop and Carter ducked inside to buy some more tobacco paper and tobacco. The stash he regularly carried had burned up with the liquid fire the previous evening. He also bought a few cigars and passed a few to Jackson after stepping back outside. Interestingly, his partner and Celeste stood talking in low voices by a telegraph pole. Something panged in Carter's gut. He liked and trusted Thomas Jackson, but seeing him, alone with Celeste Korbel, something turned in Carter's stomach. He didn't like it or the fact that he was feeling it either. Stifling the unpleasantness, he walked up, handed Jackson the cigars, and gave him a curious glance.

Jackson only thanked Carter and leaned off the pole. He and Celeste starting walking again, leaving Carter to wonder. Carter resumed his position on Celeste's right side, she being in the center of the two men.

The Waco Regional Bank occupied the corner lot and faced both streets. The main entrance, however, was on Third Street, underneath a short balcony. The overhang was only about four feet out from the facade of the building and six feet across, large enough for a few people to stand and watch the people walking along the street but little else. Once, Thaddeus Ewing told Carter he enjoyed the view from that second floor because he could see the Brazos up north and, when the sun was at a particular angle, the glint off the railroad tracks as they curved around and crossed the bridge to come into town on Mary Street.

They rounded the corner onto Third Street and were greeted with a peculiar sight. A man stood in front of the bank. He was about Carter's height and dressed in a brown suit. By the cut of the jacket, Carter could tell that the man wore a gun belt on his right side, but the suit jacket covered the weapon at the time. The man had a brown hat with a round top set low on his forehead, shadowing his eyes. Although the man tried to look nonchalant, he gave off the distinct odor of another lawman. It was likely one of Sheriff Briscoe's deputies.

Carter, Jackson, and Celeste paused at the front door of the bank and looked inside. Carter spotted Thaddeus Ewing and his assistant, Robert Gilman, talking with another man Carter instantly recognized as Sheriff Briscoe. Ewing, a thin, wiry man whose skin possessed the light pallor of a man who spent more time indoors than out was gesticulating back and forth to Briscoe, evidently telling him something vitally important.

"Help you?" the deputy asked. He had taken notice of Carter who stood just to his right.

"We're here to see Thaddeus Ewing," Carter announced.

"Bank's closed. Y'all'll have to come back."

Carter drew his brows together. "We'll only be a few minutes. We need to ask him some questions."

"I said the bank's closed. Sheriff's orders." The deputy put more authority into his voice this time.

"I'm sorry," Carter said, "but what happened?"

The deputy now rounded on Carter, Jackson, and Celeste. He looked on the two men with unrecognition. When his eyes slid over Celeste, they looked like the combination of a man wondering why the pretty lady was accompanying two men as well as mentally undressing her. She merely stood there, her eyes gazing down the street.

"Why don't y'all just move along," the deputy muttered. "The bank'll open later."

At a glance from Carter to Jackson, a barely perceptible nod took place. After that moment, Carter turned and took only a step toward the door before the strong arm of the deputy grabbed a handful of Carter's jacket and shirt and halted his progress. The plan worked perfectly as Jackson took the opportunity to pivot and place his hand on the doorknob. He turned it. The knob didn't budge.

The grin the deputy gave to Carter was more sneer than humor. "Told you the bank is closed." The man's breath reeked of coffee and tobacco.

Jackson's immediate response was to bang on the door. That got the attention of Briscoe, Ewing, and Gilman. All turned to stare at Jackson darkening the door and Carter being accosted by the deputy. Shaking his head, Briscoe walked over and unlock the front door. He opened it, blinking at the bright sunshine.

"What the hell's going on, Carter?"

With the question directed at Carter, the deputy frowned. Carter took that opportunity to yank his clothes out from under the deputy's grip. He adjusted his shirt, tie, and jacket, smoothing his hand up and down, verifying everything was in order. "We're here to see Ewing."

"Why?" Briscoe persisted.

"It's part of the case," Jackson chimed in. "We need a bank man's opinion."

"About what?"

"These." Carter shoved his hand in his pocket. The deputy half drew his gun, but Briscoe waved him off. Carter pulled out the small satchel and jingled it. He then loosened the drawstring and pulled out one of the gold double eagle coins.

It was Briscoe's turn to frown. "Where'd you get that?"

"They were on Taggart's body last night."

"And you didn't think to tell me?"

Carter was nonplussed. "It's part of our case."

Briscoe took a couple of steps and came to Carter. He

snatched the coin from Carter's grip and examined it. Without looking up, he said, "It's also part of my case."

Now Carter was taken aback. "What case?"

"Bank robbery."

The memory came back to Carter. He wasn't sure how it had slipped his mind considering Celeste Korbel was standing right next to him. He had promised Viola Wheeler to look into the bank robbery from two nights ago. It was a promise, as much as it had pained him to make, he intended to keep.

"Oh, the one from two nights ago?"

"No," Sheriff Briscoe said, "the one from here last night."

THADDEUS EWING STOOD at the central desk in the lobby of his bank. The man was in his fifties and wore a black suit, no vest, and a black tie. His shoes were shined to a high luster. A gold watch chain dangled just below the hem of his jacket. The thick lenses of his glasses were housed gold rimmed spectacles. The eyes behind the glasses were wide with worry.

Robert Gilman was perhaps a decade and a half younger. His dark hair was slicked back and perfectly positioned with a perfect part down the center of his head, the hair combed neatly on both sides. He wore spectacles as well, but these were silver-plated. His suit almost perfectly matched Ewing's to such a degree that Carter wondered if there was a dress code. The younger man's hands constantly worried the brim of his short-brimmed black hat. Premature grey flecked the whiskers of his mustache. He constantly wet and bit his lower lip.

Sheriff Briscoe locked the front door of the bank again

and came over to stand with Carter, Jackson, and Celeste. Initially, the sheriff had given her the evil eye, but with a little coaxing from Carter, the top lawman in town relented. Carter knew Briscoe didn't like or trust Celeste, but opted to let Carter dig his own grave, if that's what it came to. Interestingly, Carter watched as Celeste took in the interior of the bank.

The lobby was large as befitting a corner business. In the center of the room was a carpet. It was on this that the central desk sat. Evidently, this was Gilman's place. Behind the desk was a long counter with three separate stations. Bank tellers would stand at those positions and deal with customers throughout the day. Behind the teller counter was the safe. It was a large, black metal safe, the kind other banks throughout the west had positioned in the middle of bank lobbies, With Waco a growing town, Ewing had opted for a more secure area. No person from the lobby could get behind the teller counter without hopping over said counter. The only way to get to the safe was via a side room— Ewing's office no less. There, the bank manager would know exactly whom was behind the teller counter.

The safe's door now hung open. Inside was mostly empty metal shelves. A few stacks of papers and other non-monetary detritus stayed behind, some on the floor of the safe and just outside the door. But there was no money, neither paper nor coin. Whomever had robbed Ewing's bank had done a thorough job.

"So you got those coins off of Taggart?" Briscoe muttered. "I knew the no good son of a bitch would end up dead."

Carter nodded. He recounted the details of the previous night, now including the details he left out regarding Green Shirt. When he finished, Briscoe offered him a skeptical look.

"You know we're both lawmen, right? Had you told me about that last night, I coulda have some of my deputies scour the area, maybe find this bastard that killing everybody. Instead, you keep this information to yourself, and for what?" He actually waited for Carter to respond. When Carter opened his mouth, Briscoe cut him off. "To hog the glory to yourself, I imagine. I know you, Calvin Carter. You're the Showboat Detective. You're getting quite the reputation around the state. You better watch out. Before you know it, even the criminals will know your face, and then where will you be?"

Carter hated being called out and, ironically, in front of Celeste. He didn't know why he wanted to impress her, but he did. "I'll be careful."

"You'll be dead with a bullet in your back is where you'll be." Briscoe sighed. "Show him."

Carter handed over the double eagle to Ewing. The bank manager turned the coin over in his hands, inspecting it. "If what you say is true, Calvin, then these coins didn't come from my bank."

"The Lone Star Bank was the other one robbed, what was it? Two days ago?"

Ewing handed the coin back to Carter. "That's right. You know, that coin also might've come from other banks around Texas."

Curious, Carter asked him what the bank manager meant.

"You haven't heard the news?" Ewing blew out air between his lips. "There have been nearly a dozen bank robberies all throughout Texas. Even one up in Arkansas."

"Why hasn't it been in the news?" Jackson asked. "I think we'd have heard about it by now."

Ewing shrugged. "Would you want the world to know you've been robbed? It's one thing to have a robbery in broad daylight with outlaws and shoot-outs. That kind of thing gets noticed and can't be avoided. But robberies like this, well, you kind of want to keep a lid on it." The bank manager swore. "I thought I'd be immune, seeing as how Fleming's bank was robbed. They damn near took everything."

"Why did you think you'd be immune?" Carter asked.

"No town that's been robbed in this fashion has had two banks robbed at once. Now Waco's the first." He indicated the double eagle in Carter's hand. "You should return that, once you find out where it came from."

"We will," Carter said. He handed the coin to Jackson who pocketed it. "Tell us what happened here."

Putting his hands on his suspenders, Ewing assumed the pose of a college professor. "Whoever it was did a damn fine job, I'm ashamed to say. I opened up first thing this morning, probably around seven. Robert arrived five minutes later. We talked about what happened last night." He paused. "Did you have anything to do with that?"

"A little," Carter said, shrugging.

"Anyway, we both went to my office and into the vault area. It was when I went to engage the combination lock that I realized the door was slightly ajar. I opened it and yelled at the top of my lungs. Robert came running in and we both stared at the safe, empty!" He bit back emotion from coming into his voice.

Gilman, who had remained quiet while his boss related the story, finally spoke. "As soon as we saw what had happened, I ran to fetch the sheriff." He said those words with immense pride in his voice.

"How about the doors?" Jackson asked, ignoring the assistant. "Any sign of forced entry?"

"Not a whit," Briscoe said. "But if a man is adept

enough to crack a safe, then he'd be good enough to sneak into this building without smashing a window."

"How about a back door?" Jackson continued.

"None," Ewing said. The only entrance in or out is the front door.

"The balcony," Carter said. "Don't forget the balcony."

"I wasn't born yesterday," Briscoe said. "Checked it. That's the way he likely came in. The front door's not open. Any passerby could see a scoundrel picking a lock. But the balcony would be perfect with the railings providing cover."

Carter turned his attention up to the ceiling, scanning for the stairs that led up to the second floor. At the far side, arcing up over a second office on the east side of the room, was a thin set of stairs. They let up to a second-floor landing that spanned only the north side of the lobby. This enabled anyone to step out onto the balcony. Spying a chair and small table, Carter added a new thought: the second floor might be where a security man stationed himself during business hours.

He pointed to the chair. "No security at night?"

Ewing ruefully shrugged. "Never seen a need. Waco's a big enough town with a great sheriff not to have too many robberies."

"Well, you've had two in three days," Carter said. He moved over to the safe and crouched down to investigate the safe door and lock. Absolutely no sign of any instrument having scraped the outside. Whoever did this broke the combination. He removed his hat and put his ear up against the door. He spun the wheel and listened.

Celeste's boots clomped over to stand next to him. "You can crack safes, too?" She wore a smirk on her face.

"Not with all your noise."

She looked taken aback. "Who are you to call me noisy?"

"Well, you are the one talking." He let that last verbal jab sink in before continuing. "But I was referring to the outside sounds. With all the movement outside, I can barely hear the weights falling into place. But a skilled listener with a deft touch in the middle of the night would have no problem opening this door."

Ewing blustered. "You can't be serious."

"The first number's twenty-seven. The second is probably sixteen." Ewing's explosion of sound when he gasped was all the proof Carter needed to know he was correct. He stood and replaced his hat on his head, making sure to cock it at a rakish angle. He held his hands on either side of him, almost embarrassed, but not too much. "How do you get on the roof?"

Ewing frowned, so Gilman filled the silence. "Out back. There's a service ladder built into the wall of Bernard's shop."

Carter spun on his heel and started for the door. Celeste followed. Jackson, who had moved away to stand next to the north window, turned and looked in the direction of the next store to the west. "Son of a bitch," he muttered.

"What?" Carter asked.

"You'll never believe what's next door," Jackson replied. "A lumber shop," he paused to stretch out the drama, "that makes coffins."

18

A QUIET CONVERSATION BETWEEN CARTER, Jackson, and Celeste developed a plan forward. Jackson would go around to the rear of the furniture shop—actually the bank, the furniture shop, and other business all shared the same alley—and investigate and see if the robber left any clues. Carter and Celeste would go in the furniture shop itself and have a look around. Jackson initially balked at being shunted to the back, but Carter correctly pointed out that, if worse came to worst, he and Celeste could pose as a married couple looking for a coffin for her dearly departed aunt.

"Siblings," Celeste had said, interrupting the tale Carter started spinning.

"What?"

"We'd be siblings. Not married."

Carter stood a little straighter. "Any reason why?"

She shrugged. "Just look at us. One glance at us and folks'll know we don't' belong together."

Jackson moseyed down the street laughing so loud that an old woman chastised him for disturbing the peace.

Giving Celeste a wary eye, Carter walked with her around the front of the bank and down Third Street. The Milburn Furniture Store appeared to be a showroom for finished furniture and not, as Jackson had said, the location where the products were made. Two large windows bordered a central, recessed door. The left window displayed a kitchen table and four chairs, all doodied up as nice as could be with doilies and plates at each place setting. A bed made of pine, complete with mattress and blankets, occupied the right window. Painted in gold leaf, the name of the business arced over the front door. A bell rang when Carter opened the door. He let Celeste precede him inside. The distinct odor of fine wood and furniture polish almost assaulted his senses. He blinked at the smell, wondering if it didn't chase away potential customers or if this was the only game in town.

The sound of the bell brought a man's head up from the dusting he was doing to a particularly nice chest of drawers made out of dark oak. He wore no jacket. His shirt sleeves were rolled up to his elbows. Black suspenders crisscrossed his back, further wrinkling his shirt. His tie was cinched at the neck, a green number that matched the color of his pants. Lines of dust and sawdust lanced across his thighs as if he regularly got too close to tables. It sparked a question for Carter to ask the man, who approached them, smiling. Time had rotted one of his eye teeth and the black gap momentarily took Carter's attention away from the task at hand.

"Good morning, how may I help y'all?" The man's voice had an odd whistle to it, likely the result of the missing tooth.

Carter stuck his thumbs in his vest pocket. He had removed his badge from the garment and stashed it in his pocket. Over the years, he had discovered it was often useful to hide his true profession. Folks had a way of clamming up when all Carter wanted was information. If time or circumstances dictated it, he could whip out his badge in a heartbeat.

"Good morning. Have I the honor of addressing Mister Milburn?" Carter assumed a slight Southern drawl. He pointed ignored the eye roll Celeste shot him.

"Grady Milburn, at your service." The man bowed at the neck. "What can I do for you and your…wife?"

The arched eyebrow and half smile Carter returned to Celeste was the I-told-you-so moment he relished. On a dime, he changed his story. "My wife's aunt recently passed and we are needing a coffin." He paused long enough for Milburn to change his countenance from gracious host to somber salesman and express sorrow at the life event. "Thank you for your kind words," Carter went on. He turned around, looking for any coffins on sale. "Where do you keep them?"

Milburn waved a hand to another room. "I prefer to keep them in there. It's a bit out of the way. No one wants to come in here looking for a baby crib and see a coffin." He chuckled dryly. Carter mimicked the laugh. Celeste stayed silent, watching. "Please, follow me." He turned and let Carter into the room. Celeste begged off, instead meandering around the showroom.

"What about wife?" Milburn asked.

"Oh, she's given me carte blanche to pick out a proper coffin for Aunt Margaret. She's too distraught."

Milburn pulled out his watch from his pants pocket. "Oh, you'll have to forgive me. I have another client arriving at ten. It was a previously scheduled meeting."

Carter told the salesman it would not be a problem as he entered the smaller room. It was about eight feet long and about seven feet wide, just short of a true square. No windows let in any light. Only two oil lamps brightened the room. The daylight also shone in from the main showroom, giving Carter a good view of the room. The odor of furniture polish was decidedly less in here. Guess coffins didn't need to shine. A larger back door of this room showed Carter how the coffins got in and out of the room. Three coffins were on display, the long sides paralleling each other. Judging by the looks of the three coffins on display, they roughly corresponded to varying degrees in price. The plain one on the left was the cheapest one while the ornate one on the right was probably most expensive. The middle coffin was just that: middle.

Carter immediately went to the ornate one. He closed the open lid and studied the exterior. Whoever the craftsman was, he had engraved doves and flowers on the surface. Carter ran his fingers along the grooves of one of the flowers. The work was exquisite.

"This is some wonderful work. Very intricate. Do you do the work here?"

"No, sir," Milburn said. "The actual coffin making is done elsewhere."

"Who does it? I think I'd like to make a special request." Carter turned and looked at him down the length of the coffin lid. "I'm imagining something like this, but more ornate. Maybe even a special design raised up off the lid." He used his hands to demonstrate. "I'm thinking about flowers. Maybe a cross in the middle. I've seen some like that before. Very recently, in fact. I think Aunt Margaret would love that."

Milburn didn't answer immediately. He shifted his feet, then cleared his throat. "I use more than one craftsman here in town, and even some out of town."

"That's good. Helps spread around the wealth, I'm sure." Carter tapped the coffin lid. "But who is the one who makes the raised designs?" He jostled his pocket, then reached inside and withdrew the satchel containing the gold double eagles. "Money is no object. I might be so inclined to make a down payment."

Milburn's grin went from nervous to gracious. "That would be most generous, sir. How much were you looking to spend?"

Carter came around the coffin. He pulled out four of the gold coins. He was playing with fire here and he knew it. The double eagles weren't his to spend, much less use to buy information. They were contraband and needed to be returned to bank. For all he knew, they might've belonged to Viola Wheeler. But he pushed that aside. If Milburn gave him the name of the man who may have built the empty coffin with the air holes, then that man might be persuaded to name the person who hired him. That was all Carter needed.

"Oh, that's very generous, sir," Milburn cooed. "Very generous." He smiled, transfixed by the coins Carter held between him.

"Think that would be sufficient for the craftsman? I've got a few more for you, for the cost of doing business. Just let me know who I can contact to commission the perfect coffin for my wife's aunt."

From the front door came the sound of the bell. Milburn instantly pulled out his watch and flipped open the turnip. "My other client's here," he said, slipping the watch back in to his pocket. "Please," he gestured to the coffins, but his eyes remained transfixed on the coins, "continue looking. I'll be back momentarily."

Carter waved him off. He reached out and put a hand on Milburn's arm. "Take all the time you need. My wife and I are leaving. Who makes these exquisite coffins?"

Milburn hesitated again. On impulse, Carter placed one

of the coins in the salesman's palm. "That's between you and me, okay?" He indicated Celeste in the next room. "Please don't tell my wife. She would be very displeased with me."

Milburn shoved the gold coin into his pocket. "Luke Durham."

"Luke Durham," Carter repeated, committing the name to memory.

The footfalls of Milburn's client grew steadily louder. The newcomer wore heavy boots. Whoever he was, he must have been solid. The boots clomped along the wooden floor. They stopped, started up again, and approached the smaller coffin room.

The man who filled the doorframe was large. Ironically, it was the man's boots that Carter noticed first. They were indeed big and heavy. The man's dark gray pants were smooth and clean, as was the shirt, a blue one. But no matter the shirt color, by the time Carter's eyes reached the man's face, recognition charged through Carter's brain. The handlebar mustache that connected with sideburns. Now in the light, Carter noted the man's hair was more an auburn than straight up red. They're eyes met and the other man frowned. Carter watched as recognition swept over his face.

The man in the doorway was the man Carter knew as Green Shirt.

"Good morning, Mister Evans," Milburn said.

Those words turned out to be the last words Milburn ever spoke. In the flash of an eye, Green Shirt — Evans — drew his gun and fired.

19

Evans's bullet slammed into Milburn's body. The impact shoved him backwards, falling onto the more ornate coffin. His body scooted the coffin nearly free from the sawhorses, making the entire coffin off kilter. Milburn, mortally wounded, still had enough gumption to try and grab the coffin and right himself. He ended up pulling the entire thing down on himself with a great crash.

Carter was angled to Evans with his right side. Being a southpaw, he would have to draw his Colt, turn, and then bring his gun up. The angle was all wrong. He'd be dead within a second if he tried to draw his primary weapon.

That's why he activated his secondary weapon.

For the longest time, Carter relied solely on his Colt. He was familiar with it, was rather proficient, and it had got him out of enough scrapes that he had grown to love and appreciate the weapon. But in times like these, a backup was the better tool, even if it was only to buy him a few seconds.

Desmond Arnett served as Carter's mentor in the early years of his detective training. He also acted as Carter's shooting coach, helping to hone the younger man's skills with a gun, the type of skill Jackson learned by merely being on a ranch. Arnett was old, a veteran of the War Between the States, but he hadn't lost his touch. He also advocated all detectives of the railroad carry a special Derringer pistol attached along the forearm. It was a single-shot weapon and was only good at close range. Most of the detectives didn't bother, but Carter, ever the showman, enjoyed the moment of surprise he got when he deployed such a weapon. But he went one better. He wore it on his non-shooting arm.

Carter extended his right arm and flexed his muscles in the precise method Arnett had demonstrated. The spring mechanism activated. The small, silver-plated pistol shot out from under Carter's shirt cuff and slapped into his hand. The entire process took about three seconds, which was about the same time it took for Milburn to fall and Evans to turn his attention to Carter.

The detective had the satisfaction of seeing confusion and bewilderment on Evans's face as Carter extended his empty hand at the gunman. The bewilderment vanished when the Derringer landed in Carter's palm. Evans's eyes widened as Carter pulled the trigger.

The sound of a Derringer is distinct as being not nearly as loud as a Colt pistol or a rifle shot. The bullet is notoriously unreliable, even at this distance of ten feet. But the surprise factor often wins the day.

The bullet from Carter's Derringer sailed wide, clipping the edge of Evans's gray jacket. The tug from the bullet was enough, however, to change the trajectory of the bandit's bullet as it left Evan's gun. The much larger slug sailed high. But that was no matter for Carter had already dived onto the floor and under the middle coffin.

The legs of the sawhorses gave Carter some protection.

Unless Evans started emptying his gun in Carter's direction, the detective had a much better chance of avoiding a direct impact. He also possessed a clear view of Evans's lower body. By this time, of course, Carter's Colt was already in his left hand. He triggered twice, aiming at Evans's legs.

But the owlhoot was already on the move. One of Carter's bullets must've hit a leg, because Evans let out a guttural grunt. The boots that had entered the furniture shop in confident strides now ran out with a distinct limp.

"Green Shirt!" Carter yelled. He hoped Celeste would remember the term he had used the previous evening in describing the man who had killed the Taggart gang and pursue.

Two more shots were fired. Carter heard a short scream of pain. The pitch of the scream indicated it was a woman. There was the thump of a body landing on the wooden floor.

"Son of a bitch," Carter muttered.

He got his legs under him, rising in a crouch, arms extended in a two-hand grip. He couldn't see the front door. He also couldn't see Evans. Cautiously, Carter came out from behind the coffins and moved to the door leading into the main showroom. He kept the wall between him and Evans. He was about to turn and fire into the main showroom when he heard the front door open and the bell jingle. If Evans was going out the door, chances were good he wouldn't be shooting back at Carter.

The detective charged into the showroom, arms extended, his eyes and his gun barrel moving as one, sweeping the room. He saw a flash of gray as Evans ran east, toward the bank. Two more shots sounded from on the street. Carter nearly went after him, but the groan from the corner, stopped him. He turned and found Celeste. What he saw sent a chill down his spine.

She lay slumped on the floor, her back to one of the chest of drawers. Her fall had dislodged it from its pristine placement. A thin stain of red was on her right shoulder bicep. Her left hand covered the wound, but her fingers were covered in her own blood. In her right hand was her pistol. She looked up at him as he rushed to her side.

"Damn fool," she said. Her voice was weaker than before, but still contained a sharpness to it. "Choosing me over that man. Some detective you are."

Carter put his pistol on the floor next to her and gingerly removed her hand from her wounded arm. The bullet had snagged the fabric, ripping a jagged hole. He took the soaked cotton between his fingers and ripped. She winced at the action, but it gave him a good view of the wound.

The bullet had hit her dead in the center of the bicep. The gaping hole in the front was already clotting. With a quick apology, he felt around the back of her arm, searching for the exit wound. He found it and breathed a sigh of relief.

"It's a through and through," he said. "Can you move it?"

She tried, grunted under the pain, and slapped him across the face. "Does that count?"

Carter smiled grimly. "That'll do." He looked all around. Not finding what he was looking for, he ended up ripping the rest sleeve off her shirt. He quickly wrapped it around her arm, just above the wound, and cinched it as tight as he could.

"I knew you wanted to get me out of my clothes," she said. There was a glint in her eye despite the pain.

"If that was the case," Carter said, returning the glint, "I'd prefer a different situation."

The rear door of the smaller room slammed open. In one swift movement, Carter grabbed his gun and whirled around, eyeing the newcomer along the length of his barrel.

Jackson.

"What happened?" his partner said. He caught sight of Celeste and the blood on Carter's hands.

"The man in the green shirt," Carter said. He stood, holstering his gun. "His name is Evans. Now he's wearing a gray suit with a blue shirt. I think I nicked him."

"That would've been me," Celeste said. From the floor, she stood, her legs wobbly.

"Why didn't you go after him?" Jackson said, exasperation filling his voice.

"Sir Galahad couldn't let a maiden in distress well enough alone."

"I'd hardly call you a maiden," Carter replied. To Jackson, he said, "Did you see him?"

"Not at all. I was up on the roof." In a huff, Jackson brushed by Carter and made his way out the door. He banged it open, turned and starting running. He nearly bowled over Sheriff Briscoe who had been running into the showroom. Jackson motioned Briscoe to follow him and the two charged down the street.

Celeste looked after them. "If you catch him, I wouldn't be sad if you put a bullet through his arm."

Carter settled his hat lower on his forehead. "I'll see what I can do. Can you manage?"

Her sarcastic snort was her only response.

Carter ran out of the furniture store and after the man he now knew as Evans.

* * *

THOMAS JACKSON WAS a full block ahead of Carter. His partner's pealing commands for Evans to stop went unheeded. Sheriff Briscoe followed, the older man clearly having a difficult time with the chase. But what greeted Carter in front of the bank sent shivers down his spine.

The deputy who had been standing outside the front door of the bank lay on the ground. The man bled from two wounds, one to the throat and another in the gut. His motionless body lay on its right side, eyes wide with surprise and fear. His hands were empty, proving that Evans, in his haste to get away, shot the deputy in cold blood. Ewing and Gilman hovered over the dying—or dead—man and called for a doctor. Either one of the deputy's wounds were enough to kill him. If he had both, he was not long for this earth.

Carter inwardly chastised himself and he took off running. Why had he delayed? Was it some misplaced loyalty to Celeste? Not loyalty, per se, but another emotion that began with the letter L. For perhaps the first time in her career as a lawman, he put the interests of another person not directly involved with the case in front of the case itself. As he bounded across Austin Street, he wondered how he would write that up in his report and make himself look good. He didn't think there was a way.

Two blocks ahead, Evans turned left on Mary Street heading north. Mary Street was one of the major thoroughfares where the railroad came through the heart of downtown Waco. The Texas and St. Louis narrow gauge railroad bisected Mary Street. Jackson immediately followed.

Carter was far enough behind that he wondered what Evans's likely next move would be. He might double back and come back around to Third Street or he might traverse the alleys between the main streets. Even with Briscoe huffing at a decidedly slower pace than Jackson, unless reinforcements arrived, it was up to Carter and Jackson to apprehend Evans.

A few ideas crossed through Carter's mind. He could commandeer a horse, but with Evans on foot, the owlhoot was much more agile and could go where a horse could not. Plus, he would have fewer chances to coordinate with Jackson.

Reaching the intersection of Mary and Third, Carter slowed and came to a halt. The pedestrians and folks riding horses or wagon had taken notice of the pursuit and the panting detective that now stood in the middle of the street, his boots straddling the train tracks, and wondering which way to go.

"They ran down that way," a young girl said. She held hands with a woman, presumably her mother, and pointed north along Mary.

Carter looked at the woman. "Is there another way to catch the guy my partner and I chasing?"

The woman started to indicate a path forward, but another woman's scream charged through the air. Carter turned to the sound. It came from Franklin, the parallel street Carter had already crossed. Muttering a curse, Carter turned back and charged back the way he had come. No sooner had he reached halfway down the block than a horse and rider fled across his vision. The man held onto the reins, and gouged his heels into the horse's flanks. His hat was pulled low on his head, the brim flapping up with the wind. But Carter needed only to catch sight of the face to know it was Evans.

Carter drew his gun and made to fire. He was a split second from pulling the trigger when Evans and his horse vanished behind a building. Reason crept back into Carter's brain and he took stock of all the surrounding people and wagons that a stray bullet might have hit. He ground his teeth and hurriedly ran the rest of the way.

He rounded the corner, hoping to catch sight of Evans. He saw nothing more than what you'd typical expect to see on a busy morning in Waco. No running horse, no running man, no nothing.

Jackson, running full tilt, came up to his position. "Where'd he go?"

Carter gestured with his gun.

"You try and shoot him? With all these people?" Jackson bent over and put his hands on his knees, breathing in great gulps of air into his lungs. "First you fail to catch Evans, then you put people's lives in danger?" Jackson spat and shook his head. He stood straight and smacked Carter in the jaw.

Carter took it, mainly because he never saw it coming. The jolt smarted and he worked his jaw back and forth to verify it wasn't broken. "I deserved that."

"You're damn right you did." Jackson whirled and stomped off in the direction of the bank.

"Where you going?" Carter called after him.

"To find the sheriff and get a manhunt started."

Sheepishly, Carter looked around. Everyone on foot had stopped to watch the two detectives argue and one hit the other. Now, twice in two days, he had failed in his job. His upper lip curled into a snarl.

Calvin Carter hated to fail.

SHERIFF BRISCOE PROVED to be an efficient handler of men. Within half an hour, all of his four remaining living deputies had each recruited another two or three men. Together they started to scour the town of Waco looking for the man Carter now knew as Evans. It was a wide net, covering ten city blocks, west to east, starting at Third Street and moving south. Thomas Jackson counted himself in that number, being paired with Briscoe himself. Surprisingly, even Timothy Walsh, who had heard the commotion, found out about the manhunt and offered his services. Celeste begged off the search for the moment, instead heeding Carter's continued insistence that she see a doctor. The look of disgust she gave Carter was yet one more nail in his figurative coffin.

Calvin Carter, however, didn't join them. After trudging back to Ewing's bank and Milburn's Furniture Store where all the activity began, Carter received enough sour looks from Jackson that he didn't even bother asking what his partner had found around the rear of the building. So Carter went and looked himself.

The two story brick structure was built like most every other building in town. On the rear of the furniture store, Carter spied the freight door where the coffins were moved into the smaller showroom. Just to the right of that door was a ladder. The metal rungs, flecked with rust, were embedded into the brick and cement and went all the way to the top of the building. To get to the bottom rung, you had to go up a small set of wooden steps. This Carter did and climbed to the roof.

The roof of the furniture story merged with that of the bank. Tar and gravel acted as a barrier against the elements. In the heat of a Texas summer, the surface of the roof would be sticky, with footprints of anyone walking around up here clear and distinct. Now in January, however, the tar and gravel was firm and solid.

Carter walked across the roof and stepped over the small raised wall that separate the furniture store from the bank. Even here on the bank's roof, nothing was amiss. He made his way over to the front of the bank and looked over. The balcony that led into the bank was about fifteen feet down. An agile person could hang and land with relative ease, as long as he bent his knees on impact. More likely, the robbery used a rope to lower himself. A quick inspection of the bank's facade revealed small chinks in the cement, likely made by an iron hook. Whoever stole the money, he came this way and used a rope and hook.

He stood and inhaled deeply. Carter hated himself for failing. He hated the report he'd have to write. He'd hate talking with Desmond Arnett and telling him about his failure and having the older man chastise him. Carter decided he needed to make things right.

Quickly descending the ladder, Carter walked a block north to the country courthouse. Inside, he found the address of Luke Durham, the man who made the special coffins for Milburn. Carter thought about the furniture salesman as he walked the dirt streets across town. Milburn was meeting Evans at ten. The purpose was unknown, but clearly Milburn knew Evans, even if it was only as a client. With Evans part of the gang that derailed the train, he was probably retrieving whomever was in the coffin. Why? Carter barely had any understanding of the entire scheme much less the who or the why. It frustrated him. He pulled out one of the cigars, lit it, and smoked as he pounded the boardwalks. He kept his head down, looking up only at street corners to verify his location.

The one thing that most stuck in Carter's mind was Milburn's reluctance to name Luke Durham as the maker of the coffins. Why? Perhaps Milburn was acting as a front to some larger gang. Perhaps Luke Durham was the mastermind, the one who envisioned being able to sneak people in and out of town in coffins. That idea lightened Carter's mood considerably. That was certainly an effective way to kidnap people and offer them for ransom. Ingenious actually. He wondered why he hadn't stumbled on the idea from the very beginning.

Durham's Lumber Shop was located down on Seventh and Austin Streets. Other wagon yards occupied this city block as well. Durham's was a finely built wooden structure, a story and a half tall with the upper story appearing to be more storage than anything. The building appeared more like a large house than a place of business. The oversized front door opened onto a porch that traversed the front of the shop. Two windows looked out onto Seventh. Windows on the east and west sides also gave glimpses into the shop. The backdoor was, in fact, two doors next to each other, the better to get large finished work in and out. The back yard was where Durham kept his raw materials. Stacks of wood and other implements lined the grassless area. Tarps covered the wood to protect it as much as possible from the elements. Carter idly wondered if Durham had built his shop partly to show just how good he was.

Carter approached the rear of the house and stopped on in the street. From inside the house came the sound of hammering. The odor of sawdust and turpentine met his nostrils. He noted the stacks of wood also shielded the rear of the shop from passersby unless they stood where he was, directly to the rear of the building. Then again, chances were slim that Durham or his associates—if the craftsman was even a part of their confederacy of crime—would knowingly load a person in a coffin from inside the shop. Sure, Durham made coffins, but he sold them at Milburn's shop.

On the ground, rutted grooves told Carter how wagons backed up to the rear door of the shop. He gave a thought to tracing the paths of the ruts, then dismissed the thought as stupid. The answers were inside. So Carter went around to the front and went inside.

The sweet smell of wood was thick in the small entry way. Carter's senses were able to pick out pine, oak, and cedar. A small counter was set just in front of a doorway that led into the main shop. That doorway was covered by a black tarp that hung from a rod installed at the top. Carter pegged Durham as an unmarried man for if there was a woman in his life, she surely would have made this area more attractive. Various pieces of furniture lined the wall. All were in an unfinished state, the plain wood clearly showing the craftsmanship of Durham. Carter ran a finger along one chest of drawers and noted the types of joints Durham used. Carter didn't have a clue what the correct term was, but he couldn't help but be impressed at the nail-less methods Durham employed.

"Help you?" came a voice.

Carter turned. In the doorway that led to the main part of the shop stood a man. As expected, he was broad shouldered. The white cotton shirt was dirty and Carter suspected no amount of laundry could fully clean the grime that lined the wrinkles. The shirt sleeves were rolled haphazardly to the elbows. The blue apron he wore on his front was coated with sawdust and smears of paint from years of working. Sweat glistened on the man's thick forearms. The hands were larger and looked capable of nailing nails without the need for a hammer. Nonetheless, the man held a hammer in his right hand. Curiously, Carter noted the bulge of a holster and gun on the man's hip.

Turning on a smile, Carter asked, "Luke Durham?"

"Yeah."

"Good morning," Carter said, resuming his Southern accent. He didn't immediately know why since Durham wasn't present when Carter used it on Milburn. He chalked it up to whimsy. Why the hell not? He was an actor, after all. "My wife and I recently lost her favorite aunt and we were looking for a coffin."

Durham hooked a thumb over his shoulder. "I sell my work down at Milburn's. Go there."

"I was there. When I asked him for a particular type of coffin, he gave me your name."

Durham coughed and spat behind him. "What type of coffin were you needing?"

Using his hands to demonstrate, Carter said, "I was hoping to have one with a raised, carved piece. I want the raised piece to be of flowers. Magnolias were Aunt Margaret's favorite. Milburn said you were the only man who could do it."

A muscle in Durham's cheek twitched. "You seen something like that?"

Carter nodded. "Yes. I was at a funeral recently for an old friend. In the church, there was his body in a coffin. He was a good man, devout, loved God and his family. Great man. Anyway, his coffin wasn't one of those typical pine box jobs. He was fairly wealthy and had commissioned a special coffin with this raised carving. I took a fancy to it. So when Aunt Margaret died, I thought the best gift I could make to help remember her is to commission a coffin with one of those carvings." He spread his hands. "And here I am."

All during Carter's little speech, Durham's jaw muscles flexed. Maybe he was chewing a wad of tobacco, maybe not. But he spat into his shop again.

"Can't do it," Durham finally said. "I'm too far behind."

For the second time that day, Carter broke protocol. He reached into his pocket and withdrew the small satchel of gold double eagles. He shook the bag. "I can make it worth your while if you can slip me in. It's a surprise for my wife. I'd be ever so grateful."

Durham thought a moment, scratched the back of his head, then raised a hand and swept the tarp aside. "Come on back." He turned and disappeared back into the shop.

Carter pocketed the satchel. He came around the counter and peeked through the doorway. The interior of the shop was enormous, taking up more than half of the entire building. Stations were neatly arranged around the perimeter of the area. On the walls, tools were perfectly aligned and hung on hooks. Off to the left were stacked more pristine wood. It appeared to be most every kind, including dark ebony. The floor was coated with sawdust and the odor rushed into Carter's nose. So did the smell of turpentine. A thought flashed through Carter's brain. The last time he got a whiff of turpentine was at the cotton gin when Evans torched the place and tried to follow suit with Carter.

Alarm bells went off in his mind. Perhaps Durham was more closely associated with Evans than previously thought.

The click of the hammer of a gun put all doubts to rest. The person holding the gun wasn't Durham. He had stopped in the middle of his shop. He had turned and now stood facing Carter. No, the person holding the gun now eased out from behind the door and placed the barrel to Carter's temple. The cold steel sent a shiver down Carter's spine. He froze in place, hands slightly out and away from his sides.

"I think you have something that belongs to me," the man said. Even though he had only heard the voice from his position outside the cotton gin the previous evening, Carter knew the voice belonged to Evans.

"I'm sure I don't know what you mean," Carter said, maintaining his faux Southern accent. "I'm here to commission a coffin from this gentleman."

"Oh, you'll get a coffin alright," Evans said. He reached over and patted Carter's pocket. Locating the satchel full of gold coins, Evans reached in and retrieved them. "Thanks for bringing them back." He stepped away from Carter and came around to face the detective. The gun was still trained on Carter's forehead. "Who are you?"

Carter shrugged. "A simple man who wants to commission a coffin. If you're thinking I'm someone else, I believe you are mistaken."

Evans screwed up his face. "Kill the act. You're from the train. You shot and killed two of the men I hired."

"And you killed an old friend!" Carter spit out the words with force and venom. All traces of the fake accent were gone. Evans was momentarily taken aback. "The engineer. Did you have to kill him?"

Pausing in thought a moment, Evans said, "Probably not. But it's worth it to maintain the fear of the moment. You'd be surprised how many people don't act when someone is shot. Then there was you and your partners. Detectives, right?" He shook his head. "Leave it to bad luck there had to be railroad detectives on the train."

"There are detectives everywhere," Carter said. "There's a manhunt on. You'll be found."

"No he won't." This came from a spot behind Durham that led to the outside loading area. Carter recognized the voice even before the man walked up from behind Durham and came to stand next to the woodworker.

Timothy Walsh.

He was dressed as Carter had last seen him at breakfast in a black suit, gray pants, and gray vest. His boots were muddier than before, likely as a result of his traipsing around looking for Evans.

Confusion reigned in Carter's mind. He cocked his head, staring at the newcomer.

"After we're finished here," Walsh said, "I'll report back, tell the sheriff my area was clear. No sign of the fugitive." He held out his hand. Evans tossed the satchel and Walsh caught it. He fingered the coins though the fabric and then slipped the bag into his pocket.

Carter wet hip lips. His options appeared to be lessening by the second. "I'm not the only one who has seen his face. I described him to the sheriff and my partner. They'll find him." He gestured to Evans with his head. "He won't be able to get out of town without notice."

Walsh cocked his head, looking at Carter. "Probably not. If he's on a horse. But not if he's in a coffin. No one dares to inspect a coffin." A slow grin creased his face. "Do they?"

Carter put two and two together. The implications were many. But he focused on one in particular. "Is she in on it?"

Walsh ran his tongue over the edge of his teeth. "Stupid detective," he chided, "she planned it."

The bottom of Carter's stomach dropped to his boots. Like a talented actress, Jessica Reed had played him for the fool. No wonder Jackson was so angry with him. Even with Celeste and her getting injured, Carter seemed incapable of seeing beyond a woman's charms.

New anger swept up through Carter. He was outmanned and, even with Evans holding the only weapon, outgunned. But he sure as hell wasn't going to go down without a fight. Evans had already seen the Derringer, but it was no matter. Even though Carter had reload the small gun and slipped it back into the holster on his forearm, in the seconds it took for the gun to deploy, Carter would have a new hole in his head. His only chance was movement. Evans still had the gun trained on Carter's forehead. As skilled a shooter as Evans appeared to be, Carter knew that diving right or left would still end in a bullet. Only one option remained. Down.

Without a thought to what happened next, Carter dropped to his knees. At the same time as he hit the wooden floor, Evans pulled the trigger. Damn, he was quick. The bullet sailed so close to Carter's head that the hot slug whipped Carter's hat off his head.

The detective barely perceived how close to death he had come before he lunged forward, throwing himself at Evans. The purchase of his boots on the wooden floor was marred by the sawdust. Carter didn't get a full thrust at the gunman, but he got enough of one. He tackled Evans in the midriff. The impact sent both men backward into a table.

Tools rattled and fell on the workbench and the floor. Evans grunted in pain and astonishment and was already trying to shove Carter off of him.

But the moment also allowed Carter to act. Instead of flailing his hand around and trying to find a weapon, he already knew what weapon he wanted. The body blow allowed Carter to shove his hand into his jacket and wrap his fingers around the butt of his Colt. It was a tight fit with the weight of his body on top of Evans, who was bent over backwards on the workbench, but there was enough clearance to bring the gun to bear. Carter knew that if he backed up and tried to arrest Evans that the outlaw would merely shoot him. Or Walsh might.

The image of Elmer Osgood flashed in Carter's mind and he knew only one thing needed to be done in the moment. He shoved the barrel of his gun into Evans's gut and fired.

The flame that blossomed from the barrel of Carter's gun seared his shirt fabric and even his skin. The pain was sharp and intense, but Carter didn't care. He knew his injury would heel but Evans would die.

Something heavy slammed on the back of Carter's head. He saw stars and tried to blink away the feeling of nausea. Walsh or Durham grabbed his gun hand and yanked the weapon from Carter's grip. Another hand grabbed the back of Carter's collar and bodily dragged him off of Evans. The detective fell in a heap on the floor, plumes of sawdust rising in the air. His vision was still spinning, but he zeroed in on the sight of Evans, his face registering complete surprise, slide off the workbench and onto the floor.

"Dammit!" Durham yelled. "Now look what you've done to my shop!" He approached Carter and gave the detective a vicious kick in the stomach. Coupled with the nausea he was already experiencing, Carter wretched onto the floor. Durham kicked Carter again before spinning on Walsh. "Now what?"

Carter was nearly unconscious, but he knew he was at the mercy of Timothy Walsh. If the thief was to kill him right here and now, Carter wanted to face him with eyes open.

Walsh looked first at Evans then at Carter, worry lines lancing over his face. Then, he calmed as a new idea struck him. The lines eased and a sly grin etched itself on Walsh's face. "The new train will be here tonight. They've already cleared the track down south of here."

The last thing Carter heard before lapsing into unconsciousness was, "Why don't we make them both disappear."

CALVIN CARTER AWOKE to near darkness and the sharp tang of another man's sweat in his mouth. The acrid taste nearly gagged and he tried to close his mouth. He realized he couldn't, then figured out why. A bandana was shoved into his mouth. He moved his tongue, slowly working the damp fabric out of his mouth. He needed his hands. He tried to bring them up.

They hit something. Not only that, they were tied together, resting on his body. It was then, as he kept moving his tongue, that he took stock of where he was.

The air was stuffy but breathable. Little whiffs of fresh air mingled with the non-moving air of his confines. He opened his eyes and looked around. He wasn't necessarily surprised to discover he was inside a coffin, but that didn't mean his heart didn't hammer in his chest. Not only that, it was a coffin with air holes directly in front of his face. Faint light crept in, giving the interior of the coffin a ghostly glow.

The coffin was lined with white fabric underneath him and halfway up the sides. His head rested on a pillow. Any movement would put weight on the large bump on the back of his head and the pain that came with it. He angled his head to avoid that as much as possible.

The upper half of the coffin, roughly from his waist to his head, had greater amount of space to move around than did the lower half. He could bent his knees and raise them only about six inches before they hit on the inside of the lower part of the coffin lid. But he could lift his head nearly a foot before his forehead made contact with the coffin lid.

That was good. It gave him some room to maneuver and figure out how to get out of his predicament.

Air holes or not, Carter still shared the fear of every human on earth when it came to coffins: the fear of being buried alive. He had no way of knowing where his ultimate destination was at the moment, but he damn sure knew he was going to do something about it.

Once his eyes adjusted to the gloom, he was able to see his hands. He worked them up past the halfway point and yanked out the bandana from his mouth. He sucked in the still air in great heaving lungfuls until he caught himself. The air holes were small. Yes, they let in some air, but he was unsure how much. He slowed his breathing, inhaling evenly, until his initial panic washed away.

From outside his coffin, he heard the sound of a squeaky wagon wheel and gentle creaks of moving wood a wagon makes as it was pulled down the street by a horse team. Sounds of the city slowly came to his ears. He heard passersby talking about normal things, laughing with each other. Horses blew, other wagons passed by Carter's wagon, and children shouted and played. As far as Carter knew, this was still Waco, but he had no idea how long he had been out. The light from outside was dimmer. Maybe twilight.

Carter snaked his tied hands down to his vest and

retrieved his watch. He flipped open the turnip and held it as close to the air holes and the feeble light that came inside. The hands read 7:30pm. He had been out nearly the entire day. Inwardly, he cursed. Surely Jackson would have missed him by now. He'd probably be looking for Carter as well as Evans.

Thinking back to his altercation with Evans, Carter's jaw muscles flexed as he ground his teeth. Elmer Osgood was still dead, but at least his killer had met justice. Carter considered himself a good man, especially when he wore his badge. He didn't go off on vendettas, hunting men in order to kill them. He obeyed his commanding officer and brought back men in irons for trial. That was his job and he took great pride in following orders. But that didn't mean things happened, like today with Evans. It was kill or be killed. And Calvin Carter had done the killing.

Now, however, he needed to figure out a way of escaping his confines. The last thing Walsh said before Carter blacked out was making him and Evans disappear. That meant one of two things: burial or being loaded on a train. That it was half past seven at night and the coffin he was trapped in was on a wagon probably indicated his destination was the train. Or some other place where Carter could simply disappear, dying of thirst or hunger.

He wasn't going to have that.

Voices sounded very close to the edge of Carter's coffin and he did the obvious thing. He shouted. He called for help and banged on the lid of the coffin.

The light from the air holes darkened as something covered them. It turned out it was a person.

"Hello in there," a man said. "Good to see you're not dead yet." Carter didn't recognize the man who spoke, but it was a husky voice, tempered by years of drinking. "I was told to tell you one thing if you was to wake up: keep yer mouth shut or your partners die."

Carter gasped. Partners? Jackson for sure, but who was the other? He thought back and replayed the past couple of days in his head and he arrived at the obvious conclusion. Celeste Korbel. He stopped shouting. Instead, he talked.

"What's your name?" Carter asked.

"Peter," the man said.

"Peter, I'm a lawman, a detective. I'm being kidnapped."

"I know."

"I need you to let me out."

"Nope."

Exasperated, Carter changed tactics. "Where am I being taken?"

Peter laughed. "I ain't never talked to a coffin before." He rapped his knuckles on the lid. "Listen, lawman, I'm riding back here to make sure you don't cause a ruckus. I got told to let you know only one thing, well, two if you count the one about yer partners. You're going on a little trip."

So it was the train. Chances were good it was the newly arrived train Walsh mentioned. Carter had no idea why he was being kept alive only to be loaded onto the train, but he took it as a good sign that Walsh wanted him alive for some reason.

"Is there anything I could offer you to get you to let me out?" Carter said after a few moments.

"Naw. I'm being paid well enough. Why don't you just lay back and enjoy the ride. I don't want folks to look at me funny seeing me talking to a coffin." Another few raps on the coffin lid.

Carter laid back, thinking. His mind raced at the possibilities. Well, he thought, at least he could get his hands untied.

He worked at his rope bonds, but they had no give in them. He even tried to use his teeth to loosen one of the knots, but to no avail. It was then his mind took inventory of the tools of the detective's trade.

He felt the empty holster positioned under his right arm. His gun was likely still at Durham's shop, but that was okay. You didn't use a gun to untie rope. But you could use a knife. And he carried a foldable knife in his pocket. He reached down and felt his both pockets, wondering if Walsh and Durham had thought to empty his pockets.

They had.

Carter sighed. "This is going to be much harder now."

He moved his hands to his jacket. It had fallen open. Carter picked up the left side of his jacket and felt for the hidden pocket. There, just above the lower hem of his jacket, on the inside, he felt what he was looking for. He worked open the small flap that served to hide the pocket. He reached his hands inside and withdrew the item inside.

A coiled guitar string.

It was a low E string, made of wound brass around a central core of animal gut. In an earlier case, Carter discovered by accident just how well a guitar string could be used to cut rope. It was a long process, requiring extra patience, but he had time on his hands.

He uncoiled the guitar string. It sprang out, actually pricking him in the cheek. Holding one end, Carter slowly managed to encircle the string around the weakest point of the knot tying his hands together. He snagged the other end and pulled the string taunt until it was rubbing against the rope. Sighing again, Carter began to saw.

The entire process took at least ten minutes. Carter lost track of time. He focused part of his mind on constantly readjusting his grip and the position of the string on the rope. He did his best to ignore the biting pain in his fingers

as the guitar string did to his curled fingers the same thing it
was doing to the rope. He also kept up the tension on the
rope, and felt rewarded every time one of the rope strands
broke.

The moment his hands broke free, the force actually
made both his hands hit the sides of the coffin.

"Hey," Peter said, putting his face right next to the air
holes, "no sounds. We're getting close."

Tamping down the thrill of having his hands free, Carter
asked, "Close to where?"

"The loading dock."

Definitely the train.

He had to admire the audacity of Walsh's plan. Kidnap
a bona fide railroad detective right under the noses of the
other lawmen in town, including the detective's partner.
While he had no idea why, that wasn't the primary point at
the moment. The next objective was to get out of this damn
coffin.

In his mind's eye, Carter put himself in Walsh's mind.
He had tied up Carter's hands—thankfully, not his legs—
with the intention of loading the detective onto the train
southbound to San Antonio. Forget the why, the obvious
next question was the coffin itself. Did Walsh lock the lid?
As a rule, coffins don't necessarily need a lock seeing as
how corpses rarely try and get out. Given the pride
Durham clearly showed in his work back at the shop,
Carter assumed the craftsman would balk at putting a latch
and lock on the coffin.

Only one way to find out.

Carter brought his hands up and placed them on the lid.
Ever so gently he pushed. The wood creaked. Inside the
coffin, the sound seemed deafening. He stopped, waiting for
Peter to sense the sound and slam the lid shut again.
Nothing happened. Perhaps the sound wasn't as loud from

the outside. Perhaps also the sounds of the city dampened the sounds of the coffin.

Putting a little more force behind the effort, Carter pushed the lid a little more. Now, he had an inch of space and light. Fresh air washed over him and he welcomed its sweetness despite being laced with dirt and horse manure. He also got a glimpse of Peter's body sitting next to the coffin. Carter also spied another coffin on the other side of Peter. It turned out that the two coffins and Peter were in the back of a wagon.

The wheels of the wagon bumped over steel. The force threw the lid back down with a snap. Carter balled his hands into fists, ready to strike if Peter got suspicious and looked into the coffin. That was certainly an idea, Carter thought. Cause a ruckus and hope Peter opened and investigated. But that relied too much on chance. No, to get out of this scrape, Carter needed to act on his own.

"Peter," Carter said, "when's the train leave?"

"Eleven," the man whispered.

"Damn, that's a long time. Think you could slip me some water. I'm mighty thirsty." Carter brought his hands up to his chest. He was ready in case Peter actually opened the coffin lid.

"Maybe. Once we get you in the warehouse and out of sight of the good people of Waco, I might be able to help you."

Carter relaxed a bit. Peter wasn't going to be his savior but there was still a chance for escape.

❧ 22 ❧

THE NEXT HALF hour seemed to drag on forever. The wagon traversed what Carter seemed to be every single rut in the streets of downtown Waco. He was jostled to and fro, even banging his already sore head on the side of the coffin. He discovered rather quickly that the sides of the coffin contained no padding. The white fabric was only for show. Well, he thought, dead people don't care. Only the living trapped in a coffin care. And he wouldn't be in the coffin for much longer.

The freight depot was down south of town, on Mary Street past Eighth Street. The entire block consisted of the terminus of both railroads that came into and out of Waco. Aside from the freight depot, the passengers had their own platform and a large platform that occupied nearly a city block of space was used for cotton. Both the cotton platform and freight depot were used to store material for loading. Carter wasn't sure which one at which the wagon stopped, so he waited and listened.

In the time since Peter had promised Carter at least

some water, the detective had gone through his clothes and took stock of all the tools he had on him. Frankly, it was paltry. No gun, no knife, nothing. The only thing he had was surprise and the guitar string. The stickiness of his fingers as the blood worked in the creases of his palm gave him the idea that was his best hope. He had taken the bandana and ripped it into two roughly equal pieces. He had tied the cotton fabric around both palms to act as a barrier to the guitar string when he gripped it. He had taken his own handkerchief, ripped it into strips, and tied them around his thumbs and forefingers. That was going to have to be good enough.

The wagon halted. Carter heard Peter slide off the rear of the wagon and talk to some other people, presumably the driver of the wagon. A minute later, Carter's coffin was pulled backward. He put his hands on the interior walls of the coffin and braced himself for the awkward feeling of being carried by his makeshift pallbearers. They huffed as they adjusted their grips on the handles. One of them hollered up to the platform and Carter heard the distinct sound of a heavy door sliding open on metal runners. The angle of the coffin was changed. It tilted down precariously when the men made to haul the coffin up onto the platform. He banged his head on the top as gravity pulled him downward. He fought back a curse as the bump on his head was again smacked.

Moments later, the sounds of the city almost disappeared. Carter then knew Peter and his compadres had brought him into the freight depot. Carter had been inside only once. It was a simple rectangular structure with a wide platform surrounding the wooden building on all sides.

Carter tensed. He knew the time was nigh. He fully expected Peter to be surprised when he opened the coffin

lid and Carter sprung his attack. The detective just hoped
that Peter was alone or that he could talk his way out of the
bad situation with anyone who happened to be around.

"Over here," Peter said. He was closest to Carter,
holding one side of the coffin. The trajectory of the men
changed. Carter felt himself being lifted up and then back
down, settling finally onto the floor.

"Damn he's heavy," one of Peter's compatriots muttered.

"There's one more," Peter announced. "Let's go get it."
Footsteps traipsed away, fading back into the sounds of
the city.

Hope scorched through Carter's heart. Was it going to
be this easy? Not wanting to take anything for granted, he
curled the guitar string around both palms. He hoped to
convince Peter to let him walk. Carter didn't necessarily
want to kill the laborer. He was just following orders. But
when the only weapon on hand was a makeshift garrote, the
choice might be made for him.

He edged the coffin lid up and inch. He peered out,
trying to catch a glimpse of legs or people in general. Carter
knew he had surprise on his side and perhaps the workers
here at the depot might be predisposed to help a lawman.
Then again, the sight of a man rising up out of a coffin
might also send them into a state of shock. Carter actually
smiled at the thought. The theatricality of that moment
would be so good.

Carter opened the lid a little more. Still no sign of
anyone. Could he be this lucky? Steeling himself for a fight,
the trapped detective opened the lid all the way.

The interior of the depot consisted of crude, unpainted
wood. Crates of various sizes lined the walls and were
stacked in rows. Most of them had paper tags tied onto
them, directing any worker who may handle them as to the

proper destination. The ceiling was a good ten feet above him. The one door which he had come through remained open. He heard the huffing of the workers as they brought up the other coffin—likely with Evans's corpse—into the depot.

Without another thought, Carter sat up in the coffin. He got his legs under him and stepped out onto the floor. Gingerly, he closed the lid. The view to the loading door was blocked by a couple of other crates. He had only seconds to find a place to hide or a position from which to launch an ambush.

The forms of the men hauling up the other coffin came into view. Their backs were to Carter and he suddenly had no time. He leapt over the coffin and put himself against the south wall of the depot. He was exposed, but it was the best he could do considering the circumstances.

The face of the man nearest Carter was red with the effort of carrying the second coffin. Idly, Carter wondered if Evans's corpse weighed more than his living body. He'd have to ask a scientist that question at a later date. The men already on the platform hadn't seen Carter. The two men still on the ground were scrambling up the steps, trying to maintain their balance and not drop the coffin.

A cruel grin creased Carter's face. This might be better than he expected.

Carter braced himself. He uncoiled the guitar wire from his left hand, but still held onto it with his right. He raised his right arm and brought the guitar wire down as hard as he could on the exposed forearm of the nearest man. The wire acted as a whip, swishing through the air and snapping around the man's arm. The wire lacerated the skin. A line of blood appeared on the man's arm.

He cursed and let go of the coffin, using his free hand to cover the mysterious wound that suddenly appeared on his arm. The remaining three men tried to take up the shifting weight of the coffin.

"What happened?" Peter called. He was on the steps on the same side as the wounded worker. Peter now had to hold more of the weight and he was struggling.

Carter stepped around the edge of the door. Peter caught sight of the detective at the same time Carter planted a boot on the coffin.

"What the hell?" Peter muttered a second before Carter shoved his boot forward. The coffin lurched to the side and downward. Peter lost his footing on the step and fell backward. He tried vainly to maintain his grip on the coffin, but that only served to guide the heavy object down upon his legs. The end result was that Peter was wedged under the coffin. His head smacked on the dirty ground. His eyes fluttered then shut.

The other two workers who still gripped the coffin fell with Peter. The only man still on his feet was the man who Carter had whipped. "Where the hell did you come from?" he cried.

"From the dead," Carter said. He punched the man directly in the middle of his face. The man staggered backward, but didn't fall. Being a burly freight worker, it was going to take more than a single punch to bring him down.

Which was why Carter hopped to the ground. He didn't have time to screw around with a fist fight. He needed to rendezvous with Jackson and make sure he and Celeste were okay. That meant flight.

But not before reaching down and snatching Peter's gun from its holster. He swung the gun up to the platform, aiming it at the worker's midsection.

"I'd be much obliged if you didn't follow me," Carter said. "You in on it?"

"In on what?" the man said. He again held his forearm. Blood trickled down the man's arm.

"That's all the answer I need." Carter spun on his heels, then stopped. "Oh, and if you don't mind, don't raise an alarm. You'll only get caught in the crossfire. Okay?"

Calvin Carter didn't wait for an answer. He was already charging down the street to his destination.

But Carter made a detour. The McLelland Hotel was
on Fourth Street, four long city blocks from Eighth where
Carter now found himself. As he quickly dashed away from
the train depot, Peter's gun in his hand, Carter got his bearings and decided to make another stop first.

Durham's Lumber Shop was only a block away. Much
easier. Besides, his gun might still be there. He didn't mind
using Peter's gun in a pinch, but Carter much preferred the
feel and handle of his own Colt. Besides, he owned Durham
for the vicious knock on the back of his head.

The time was nearly eight and most businesses in this
district were closed and boarded up for the night. Durham's
shop was no exception. All the windows showed no light
from inside as Carter approached the building. He toyed
with the idea of just skipping the detour, but he couldn't let
it go. He flat out wanted his gun and he was damn sure
going to get it.

Carter circled the entire building, scouting out doors
and windows. All were dark. Durham was either inside and

sleeping or outside. One way or the other, he was about to
find out.

Finding a piece of sturdy wood from a discard pile,
Carter picked it up and hefted it. He nodded and
approached the front door. After a quick look around,
Carter jammed the wood directly into the window. Glass
shattered and tinkled inside. He paused, listening. From
somewhere inside the shop came a rustling sound. Carter
dropped the wood and flattened himself along the exterior
wall. The footsteps grew louder. They were joined by a
muttered "What the hell?" A moment later, a head poked
out from the shattered window.

Carter's arm lashed out, grabbed the back of the man's
collar, and yanked him forward. Momentum carried the
man fully out of the window, landing in a heap on the short
front porch. Before the man could even make sense of what
had happened, Carter shoved the barrel of the gun into the
man's face. He raised his hands in surrender.

"Hello, Durham. Let's talk."

What the other man blubbered actually made Carter
laugh.

* * *

TWENTY MINUTES LATER, Carter barged into the Wheeler
Saloon. The crowd was as boisterous as usual. The shouts,
the jeers, the laughter filled his ears. Men and a few women,
dressed in finer clothes, still mixed, mingled, and played
poker. The only difference from the previous night was the
occasional word or phrase exchanged between people about
all the excitement that had been in town the previous two
days. Upon hearing one especially tall tale version, Carter
stepped over to the two men and corrected one particular
fact.

"No, the railroad detective most certainly shot that man. It wasn't just Miss Viola's woman."

The two men looked skeptical and Carter let it slide.

He spied Viola Wheeler walking among the crowd, still dressed like a queen in a dark purple gown, talking with players and directing some of the ladies to particular marks. Nicholas the Giant was close in her wake. It was he that first spotted Carter. He tapped Viola and pointed. The look of surprise on her face appeared genuine, and the shrill shriek of his name certainly meant good things. She beelined her way up to Carter, who kept moving to her.

They met and she actually hugged him. Her scent was a mixture of lavender, makeup, and perfume.

"Calvin, my boy, we thought you were gone."

"I was, but I'm back from the dead now." He grinned at her. "Literally. Where's Celeste?"

Viola pursed her lips and arched an eyebrow. "Why the concern for her?"

He waved his hand, silencing her. "Is she okay? The bastard who's behind the robberies said she and Tom might be in danger."

Viola, clearly miffed at Carter's dismissive way to shut her up, nonetheless turned him around and pointed to the far corner. There, dressed in the same type of clothes he had only seen her wear, stood Celeste Korbel.

Carter's heart skipped a beat upon seeing her safe and sound. It skipped two when she turned in their direction and their eyes met. He watched as her mouth opened in shock at seeing him. Then, realizing her employer was standing right next to him, closed it and stared hard at him. Upon a beckoning wave from Viola, Celeste leaned off the wall and came to them. She didn't lose eye contact with Carter the entire way.

"Where the hell have you been?" she said once she stood next to Carter.

"Good to see you, too," Carter said. He gave them the briefest of descriptions of what had happened to him. He ended with, "Where's Tom?"

"Last I checked, he was with the sheriff."

"And Jessica Reed and Timothy Walsh?"

She looked surprised and not a little annoyed at the mention of Jessica's name. "Why do you care about them?"

Carter made a mental note of Celeste's tone. Did he detect jealously? "Because they stole you're money, Miss Viola."

"Preposterous! What proof do you have?"

He gave her a lopsided grin. "Would you mind loaning me Celeste for the evening?"

"Loaning?" Celeste blurt out. "What the hell?"

"You want your money back?" Carter asked Viola. "I need a little assistance."

Viola's eyes went from Carter to Celeste and back again. "You can have Nicholas as well if you think you need him."

Carter shook his head. He swept his arm toward the front door. "No, ma'am. Celeste is all I need. Care to join me?" He raised his eyebrows in a silent question.

Celeste thought a few moments, her jaw muscles flexing. With a sigh that wasn't necessarily upset, she started moving to the door.

"Is this your idea of a date?"

"Believe me, you'll have a blast."

* * *

TRUTH BE TOLD, Carter needed Thomas Jackson as well as the sheriff and his men. Moreover, Carter owed Jackson the courtesy of letting him know his partner was alive and well. But as he and Celeste exited the Wheeler Saloon and started making their way over to the McLelland Hotel, he asked her about Jackson.

"He apologized to Walsh and Reed for not only not finding her father's body but also for you apparently disappearing and not helping the case."

Carter winced. "Really?"

"What else were we to think? You didn't join in the manhunt and the next thing anyone knows, you can't be found."

"Hey, maybe I was working a lead and needed complete freedom?"

"Or maybe you just got so embarrassed you let Evans escape that you found a saloon and drowned yourself. He said you did that once before."

Carter screwed up his face again. "Yeah, well, I was younger then. I'm older and much wiser now."

She sniffed. "I'll grant you older, but wiser?"

In a few minutes, they reached the lobby. He asked the desk clerk if Jessica Reed and Timothy Walsh were in their room.

"No, sir, they checked out earlier this evening."

"And Detective Jackson?"

"He went with them."

Frowning, Carter said, "Where?"

The clerk gestured west. "To the opera house. They were going to see the play before the eleven 'o clock train departs."

Another huge grin creased Calvin Carter's face.

"What?" Celeste asked, warily.

"It's show time."

❧ 24 ❧

THE MCLELLAND OPERA HOUSE was a mere half block away from the hotel of the same name. A new structure built in the classical style, it was the largest opera house in central Texas. Touring troupes came through Waco and brought not only the classics to life, but modern stories as well. Carter had appreciated the performance of Julius Caesar a few nights ago upon the completion of their previous case and had met many of the actors backstage for drinks and to swap tales of the stage. So when Carter and Celeste knocked on the rear door and made their request of the actors, they all gladly agreed.

Celeste gave Carter a sidelong glance. "Are you sure you have to do it this way? Can't you just arrest them?"

"Sure," he replied, "but what's the fun of that? Besides, with you up in the box ready to nab them, you'll get to see just how good an actor I am." He winked at her. "You know, when this is over, maybe I can regale you with a discussion of the classics of the stage and my talents as an actor."

She gave him a look that was probably the softest she

had ever given him. Carter took that opportunity to lean over and kiss her. She kept her mouth in such a hard line most of the time that he expected to be greeted with a firm kiss. Instead, her lips softened under his. They felt wonderful. He pulled back before he got lost in the moment.

"Work first," he said, his voice a little hoarse. "We'll continue that later."

"That confident are you?"

"I am. But let's catch the bad guys first."

With her own wink at him, Celeste turned and made her way to the front of the opera house. Carter climbed the back stairs and vanished inside.

The play was in full swing and Carter couldn't have planned it any better. Julius Caesar was already dead and Mark Antony was due to go on in another scene. To make the reveal as powerful as possible, Carter chose to wrap himself up in one of the toga costumes. The actor who played Mark Antony initially balked at what Carter asked of him, but when the detective mentioned he'd be nabbing bank robbers, "Mark Antony" relented. Carter got himself ready, making sure the toga didn't interfere with his ability to draw his weapon if things went down badly. He rehearsed his lines—he had memorized Antony's speech earlier in his acting career—and figured out just how far in the speech to go.

In costume, he moved to the edge of the curtain and peered out. Not every seat was filled tonight, but it was almost three quarters. After what he did later on, he expected the entire town to think they witnessed it. Based on the directions the other cast members gave him and remembering his visit, Carter found the special box seats up on the balcony. In the ambient light from the stage and the lamps suspended from the ceiling, he made out Jessica Reed's face. She sat in rapt attention, staring at the stage, not realizing her freedom was mere minutes from vanishing altogether. Then there was Timothy Walsh. The smug bastard wore a nonchalant expression, almost as if he wished to be somewhere else. Judging by what he had planned for Carter, the detective knew Walsh's thoughts were likely on how to spend the stolen money.

And Jackson sat on Jessica's right. Carter's heart swelled with pride at seeing his partner safe and sound. Jackson looked bored. Carter wasn't surprised. He personally had to drag Jackson to see the show just a few nights ago. Now, Carter liked to think that his partner was worried for Carter.

From behind Jackson, Carter saw Celeste open the door that led down into the box. She bent down and whispered in Jackson's ear. He turned abruptly, but a steadying hand on his shoulder calmed him. The smirk on Jackson's face was his way of showing relief at Carter's safety.

"It's time," a cast member whispered.

Carter nodded and moved around to where the actor who played Caesar lay on the floor. The scene called for Mark Antony and others to carry the dead Caesar on stage and complete the scene. Caesar, his toga red with some sort of prop paint to resemble blood, stamped out the cigarette he was smoking. As one, Carter and the other three cast members each grabbed a limb and carried the dead emperor out to the middle of the stage.

When the lights swept over Carter's face and the protection of the curtain was behind him, a thrill coursed through his body. It had been nearly a year since he last acted in a play. He missed it. In fact, he considered it his true calling, the craft for which he was the most suited and the most gifted. It was also likely the reason he conducted his investigations in the manner he did. He loved the thrill of the show and the splendor of being at the center of attention.

And here he was again. In his mind, another Shake-speare quote came to mind: Once more unto the breach, dear friends, once more.

Interestingly, not all the cast members were in on the duplicity. Those that were already on stage when Carter decided to make his entrance stopped and frowned at him. But when the detective delivered his lines without missing a beat and when the other cast members, hidden offstage, motioned for them to keep going, they hesitatingly went along until it was time for Carter to delivered Mark Antony's big speech.

He moved to the center of the stage. He gazed out at the audience, pointedly not looking up at the box where Jessica and Walsh were sitting. All the eyes in the opera house were on him. He steadied his nerves and began speaking.

"Friends, Romans, countrymen, lend me your ears. I come to bury Caesar, not to praise him. The evil that men do lives after them. The good is oft interred with their bones. So let it be with Caesar." Carter's voice was clear. He projected to the cheap seats in the back. All who were in the opera house had no difficulty hearing him. He continued the soliloquy until he reached the part where he decided, on the fly, to veer off script.

"I speak not to disprove what Brutus spoke, but here I am to speak what I do know." With those words, Carter swept up his arm and aimed it at the direction of the balcony box. The stage lights weren't so bright that they blinded him. He clearly was able to see Jessica and Walsh. "You all did love him once, not without cause: What cause withholds you then, to mourn for him? O judgment! Thou art fled to brutish beasts, and men have lost their reason. Bear with me; my heart is in the coffin there with Caesar, and I must pause till it come back to me." He waited a few beats before continuing.

"But that's not all that was in the coffins, was it? All the money you have stolen is in the coffins, isn't it. How many banks has it been? I heard a dozen, all up and down the rail line. It was the perfect setup. Three coffins, all being shipped together down to San Antonio. One had air holes. Why, you may ask? To smuggle in or out a living man. Evans, by my guess. He was y'all's third partner. If things got too tight, he would escape inside the coffin. No one would ever think to search the coffin of a young lady who just recently lost her father, would they? Because if they did, they'd find not only an outlaw and bank robber but all the money that had been stolen. It was a good scheme, dear Jessica, but you and your "cousin" made three mistakes."

Carter waited for the audience rustle to die down. Jessica's face registered shock. Walsh sat mutely. "Your first mistake was your hands. Normally, letting a man hold your hand isn't a mistake, but normally, that man isn't a detective like me." With those words, Carter shrugged out of the toga costume and let it fall to the stage. The audience now was considerably surprised, but a gesture from Carter tamped down their noise.

"You see, those hands are strong and delicate. They enable you to climb down the sides of buildings, specifically the Waco Regional Bank, and sneak in. But that's not your only mistake. You're second mistake was revealing just how good your ears are."

The audience, realizing what they were hearing, now sat in rapt attention. A few craned their heads to get a glimpse at the people to whom Carter was speaking. Jessica, for her part, sat still. Walsh's face seemed to be growing redder by the moment with anger.

"When my partner and I arrived back at the McLelland Hotel the other night after the cotton gin burned to the ground, it was past midnight. I take pride in being able to sneak into rooms with nary a sound. I've even trained my partner in the same manner. We were quiet. I barely heard our footfalls. Yet you, from behind a door, said you heard us. Your ears must be exceptional, exceptional enough to hear the gears of a safe fall into place. Isn't that right?"

With that utterance, the audience actually gasped. Murmuring filtered throughout the people in the seats. More and more of them moved to get a better look at Jessica and Walsh.

"And your third mistake wasn't even made by you, dear Jessica. It was made by your compatriot, Timothy Walsh. Do you know what it was? You left me alive." Here, Carter put a sharpness in his voice. "You should have killed me when you had the chance. Because your man, Evans, also killed a good friend of mine. As soon as he did that, I was never going to give up until I brought that murderer to justice. That I've done. Now, it's your turn."

Jessica made to rise. A steadying hand from Jackson brought her back into her chair. Walsh had no such barrier. He scrambled to his feet. In his haste, he tripped, falling on the few steps that led from the box up to the balcony door. He got up and started back up the stairs. A figure filled the doorway. Carter recognized the smooth form of Celeste Korbel, her hands on her hips, blocking his path.

With a roar of frustration, Timothy Walsh turned back to face the stage and Carter. "Damn you!" In one swift movement, his gun was in his hand and it was aimed at Carter. He got off two quick shots.

Carter saw the movement—had anticipated it even—and dove to the side of the stage. The hot lead slugs chewed up the wooden stage floor in arcs of splinters. He kept rolling until he hit the edge of the stage. The ladies in the audience screamed. Men and women both started to flee.

Another shot sounded inside the opera house. A sharp

cry of pain pierced the ears of everyone in attendance. Carter looked up. Timothy Walsh's body now law slumped over the edge of the balcony. His gun, now free from his grip, tumbled end over end to the first floor.

In the ambient light from the stage, Carter noted the smoke rising from Celeste Korbel's gun. She moved down the few steps until she reached Walsh's body. With her gun trained on him, she grabbed his collar and heaved him back into the box. Jessica screamed at the sight of the lifeless form of Timothy Walsh.

With that, Carter stood and approached center stage. "It's all over, folks, it's all over. The sheriff has already been contacted. The coffins and all their baggage, so nicely ready for the eleven o'clock train, should be confiscated by now. The money will be returned to the proper banks, starting with the local money here in Waco. And you, dear Jessica, are going to jail."

Spontaneously, the audience began to applaud. Carter held out his arms and bowed at the waist. Up in the balcony, Jackson merely shook his head. From the posture of Celeste Korbel, Carter thought that he had finally had done something to impress her. That thought warmed his heart.

THE WHEELER SALOON was in full swing by the time
Calvin Carter arrived just before midnight. The crowd
appeared more boisterous than ever. The cheers sounded
more joyous, the jeers more discouraged, and the calls for
drinks more insistent. The smog of smoke hovered near the
ceiling as men enjoyed celebratory cigars. The ladies
dressed in their finer clothes, and the ladies who worked at
the Wheeler Saloon also came dressed for the occasion. In
short, it was like a festival at the saloon.

And why not? The owner's stolen money had been
found. Viola Wheeler was in high spirits. Attired in what
Carter suspected was the best dress she owned, Viola all
but floated between the tables and the patrons of her
saloon, waving at old friends and making new ones every
step of the way. Nicholas the Giant followed in her wake.
Even he was smiling.

"I don't think I've ever seen her this happy," Celeste
Korbel said. She stood next to Carter just inside the
front door.

After Carter's big show at the opera house, Sheriff

Briscoe had arrived. Word had indeed gotten to him about the coffins, and he and his deputies had confiscated and searched the coffins bound for the train. Aside from the two coffins that were supposed to carry Evans's corpse and Carter out of town, the three original coffins were filled with stolen cash and coins and not a few legal documents. Jessica Reed, unnerved by the killing of her partner, Timothy Walsh, had put up a stoic front for a while, but crumbled into tears. She confessed that they started to acquire various legal documents as collateral in their long trial of robberies mostly for extra blackmail potential.

When the time came for Briscoe to haul her away, Jessica had wrenched herself from the sheriff's grip and flung herself at Carter. "Please help me," she had said. "Don't I mean anything to you?"

Carter, keenly aware that Celeste had been standing within earshot of Jessica's pleading and paying heed to Jackson admonition that he, Carter, was too enamored with the ladies, merely looked at Jessica. "Yes, you do. You'll be a key character when I write up the report for this case."

The fury in her eyes told Carter that Jessica was likely to strike him. He had the wherewithal to raise one of his arms and block her open palm in mid-flight. He grabbed her arm and threw it aside. "Take her away."

The sheriff had nodded to one of his deputies and Jessica Reed was taken to jail. Carter caught Jackson's face which didn't hide his pride at his partner's decision. Carter also noticed Celeste's expression, it was one similar to that which he had witnessed from the stage. Up close, it was even more enchanting.

Now, standing back inside the Wheeler Saloon, Carter agreed that he had never seen Viola Wheeler so happy. He also enjoyed standing next to Celeste. He had angled himself so that he was able to see her without appearing to stare at her. With her boots on, she actually came to his height. She had washed her face from the day's activity of searching for Evans and then him. He hadn't been this close to her so far and, with the pressure of the case over, the worry lines around her mouth and eyes had softened. Carter found himself intoxicated just standing next to her, a warmness swimming around in his stomach.

"Shall we tell her?" Carter asked.

"Let's," Celeste replied.

Carter held out his arm, beckoning her to precede him. She cocked an eyebrow. "Ladies first," he told her. With a slight bow at the neck, Celeste led the way to Viola.

When the saloon owner saw them, she squealed like a little girl. "Calvin!" Many eyes and faces turned to Viola and watched as she took Carter's face in her hands and planted a massive kiss on first one cheek then the other. Surprisingly, the older woman's lips were firm yet giving. They left wet patches on his skin where they touched.

"I'm so proud of you, Calvin, my dear."

"You sound like my mother," he replied. His grin was wide and broad. "I just did my job." He turned to Celeste. "And I wouldn't have been able to do it if not for Celeste saving my ass."

"Oh," Celeste said, "you finally acknowledge the truth?"

Carter shrugged. "I didn't have a good angle. You had the better position. You plugged him."

Celeste again bowed at the neck. "Thanks."

Carter turned to Viola. "Sheriff Briscoe has already returned your cash to the bank. Celeste here can testify to that."

"I know." Viola hooked a thumb over her shoulder. Over on the far side of the saloon, a cigar in his hand and a glass of whiskey within arm's reach, sat Sheriff Briscoe at one of the poker tables. In his hands he held cards, fanned out. Conspicuously he wasn't wearing his badge. He caught sight of Carter and waved nonchalantly.

Next to him, with a large pile of chips in front of him, was Thomas Jackson. He had a grin on his face, but Carter couldn't tell if it was from the cards in his hand or the pretty red head who had pulled up a chair and sat next to Jackson. She had a hand on his shoulder and was looking at his cards. She said something, and Jackson laughed.

"News travels fast," Carter said.

"Good news travels faster," Viola replied. "Have you had a drink on the house?" she gestured to the bar. "Anything you want, Calvin, dear. Anything you want."

Carter turned to Celeste who regarded him with a peculiar look. "Care to join me? My treat."

Celeste cocked her head. She gave her boss a quizzical look. The saloon owner merely gestured to the bar and, without another word, eased back into the crowd to mingle among her patrons.

"I think I'll take you up on that offer," Celeste said.

"What offer was that?" Carter asked.

Celeste Korbel leaned in and brushed her cheek along his. Where their skin touched, lightening sparked along his face and down his side. She reached his ear and spoke, her lips and warm breath sending chills all throughout his body. Despite the cacophony in the saloon, Calvin Carter only heard the words she spoke.

"I think I'd like some *private* lessons in the classics."

KEEP READING for a sneak peak at the next Calvin Carter: Railroad Detective novel…

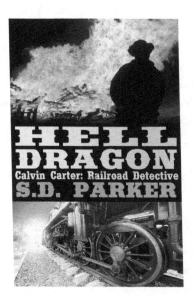

Coming 1 March 2019 from Quadrant Fiction Studio

HELL DRAGON PREVIEW

WHEN MALCOLM WHEELER was a young soldier during the Late Unpleasantness, he found himself unprepared for battle. It wasn't in the fervor of the cause. Being a soldier from northeast Texas, he knew the war was about defending a particular way of life, his way of life. No, he didn't own any slaves, but he benefited from that situation. He wanted things to go back to the way they were. They never did. His unpreparedness actually stemmed from the lack of adequate weaponry and equipment. When he was asked to march across the battlefield and take the hill, his rifle barely worked. The men around him fell. He didn't. He was captured and he learned of the events of Appomattox from a prison camp. But he had already vowed never to be unprepared again.

Now, as Wheeler gazed up at the blackest of night, he marveled at the stars and how many other people or things must be up there. He wondered if there were other people like him who made a decision about their life and enacted it with a constant thought like he did. He reckoned there were because if there's one constant in life, it's that everybody has the opportunity to learn and improve their station.

The stagecoach upon which Wheeler sat rocked gently along the rocky terrain. One wheel squeaked with every turn, having lost its lubricant hours ago. Wheeler told himself when he and Frank took a break in another hour, more lubricant would be applied to the wheel. He had made sure to load some on the stage ahead of time because he knew that this particular coach always squeaked when pushed into service for this long.

Preparation.

The surrounding countryside of the New Mexico territory was rough. The dark shapes of mountains appeared like black shadows against the even blacker palette of the night sky. The only way Wheeler could tell when the sky stopped and the mountains started was when he saw no more stars. The air was still filled with the odor of hot sand from the day's heat. Sagebrush and mesquite mingled with the heat, making a peculiar smell for his nose to breath into his lungs. He almost tasted the coppery air on his tongue.

Frank Jones was the driver. He was an old timer, his gray beard, neatly trimmed, covered his cheeks and face. The only skin that appeared out from under the whiskers were his lips. An unlit cigar hung from between his lips, the teeth wetly working the tobacco and sucking in the juice. His brown shirt and pants were engulfed in the darkness. The gloves he wore were leather, and they loosely held the reigns to the six horses pulling the stagecoach out from El Paso and over to the settlement of Burroughs. It was the last stop before they reached Texas and the railroad there that would connect them to the rest of the state.

And bring in the silver housed in the crates stored in the stagecoach.

The owners of the mine were fed up with the robberies.

The thefts were not regular. That irregularity proved the hardest part of shipping silver ore down from the mountains and back into banks in Austin, San Antonio, and on to Galveston. Some stages crossed the terrain without incident. Several in fact. But lately, the number of stagecoaches held up had increased. Rumors abounded as to the identity of the owlhoots responsible. The one name that kept being mentioned was Angus Morton. His gang of robbers had a pretty good reputation, but they hadn't been seen in the area for over a year. Some say they took their loot down into Mexico to escape American law and justice. No one dared pursue them. As long as the shipments got through okay, no one cared.

But things had changed. The robberies had increased. Silver and other valuable assets slowly had been stolen. With the mine owners desperate to secure their investment, changes had to be made. Special men, like Malcolm Wheeler, were deployed to guard against theft and robbery. Men who wouldn't think twice about shooting an outlaw in the back if necessary, the law be damned. Wheeler wasn't exactly as hardcore as that, but he was hired because he was the best. The reason he was the best was because he was always prepared.

Wheeler sat atop the stagecoach and waited. He wasn't worried. His clothes were finer than Frank's. The brown suit was tailored to fit his muscular body. Wheeler had large shoulders, broad and firm. The shirt was black, a concession to the manager of the stage line. When Wheeler told the manager he wanted to wear a white shirt so Morton would know where to aim. When Morton did, the fire from Morton's gun would serve as a beacon for Wheeler to shoot the son of a bitch. The manager didn't approve and insisted Wheeler wear dark clothes. Wheeler merely shook his head...but wore the dark clothes anyway. The sound of the stage itself was more than loud enough to draw the attention of anyone around. Wearing white wouldn't be an issue. But the manager--a scrawny little pipsqueak whose only worldly knowledge revolved around numbers in a book-- had insisted. He was paying so Wheeler complied.

His lack of worry came from his being prepared. He wore holsters on each hip, each cinched to his thighs with leather straps. In each holster was a Colt .44, the dark metal of the guns also muted against the night. In the boot to his immediate left was his Winchester. On daylight trips across the country before the robberies dictated night shipments, Wheeler could shoot a man from fifty yards while still on the moving stagecoach. Here in the night, it wasn't as much good as the shotgun that lay across his lap. His fingers caressed the barrel, up and down its length. Any bandit who tried to get him would get a face full of buckshot.

"It's pretty quiet tonight," Frank said around the cigar. Even his voice sounded wet. Air hissed out from between a missing tooth.

Wheeler nodded sagely. He was younger than Frank by about ten years. Wheeler respected Frank, but the other man had taken different lesson from the Late Unpleasantness. Frank's response was to run away. This Wheeler had learned from numerous trips with Frank. A lot of time needs to be passed, but Frank seemed to have run out of stories. Wheeler sometimes wanted to come out and ask Frank if he was a deserter, but he never did. If Wheeler found out the truth, there would be an uncomfortableness between them. Wheeler couldn't abide a deserter. It was a special type of coward who fled and left his fellow soldiers in the heat of battle.

"Yup," Wheeler muttered. He had told most of his stories, too. They passed the time in amiable silence for most of the night. As loud as the stage actually was, when they entered the small valley bounded by short rises on either side, they both had just quieted down. If Morton or any other varmint was going to try anything, it would be here.

Wheeler's eyes were attuned to the night. He saw the contours of the rocks along the road. Even the scrub bushes dotting the landscape were clear to his eyes. The six team in front of him--all with dark coats, naturally--were discernible. There was ample evidence of him earning his nickname of Night Owl.

As good as his eyes were, they immediately fixated on the bloom of fire that erupted from their right. The light flashed in the night, bright against all the darkness. Wheeler barely had time for his brain to acknowledge the light source before the sound met his ears. And the lead slug slammed into the side of the stagecoach. It thunked into the wood, chewing splinters and gashing a hole in the side of the coach.

"What the hell?" Frank muttered.

"Go! Now!" Wheeler ordered. He slapped Frank's arm to prod him into action.

The old timer was slow to react. The few seconds nearly cost him his life.

Wheeler yelled at the horses to go. His hand shot out, grabbed the reins, and urged the team forward. Frank, surprised at the shot, quickly got his head back in the game. He hadn't fully released the leather reigns from his grip, but now his hands tightened around them again and he took control. The horses, tired at pulling such a heavy load and accustomed to the slow movement through the area, were also slow to react. But they stepped up their pace and charged forward. Frank was momentarily thrown off balance, but he set his feet along the sides of the stagecoach and braced himself for the charge.

From the side window of the stagecoach, Luke Gregson stuck out his head. "What that a shot?"

Wheeler crouched low, bringing the shotgun to bear in his left hand while also drawing one of the Colts with his right. "Reckon so. Came from our right, maybe thirty yards. If these skunks are smart they'll..."

Wheeler never finished his sentence because what he feared came true. Another flame flashed in the darkness, this time from the left side of the stage. And it wasn't alone. Two, three gunmen opened fire on the stagecoach. The bullets chewed holes in the side of the stage. Luke actually cursed.

"You hit?" Wheeler yelled.

"Naw," Frank yelled.

"Luke?"

"I'm good," came the reply. Amid the cacophony of the stage charging forward over the rough terrain, Wheeler heard Luke scramble inside the stage. He must be moving to the other side.

Wheeler holstered his Colt and shucked the shotgun in the boot. He pulled up his Winchester and put a round in the chamber. He had good eyesight and he still could pinpoint where those gunmen likely were. Even if he missed his mark, Wheeler could still give those bastards a second to think things over. Not like it would ultimately do any good. There were four bandits so far. Who the hell knew how many more there would be.

The stagecoach crested a small rise and the plain down below came into view. The starlight illuminated the terrain, the scattered bushes and trees, the rocks and boulders from when God himself set them down eons ago. Wheeler also spied what he knew was there. Snaking through the land, the twin steel rails of the track caught the light from the stars and reflected it back to Wheeler's eyes. The rails rounded another rise and disappeared, but the shack was still there and reinforcements, too.

A part of Wheeler's mind wondered why Morton's men picked this spot, so close to the rails and the house. Two more of the stagecoach men were in there, ready to ride out at a moment's notice. Wheeler took in the sight, saw the light emanating from the house, and waited for the door to open and the two men to come and help.

Curiously, the door remained closed.

Wheeler turned and triggered two rounds back in the direction of the gunmen. Who the hell knew if any of his bullets had hit their mark, but the return fire ceased for a few moments.

Frank continued to steer the horses as they ran down to the rail line. The man may be old, but he was a veteran horseman. He maneuvered the beasts with excellent precision and made sure they didn't crash.

From inside the stagecoach, Luke fired off rounds from his Winchester. Two more gunmen opened fire on the right side. The bullets made new holes in the stage. A moment later, a sharp cry pierced all the noise of the stage and the horses. Luke had been hit.

"Luke!" Wheeler yelled. He waited a few moments then repeated himself. "Are you okay?"

No answer.

Wheeler swore. He turned and climbed up onto the roof of the stage. Along all sides was a short metal railing, usually meant to keep packages from sliding off and around which rope could be used to secure baggage. Tonight, it was empty. Wheeler had insisted on it, and for this very reason. He needed the room.

He lay flat on his stomach and spread his legs so that both boots anchored him to the railing. Frank was doing his best to keep the stage from crashing, so he wasn't too concerned about how bumpy was the ride. Wheeler didn't care either, but he certainly wanted to have as level a shot as possible back at the bushwhackers.

"Stay low!" he yelled over his shoulder.

Wheeler brought the Winchester to bear, resting it on the rear rail. He waited. Knowing outlaws the way he did, they would sooner or later reveal their position. They were most likely an impatient lot, ready to get the business concluded and the loot in their pockets. When they fired again, Wheeler would be ready.

The fire from five or six barrels flared in the night almost at once, as if it were a coordinated attack. All Wheeler saw was little pricks of light, more or less in a line at their rear. The slugs slammed into the back of the stage where some of the burlap bags were tied. The bullets did no damage, but Wheeler now had the positions of some of the owlhoots.

He triggered twice, aiming at a single spot. Two quick shots. He was rewarded with a scream. A grim smile creased his lips. If he met the Lord tonight, Wheeler told himself, he'd have sent at least one of the bastards to hell.

The angle of the stage changed and Wheeler slid forward. Frank had reached the top of the rise and was now angling the horses down to the house. With the rear of the stage now covering him from the front, Wheeler knew he had a few precious seconds to reload. He shoved his hand down into the jacket pocket and thumbed fresh cartridges into the Winchester. His fingers acted independently, having performed this task since he was a youth and before the Late Unpleasantness. It allowed Wheeler to clear his mind and assess the situation.

If Frank could get the stage down to the house, he and Wheeler might have a chance to dash inside for cover. With the other two men who were supposed to be inside, the four of them should be able to hold off the varmints. The outlaws numbered five or six, but they were down at least one. Wheeler vowed that he would subtract another before the stage reached the flat plain that led to the railroad.

He wasn't sure if the shooters were on horses or not, but he trained his fully loaded Winchester up along the ridge line and waited. He suspected the ambushers would charge over the rise, guns blazing. In another moment, his prediction proved correct.

The men were on horseback, their darkened shadows silhouetted against the horizon and blotted out stars as they charged. Wheeler counted five through the dust plumed up by the fleeing stage. The dust caught the starlight and actually provided a ghostly sheet against which Wheeler's excellent eyesight easily picked them out. He sighted one along the barrel of the Winchester, adjusting downward to increase the odds of striking the man or his horse, and fired three quick shots. The silhouette fell off the horse. Now they were down to four.

Wheeler didn't dare look behind him to see how close they were to the house. His eyes were fixated on the outlaws. But in the back of his mind he kept wondering when the reinforcements would emerge from the house. Surely, they could hear the stage storming down the lane if not the gunfire. What the hell was taking them so long?

The stage leveled out on the flat plain and Frank pressed the horses even more. Perhaps a hundred yards now separated the stage from the house. The bandits behind the stage had closed to about thirty yards, close enough for then to fire another fusillade of lead at the stage. Most of the slugs either struck the stage or sailed overhead.

Down east of the house lay the train track, disappearing in the distance. On the west, however, the track curved around a large rock outcropping the rail engineers clearly considered too expensive to explode. So they had veered the rails around the rocks. The end result was that the thing that emerged from behind the outcropping appeared almost out of nowhere.

"What the hell is that?" Frank cried.

Wheeler spun around and looked at what had gotten Frank's attention. The object's size was difficult to discern considering he was bouncing along on top of a stagecoach, but Wheeler thought it was the size of a small locomotive. It moved slowly out from behind the outcropping, inexorably to the house. Wheeler thanked the Lord that a train was approaching. It didn't matter from where it came. It meant that there would be men on that train, men with guns who could help him and Frank stave off these ambushers. He felt a glimmer of hope pass through him. He didn't breathe a sigh of relief, but there was hope.

That hope was dashed when two things happened one right after the other. First, the door to the house opened. Bright light streaked out into the night. A rectangle of light slid over the ground in front of the house. A figure emerged from the house. Wheeler squinted at the man. He had met the railroad men a few times, but this man didn't appear to be either of them. This man was dressed in a rumpled jacket over loose pants. The hem of the pants were shoved into calf-high boots. The man's head was shadowed by a large brimmed hat. Even if Wheeler didn't recognize the man standing in the doorway, he couldn't escape the sight of what lay on the floor of the house behind the man.

Two bodies, both with blood stains on their chests.

Wheeler had enough time to wonder what it all meant and arrive at a dreadful conclusion: no one would be coming to help. He and Frank were on their own. It also meant that they didn't have a refuge in the house.

Apparently Frank had reached the same conclusion. He

already was turning the team away from the house and toward the locomotive now approaching the house.

That was when the man who stood in front of the house signaled the approaching locomotive with a wave of his hand. Wheeler's eyes followed the motion and he gazed at the approaching machine. The front of the locomotive did something completely unexpected: a door swung open at the front. What was revealed was a short, flat platform. On the surface stood a man behind a shape Wheeler's brain recognized as a Gatling gun at the same time the gun began to spit lead into the night. If Frank recognized the shape, he never had a chance to respond.

The Gatling gun opened fire, but the hail of bullets wasn't directed at the stage. The bullets peppered the lead horses of the team. The high-pitched squeal of the beasts was a sound Wheeler hadn't heard since the battlefields of Pleasant Hill and Mansfield in Louisiana. The bullets punctured the lead mounts, killing them almost instantly. They fell to the ground, the other horses running directly into them, a great mass of dead and wounded animals. The end result was a near sudden stop of the stagecoach, which slammed into the back of the rear horses.

But that wasn't the end of Frank and Wheeler. Both men sailed through the air as their momentum continued. Frank fell head over heels down into the pit of the dying horses. His muffled cry was silenced by a combination of the bullets and the hooves of the beasts. With his position on top of the stage, Wheeler flew over the mass completely unscathed. He lost his grip on his Winchester as he vainly tried to steer his trajectory through the air. He landed on a shoulder. He both felt and heard his collarbone crack. His right side went numb, his right arm flopping and useless. He screamed at the pain. He continued somersaulting until he came to a rest at the foot of the porch. His eyes, wide with fear and pain, stared at the sky.

The sounds of the wounded horses filled his ears. So, too, did his own screams and grunts. Amid those sounds, Wheeler heard the approaching rataplan of horses from his rear. He knew the bandits that had chased him approached. He also heard the crunch of dirt and gravel under the boots of the man who had signaled the train. He approached, the light from the house illuminating one side of his face.

The man wore a French goatee, the ends of his mustache curled to points. A scar furrowed its way along a cheek. The light shining in the man's eye showed delight at what had happened. In his teeth was an unlit cigar, one end soddened with saliva. Wheeler had seen broadsheets with this man's face and he realized the man was Angus Morton.

"Evening, suh," Morton said. His thick Virginia accent pronouncing the word "sir" as "suh." He didn't remove the cigar as he spoke. "I'm glad you could join us." His eyes smiled down at Wheeler.

When the riders slowed to a halt, Morton surveyed them. Concern crossed his face. "Where is Rice and Dodge?"

"Dead," came the reply. Wheeler couldn't turn his head to see who spoke and realized he didn't care.

Morton returned his attention to Wheeler. "You managed to kill two of my men riding on top of a stage-coach, at night? I have to say your reputation remains intact, Mistah Wheeler." When Morton said his name, it came out "Wheelah." "When I heard it was you we were to face, I relished the challenge. But I have beaten you. Again."

He turned, removed the cigar, and spat on the ground. "Okay, boys, let's get what we came for." He signaled one of them. "John, come here and give me a hand with Mistah Wheeler."

Wheeler didn't know what Morton meant, but in a moment, the outlaw and one of his men each grabbed a shoulder and yanked Wheeler up and dragged him over to where one of the horses lay. The pain was excruciating. Wheeler howled. He weakly tried to reach for the gun on his left side, the arm that still seemed to work.

Morton reached over, withdrew the pistol in Wheeler's left holster, and tossed it away. "Ever the lawman, I see. I admire that, more than you know. But I'm gonna reward your tenacity to your duty with knowledge that few men know." He deposited Wheeler in his place. "You just sit tight and you'll see."

Amid the pain that creased through his vision, Wheeler watched as the men rummaged through the remains of the stagecoach. They hauled out Luke's mangled body. Wheeler noted the mass of blood along Luke's neck and realized the bandits had had a lucky shot. Luke likely bled to death before the crash. The injured horses moaned under their own weight, but the outlaws didn't seem to care. They busied themselves with removing the several thick bags from inside the stage.

Wheeler's only pleasure was seeing them struggle under the weight of the silver ingots inside those sacks. One of the owlhoots even tripped and fell. His bag fell open and little chunks of silver spilled out. Morton cursed the man, but also scurried over to him and helped pick up all the pieces. In an odd gesture, Morton brought one of the silver ingots over to Wheeler and placed it in his hand.

"There," he said, "now you have fulfilled your duty. You've saved one piece of silver. I hope when you meet the Lord, you can say you did your best. But tonight, your best wasn't as good as mine."

Wheeler tried to speak but his voice gurgled. The thick coppery taste of blood filled his mouth and ran over his tongue. He turned, fought through the pain, and spat, clearing his mouth. "Why?" was the only word he managed to utter.

"For the Confederacy, of course," was Morton's answer.

The response meant nothing to Wheeler. True, he was a Texan and his state lost the war, but life went on.

When the men had finished gathering up all the loot from the stagecoach and taking it to the locomotive which had come to rest just to the side of the house, Morton returned to stand in front of Wheeler. He snapped his fingers. "You still with us? I'd hate for you to die not knowing your ultimate answer."

Wheeler's eyelids fluttered open. In the intervening minutes, he had taken in the scene inside the house. Both men had been gunned down in their long johns. Each man didn't even have a weapon in their hands so swift was the invasion of the house by Morton. It seemed the outlaw's own reputation as a ruthless and cunning bandit was also secure.

Morton kneeled next to Wheeler. "I'm gonna take my leave of you now, Mistah Wheeler. I know this is a matter of honor for you, but it's only business for me. That's why you get to see what you're dying for." He put fingers to the brim of his hat and nodded at Wheeler. He stood and walked back to the locomotive.

Within a few minutes, Wheeler heard a massive roar. It reminded him of the sound a locomotive engine makes when it's ready to move. But instead of moving, something else happened.

A great stream of fire lanced through the night. It arced up from a position up above the platform upon which sat the Gatling gun. The doors to the Gatling platform were again closed. The fire appeared to be liquid. It wavered in the slight breeze. Wheeler's suspicions were confirmed when the fire landed on the roof of the house and splashed about. Wherever the liquid fire touch, new flames sprung to life. Within seconds, the house was ablaze.

Wheeler stared at the conflagration in wide-eyed wonder. The thing that had spewed out the liquid fire could better be seen now. It was indeed a machine, more like a modified locomotive. Instead of the black and steel of a typical locomotive, however, this machine was painted.

It resembled the face of some large, mythical beast, the kind of creature that populated the nightmares of little children. One orb resembled an eye. It glowed red from within. He saw shadowed figures working levers and gears. He traced the line of fire back down to a nozzle on the roof of the contraption. He found himself amazed at what his eyes beheld.

Malcolm Wheeler's amazed wonder turned to sheer terror when the streaming line of fire began to pivot and move. The outflow of fire changed its trajectory. The house was a raging inferno. Now the liquid splashed onto the ground at his feet.

The last thoughts Malcolm Wheeler had on this earth was that he hoped he had lived a good and decent life, that he would be forgiven for the sins he committed in the Late Unpleasantness and admitted into heaven because right at that moment, he knew what hell felt like.

THE ORIGIN OF CALVIN CARTER

HARD TO IMAGINE but it has been ten years since Calvin Carter was born. But his origins emerged from things even older.

Back in 2008, I helped my dad clean out a trailer home he and mom had on some land they were about to sell. In the process, we discovered the boxes of my grandfather's (dad's dad) paperback westerns. They were divided into a Louis L'amour box and an everything else box. In that box were dozens of westerns by authors I didn't know at the time. One was Mascarada Pass by William Colt MacDonald. It's a novel featuring Gregory Quist, a railroad detective. That aspect was one my limited knowledge of westerns told me was rare.

Around the same time, I visited a local Houston gun show. I went for research into modern weapons but became enamored by all the historical guns and paraphernalia. I saw a Texas and Pacific Railroad Special Police badge and, thinking of Quist, bought it. That's probably where the seed of the idea to write a story was born. Another seed was to write a story my grandfather would have liked.

The story in question turned out to be "You Don't Get Three Mistakes." It was first published on David Cranmer's Beat to a Pulp webzine. What makes the story special was that it was my first published tale for others to read. Not surprisingly, the origins of the story remain elusive.

I've pored over all my files, paper and electronic, and can find no trace of any notes I made prior to the writing of "You Don't Get Three Mistakes." The story was written in one session, pretty much as it was published, with nips and tucks here and there based on editorial suggestion. A writer friend of mine suggested the title, which was great considering the working title of "Job Interview" was pretty lame. I have notes written afterwards when I realized how much I liked the story and the chances that I might have a character on which I could hang a few more yarns.

Interestingly, his original first name was Caleb and I had no last name. When I came time to submit the story to Beat to a Pulp, I still had no last name. I scanned my writing room, searching for a name. My eyes landed on Max Allen Collins' first Hard Case Crime novel, Two for the Money. But, as you can see from the previous sentence, I didn't want a character with an "s" in his last name. Somewhere, Carter popped into my head, likely the result of me seeing all eleven volumes of Edgar Rice Burroughs's John Carter stories on an upper shelf. As for the first name, it was likely the number of volumes of the collected Calvin and Hobbes comic strips. More than likely, "Calvin Carter" owes his name to Burroughs and Watterson.

When it came time for the character to be born, Calvin Carter had a few fathers. I love the "Wild Wild West" television show from the 1960s specifically for its mash-up elements. Pitched as "James Bond on horseback," The Wild Wild West ended up becoming a steampunk television show. I dug all the gadgets Jim West had at his disposal. I also liked Artemus Gordon's ability to impersonate anyone. Naturally, railroad detective Gregory Quist was part of the mix. And I was reading the first Doc Savage novel when I wrote that first story. I had just met Charles Ardai at Murder by the Book in Houston and he had given us a preview of Gabriel Hunt. All of that swirled together and out popped Calvin Carter and his first tale, "You Don't Get Three Mistakes."

Carter's second tale, "The Poker Payout"—originally published in *The Traditional West*—introduced his partner, Thomas Jackson, a New Yorker whose father came to Texas to operate a ranch. A running joke between the two men is that Jackson, the Yankee, is more Texan than Carter, a native son. This second story changed the tone of Carter a bit. It was lighter, funnier, and edging close to over-the-top. Which was fine by me.

After a third story was written, I started his first novel. No, it's not the one you just finished reading. The first attempt at a novel-length story started off quite well, but it hit a few snags and, as of this writing, remains unfinished. But fear not: the components of that story will make its way to you someday.

The novel-length stories of Calvin Carter had a specific and direct influence: the Longarm novels as written by James Reasoner. Debuting in 1978 and created by Lou Cameron, Longarm was a major title in the adult western market. Using the house name "Tabor Evans," the publisher hired multiple writers over the years to contribute to the monthly titles. My grandfather had only a few. My dad's recollection of why my grandfather read those novels was that he had read everything else, probably more than once. Now, I wasn't a dummy back in the day, but a cowboy book with a pretty lady mostly undressed meant something. There was sex in them thar pages! It was a small miracle I never scanned those books on summer nights, trying to find those particular sex scenes. Heck, if I'd have actually read the books, I would have discovered just how entertaining the stories actually were.

The first Longarm novel I read was *Longarm and the Bank Robber's Daughter*, the 301st entry in the series. Why this one? Well, the actual writer was James Reasoner. Among all the folks I have met online, James is special. Not only is he a modern pulp writer whose writing output is a marvel, he likes the things I like and writes the kinds of stories I enjoy both reading and writing. Why not discover Longarm via James's particular lens?

I was sold in three paragraphs. I could barely put the book down. I kept reading James's entries and, other than a couple of other ones, the only Longarm novels I've read to date are those by James Reasoner.

But as I kept reading these books, I also saw the structure. Each novel is approximately 180 pages, each has approximately twenty chapters. And it dawned on me: could Calvin Carter novels be written with a similar style?

Well, you hold the answer in your hands. With that idea in my brain, I started *Empty Coffins*. And I didn't look back. Having this scaffolding in place, the story all but wrote itself. It was a blast to write. I hope you enjoyed reading it.

From the end of *Empty Coffins*, *Hell Dragon* emerged. But that's a story for a different book.

SCOTT D. PARKER
   1 January 2019

"YOU DON'T GET THREE MISTAKES"

"ROBERT PRESCOTT?"

Prescott tied the reins of his painted horse around the hitching post and cocked his head. In his peripheral vision, a man stood not ten feet away. The late afternoon sun cast the man's shadow onto the porch of the hotel. Prescott turned. Casually, out of sight of the man, he moved his suit jacket away from his gun. He turned and removed his riding gloves.

"Who wants to know?" Prescott noticed something shiny dangling from the man's right hand. The sunlight sparkled off the metal chain.

"Robert Irving Prescott?" The stranger shuffled a pace or two forward, limping, the dust curling around his feet. Carved in the dirt street behind the man, in a sort of Morse code repeating the same feeble refrain, Prescott saw foot-prints — one longer, ragged rut where the man dragged his left foot for each clean boot print of his right — trailing back across the street.

A muscle in Prescott's face twitched. He narrowed his eyes and took full notice of the newcomer. Trapped under some invisible weight, the man's shoulders sagged and his right shoulder was lower than his left. In a town with enough dust to make dressing up for Sunday services an exercise in futility, the man's collar was dirty around the neck and wrinkled. His black ribbon tie drooped over his brown suit. The brim was pulled low but Prescott noticed the glint of spectacles. The man carried no pistol.

Prescott hung his thumbs inside the pockets of his vest. He sized up the man and stifled a laugh. This wasn't a bounty hunter after the price on his head. This man was small, meek, and lame. Prescott knew he could kill him, just for the hell of it. No one would care. All around them, the locals milled, their rapid Spanish too fast for Prescott. They took no notice of the two gringos staring at each other.

With an air of near boredom, Prescott dismissed the lame man. Surely this wasn't another agent sent by the railroad after the bounty hunters came up empty. He suppressed a grin of pride. The getaway was too good, too clean and precise. No one could have followed his trail. Well, no one except that railroad detective. And Chet. Neither made it out of Texas alive. Not for the first time did Prescott wonder if either body had been found.

Too bad about Chet, though.

He allowed a smile. He felt no fear. "Yeah, I'm Prescott. Who the hell are you?"

The man stood still, not moving a muscle. After a few moments, Prescott gave the man his back, waving a hand over his shoulder. "Don't hassle me, cripple. I'm hungry."

"I believe this is yours."

Prescott frowned. Turning around, he stared at the man who held out his right hand. The dangling thing appeared to be a pocket watch chain, the kind gentlemen wore in their vest pockets. A fob swayed in the light breeze, twirling back and forth. It took a moment before Prescott made out its shape. His blood ran cold.

The little fob was shaped like a tombstone, the letters "R.I.P." engraved on the front. Instinctively, Prescott's hand went to his own vest. He felt the replacement chain and fob he bought after he lost his original chain during the train robbery. Through the fabric of his vest, his finger traced the outline of the replacement fob.

Prescott heard shuffling. The stranger had moved a few steps closer.

"Need a closer look, Prescott?" he said. Something about the man's voice, his tone, unhinged Prescott and he caught his breath.

Someone had found him.

Energy surged through him. Prescott's hand flashed to his Colt .45. He prided himself on his speed. It saved his life countless times, especially when Chet got wise. He almost lost to Chet. But he wouldn't lose here, today, to this cripple.

The stranger's left hand blurred into his suit. Prescott watched as if underwater as the lame man pulled out a short barreled revolver and aimed it at Prescott's middle. Prescott had barely cleared his Colt when a bullet ripped into his side, knocking him backward onto the hitching post. He half fell into the water trough. His Colt thudded onto the dirt at his feet.

Hot pain seized his right side. Prescott pulled his arm out of the water. He blocked the sun and stared at the stranger, still slouched, but with the gun, clutched in his left hand. The smell of gunpowder bit Prescott's nostrils. It was usually a smell he associated with exhilaration. That was before he was the victim.

Not breaking eye contact, Prescott felt his torso. Warm and wet. He held up his hand in front of his face and watched as light, tan dust, floating in the breeze, embedded itself in the bright crimson of his own blood.

The townspeople stopped and stared at him and the cripple. The boy who worked at the livery stable stood, mouth agape, awesome wonder in his eyes.

Anger swelled in Prescott. "Who sent you?"

"You didn't answer my question," the cripple said. He held the fob and chain out to Prescott. "Need a closer look?" He tossed the fob toward Prescott who flinched in spite of himself.

Prescott picked up the chain and examined it. Yes, it was his, the one he'd lost during the train heist. He remembered exactly when, too. The railroad detective, traveling to investigate an unrelated case, had surprised Prescott and Chet. In the brief struggle, the detective had grabbed for Prescott. But he only got the watch chain and fob. Prescott had fired then, but only grazed the detective. The son of a bitch had followed Prescott and Chet for half a day, bleeding slowly to death. The same night, in order to make sure he wasn't followed anymore, Prescott had doubled back and slit the detective's throat. Then, he'd dispatched Chet.

Poor Chet. He was a good brother.

Prescott held up his hand in deference and began to make his way up to a standing position. So someone had found him. It was inevitable, really. And not surprising when once he decided to abandon the original plan for a new one. But he still had a trump card.

"You the best man the railroad could find? You're a damn cripple."

The stranger allowed a little taunting to enter his voice. "Found you, didn't I?"

Prescott's pride got the better of him. "How?"

The stranger took a step to his right, dragging his foot in

the dirt. "It wasn't easy. I'll give you that. Your first mistake was the railroad detective. You shouldn't have killed him. The railroad put a price on your head so high that any school boy with dreams of an easy life would've rode to find you."

Prescott smiled. "They didn't."

The stranger shook his head once. "They didn't have the proper motivation." He paused. "But two did. What happened to them?"

Prescott smirked as he remembered the ambush against the two bounty hunters a few weeks ago. "Not telling all my secrets, cripple."

The man shrugged. Prescott was momentarily taken aback. He wanted to brag, to have the stranger plead it out of him. The man's refusal unnerved him.

Prescott pushed up from the water trough, trying to stand his full height. The livery stable boy backed up a step. A few women hurried their children away. Blood seeped downed his leg. Prescott knew he needed to get a doctor soon or he'd bleed out.

The stranger continued. "I was looking for you when I got news of the bounty hunters. They helped me narrow down where you might be." He took another step to his left and lowered the gun to his side.

"The fob did it. Unique. Signed by the maker. With the right amount of persuasion, the maker told me your name." He chuckled and pointed with his chin toward the blood on Prescott's vest. "A tombstone. Not the best of charms."

"My little pun on life." Prescott tasted coppery blood in his mouth. His vision wavered. The bullet must've struck something vital. He needed a doctor. He didn't need to be wasting time with this cripple. He let go of the hitching post and stood on wobbly legs.

"Killing your brother was another mistake."

Prescott arched an eyebrow. He didn't see how. He had searched the body and taken away the map to Mexico. He'd even taken the Army discharge papers. He frowned.

"The gun, Prescott," the stranger said, "the gun. You gave your brother the dignity of dying with his gun. Honorable for a Cain like yourself. But you forgot the holster belonged to your father. Once I figured out who he was, I spoke with your mother…"

"What did you do to her?" Prescott boomed. A small spray of blood shot out of his mouth.

The stranger pursed his lips. "Not a damn thing. After I informed her that you killed her baby, she told me everything I wanted to know, how you and Chet dreamed about living in Mexico, which towns y'all selected, depending on how much money y'all had, that kind of thing." He shook his head and let his teeth show in a full grin. "Don't think she takes kindly to fratricide."

Prescott's vision grew red. The sound that escaped his throat was louder than any since he pealed the Rebel yell. He raised his right arm at the cripple. With a practiced movement of his forearm, the small Derringer slipped out of its arm holster and into his grip. He heard the sound of a gunshot and, seconds later, realized it didn't come from his own gun.

He fell backwards, banging his head on the front step of the hotel, the Derringer still clenched in his hand. The second bullet struck him low enough to puncture a lung but not enough to kill.

Prescott squinted up at the stranger. He knew he must be imagining things because the cripple appeared to grow taller. Like a cobra uncoiling itself and rising to attack, the stranger rose to his full height, shoulders squared, a man fit as could be. He pulled off his spectacles with one hand, folded them, and placed them inside his jacket.

Like a school teacher, the stranger wagged a finger at
Prescott. "That was your other mistake, Prescott. You took
the railroad detective's arm holster. Once I saw it was missing, I knew his killer had taken it. It was an easy deduction
to learn your location once I heard about the two bounty
hunters being killed by a man with a gun up his sleeve." He
put his pistol back into his shoulder holster and spread
his hands.

Then the cripple walked. Not with a gimp leg but with a
gait that was strong and able. Prescott's mouth hung open,
not to gasp air but in astonishment.

The stranger loomed over Prescott. With his foot, the
one Prescott took for lame, the man stepped on Prescott's
right hand, the one that still held the Derringer. He winced.

The stranger grinned. He kneeled down and reached
across Prescott's body. He picked up the watch chain and
fob from the dirt. He held it for Prescott to see then put it in
his own pocket.

"A souvenir," he said. "Something I can take back to my
new bosses." He shrugged. "My uncle, one of board
members of the railroad, didn't think I had it in me to locate
you. I was just an actor, you know. What the hell did I
know about tracking a fugitive from justice?" He cocked his
head and stared off in the distance. "The president of the
railroad offered me a job if I found you and brought back
the money." He looked down at Prescott. "I guess you could
consider this sort of a job interview." His smile was thin and
humorless. "How'd I do?"

The man unsheathed a knife from inside his jacket. He
twisted it, letting the sunlight reflect from the smooth blade
into Prescott's eyes. He placed the point on Prescott's throat
and moved his face closer. "I understand the robbery part,
the desire for money. I do, really."

Through eyes growing dim, Prescott watched a bead of

sweat flow down the stranger's nose and hang, suspended. The bead caught the sun and glistened like a prism. Finally, gravity won and the bead fell. It landed on his lips. He tasted the other man's salt.

"I understand why you had to kill the railroad detective. And, as abhorrent as it is, I understand why your greed forced you to kill your brother." He dented Prescott's neck with the tip of the knife. Blood pooled around the tip and ran down his neck. "Why the train engineer? He did exactly what you asked of him. And you killed him anyway."

Prescott frowned. He remembered the heist, stopping the train, stealing the money. He did exactly as he was told. No one on the train got hurt. The railroad got it but that was in the mountains and hours later.

The train engineer. Of course Prescott knew the train engineer. His thoughts swirled in his addled brain. Coldness started to creep along his fingers. Prescott knew he would die if he didn't get medical help. He didn't want to die. He had to make this man help him.

Prescott gurgled.

"Sorry," the man said, "you'll have to repeat that."

With effort, Prescott said, "You still don't know where the money is. Help me and I'll take you to it. You can have it all."

The stranger's countenance changed. It grew hard. "Ain't mine. It's company money. Besides, I wouldn't take it even if it was yours to offer."

Prescott's mouth opened in shock. He turned questioning eyes up at the man. "Why? Who are you that won't take money?"

The man's lips curled into a snarl as he roared into Prescott's face. "My name is Calvin Carter, you son of a bitch, and I just want my father back."

ACKNOWLEDGMENTS

Calvin Carter is a railroad detective in the Wild West. History major though I am, I know a decent amount about 19th Century America, but I don't know much about railroads. But I have an excellent source.

John Frank, a cousin of mine, is a railroad guru. As I grew up, I quickly learned about John and his love for trains. In fact, he built out his entire garage into a model train landscape. It was the coolest thing, especially because you had to go under the table and emerge in the middle just to see some of the detail John had used. John has traveled the world just to ride on certain trains. He has forgotten more about trains and railroads that I'll ever learn.

When it came time to write about Calvin Carter and the railroads in the old west, I had the best source. If I needed to know how long it took for a train to travel from city to city, John would supply time tables and other valuable resources. He is a treasure, and he helped ensure the details in these books are as accurate as possible. Any errors in this book or the subsequent Carter novels are mine.

Thanks, John.

ABOUT THE AUTHOR

Scott D. Parker lives and works in his native Houston, Texas.

The westerns I write using the **S. D. Parker** pen name draw their inspiration from classic TV shows like Maverick, The Wild Wild West, and the Adventures of Brisco County, Jr., and authors such as James Reasoner, Bradford Scott, and Louis L'amour.

As **Scott Dennis Parker**, I write Mysteries that evoke smoke shrouded streets, the glint of a gun barrel in the night, private investigators, police detectives, a dead body slumped on the floor, and stolen treasures. James Patterson, Erle Stanley Gardner, and Clive Cussler are among my influences.

I am the Saturday columnist at DoSomeDamage.com.

Visit my website where you can learn about my other books, watch videos, and join my mailing list to keep up-to-date on new books. **ScottDennisParker.com**

Newsletter

Join my email list to receive updates on new books and videos, and get an exclusive **Catalog Sampler for 2019** with a special offer: *Buy One Book (of your choice) and Get a Second One Free.*

Sign up at ScottDennisParker.com

 facebook.com/scottdparkerstoryteller

 twitter.com/sdparker7

WESTERNS BY S. D. PARKER

What would you do if your spouse was murdered?

Isabella Gilmour woke one morning thinking it was just another
day. It wasn't. It was the day the horrifying news thundered down
on her: her husband had been shot dead by Bart Conway, the
scion of the biggest cattle rancher of Junction City, Texas. In her
moment of anguish, she invokes Mosaic Law: an eye for an eye, a
life for a life. She makes a simple request of her father: "Go get
Stephen's rifle."

Her desperate father begs her to let the legal system work. Will
she, or will she let justice come in the form of a bullet?

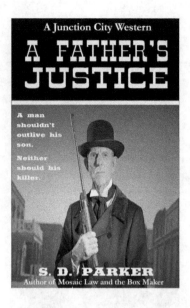

A man shouldn't outlive his son. Neither should his killer.

In a searing new western from author S. D. Parker, you will discover all a father will endure to see justice done right by his murdered son.

Luke Russell was a cowpuncher, making an honest way in the world at one of the biggest ranches outside of Junction City. But he got himself in trouble over a girl, and he paid the ultimate price.

Now, a stranger's in town, asking after Pete Davidson, the man who put a bullet in Luke Russell's gut. This stranger is old, and folks realize it's Luke father, come to kill Davidson. The gunslinger is young and vibrant, just like Luke Russell was. The old man doesn't stand a chance.

Or does he?

A Triple Action Western

THE BOX MAKER

A simple request turns deadly

S. D. PARKER
Author of Mosaic Law and The Agony of Love

Imagine you are a carpenter and a gunfighter asks you to build a coffin…for him. What would you do? And how many coffins would you have to make?

The answer comes in an exciting new Junction City novelette from author S. D. Parker in the style of Louis L'Amour, James Reasoner, and C. K. Crigger.

Emory Duvall practices his simple carpentry trade, knows everyone in town, and stays out of trouble. But when a young gunslinger pulls iron on him and makes an unusual request, trouble lands in Duvall's lap.

Now, the carpenter must figure out how to avoid getting shot… and how many coffins he will have to make.

This exciting new Western from S. D. Parker will have you asking a simple question: what would you do in Emory's position.

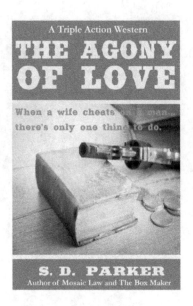

What would you do if your wife cheated on you with a dandy of a gambler?

John Hardwick answered that question for himself. Now, he's about to act on it.

John loves his wife like a Shakespeare sonnet: full, complete, and without equal. Unfortunately, John now finds himself in the crucible of infidelity. He knows the other man's name: Alton Raines, a professional gambler.

John is a good man, not prone to violence, but the images in his mind's eye—of his wife in Raines's bed—puts murder in his heart and a gun in his hand.

A Triple Action Western

THE NAKED CON

Sometimes a man hides
something in plain sight.

S. D. PARKER
Author of Mosaic Law and The Box Maker

Sometimes a man hides something in plain sight. When that man
is naked, what he's hiding is even more difficult to see.

Taking inspiration from movies Maverick and Butch Cassidy and
the Sundance Kid, "The Naked Con" is the exciting new western
short story from author S. D. Parker.

It's not every day that the passengers of a stagecoach in the Old
West see a naked man cowering behind a rock. But the motley
group of people bound for Uvalde, Texas, stop and question
Finnegan McCall, naked as the day of his birth. He claims he's the
new manager at the bank in town and a thief stole all his clothes
and money.

But if McCall is telling the truth, then who is the stranger at the
bank claiming he is the new bank manager? And why is this
stranger asking the assistant manager to open the safe?

This humorous new Western from S. D. Parker will have you
questioning who is whom and what it all means.

MYSTERIES BY SCOTT DENNIS PARKER

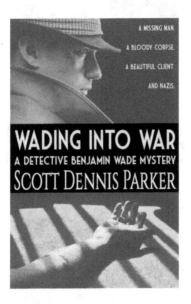

When bullets burst through a door, unarmed gumshoe Benjamin Wade knows his case just got a hell of a lot more difficult.

The smoke clears, the shooter escapes, and Wade finds a corpse. It's the man he was hired to find. His client would not be happy.

Beguiling and enigmatic Lillian Saxton asked Wade to locate a missing reporter who claimed to possess information she craved: whether or not her brother had died in Europe during the early days of World War II. The reporter vanished soon after his ship docked in Houston and she's desperate.

Wade, a laid back former cop, accepts cases so mundane he rarely carries a gun. Now, Wade must unravel the truth about the reporter's murder and the cache of missing documents that reveal a shocking story from Nazi-controlled Europe and an even more sinister secret on the home front.

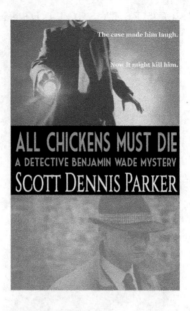

The case made private eye Benjamin Wade laugh. Now, it might kill him.

May 1940, the last days of the Great Depression, and laid-back gumshoe Ben Wade isn't exactly rolling in the dough. He doesn't even have a secretary. He's so bad off, he can't refuse any case.

Elmer Smith is a local farmer. A few days after the police chased a hoodlum through Smith's farm, he receives a court notice: his chickens are infectious and scheduled for slaughter. Desperate to save his livelihood, Smith hires a lawyer to slow the process, but time is running out.

With his coffers nearly empty, Wade suppresses his pride and takes the case. Curiously, the police have no record of the incident. The nervous health inspector is suddenly evasive. And the inspector's beautiful secretary thinks she's being followed and seeks Wade's help.

To unravel the mystery, Wade obsesses on the central question: What really happened the night police chased someone through Smith's chicken coop? Wade isn't the only one asking the question, but he might be the only one who dies for it.

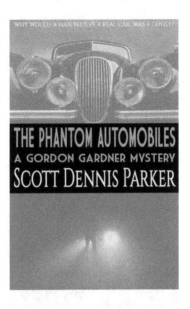

Witnesses all said the same thing: the lunatic who jumped in front of a moving car claimed the vehicle was a ghost. His death proved him wrong.

Why would a man do this? That's the question ace reporter Gordon Gardner asks. What started out as a basic police blotter story initially depressed Gordon. As a reporter second to none, how could a simple accident be worthy of his considerable talents? Even his pairing with a beautiful photographer didn't lighten his mood.

But when Gordon learns the truth about the crazy man's last moments, he digs deeper and zeroes in on a fundamental question: what made Victor Tompkins, a traveling salesman, leap in front of a car?

The police don't care. They've already closed the case. His editor wants the piece yesterday. His rival reporter can't wait for Gordon to fail. Even his new partner, the beautiful Lucy Barnes, thinks Gordon is barking up the wrong tree.

Yet Gordon Gardner didn't earn his bulldog reputation by giving up and walking away. Too many oddities exist. Why would someone break into Tompkins's house after he died? What happened to Tompkins out in the country? Who were the killers who just gunned down one of Gordon's witnesses? As the footsteps approach his position, Gordon Gardner fears he'll never uncover the real truth of the phantom automobiles.

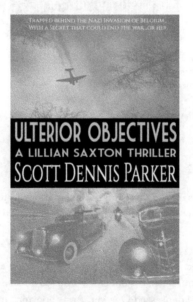

What if the only way you could discover who killed your brother was to lie to your commanding officer?

May 1940. Western Europe is on edge, wondering when the Nazis will strike. America is neutral, woefully unprepared for war, and President Roosevelt tries to steer the dicey waters of international diplomacy and keep the United States out of the conflict. Army Sergeant Lillian Saxton receives a cryptic message from an old flame who now lives in Germany: meet in Belgium and he will not only hand over the key to the Nazi codebooks but also information about the man who murdered her brother.

Lillian conducts all her missions with panache and confidence, even when bullets start to fly and enemy agents zero in to kill her. She's more uncertain of how she'll react when she sees the man who broke her heart or how she'll get out of Belgium when the Nazis launch their invasion.